TO RECLAIM A KINGDOM

BOOK 1 IN THE RED WOOD SERIES

CLAIRE BUTLER

Page Turner Publishing

https://www.clairebutlerauthor.com/

This is a work of fiction. Names, characters, places, and incidents either are the products of the authors imagination or are used fictitiously. Any resemblance to actual persons, living or dead, places, businesses, companies, events, or locales is entirely coincidental.

Cover by 100covers

Editing by Emily Marquart

E-book ISBN: 978-0-6457948-0-9

Paperback ISBN: 978-0-6457948-1-6

For my literary soul sister, you know who you are

CONTENT WARNING

CHAPTER ONE

B rielle surveyed the ladies sitting around her, each one perched prettily with backs straight, their colorful skirts splayed in neat arcs. The most beautiful young ladies at court, the wealthiest, from the most powerful families; that was what her ladies' court was famed for across the land. Dare she say, across the kingdoms. And why not? Surely no other kingdom had a ladies' court that could compare.

Of course, none of her ladies were as beautiful or wealthy or powerful as she. A princess by birth and soon to be queen by marriage, her ladies were poor imitations, mere pretty adornments to her great destiny. Brielle looked on as the ladies shuffled their playing cards and nervously peered at each other.

"I am aging prematurely waiting for you to make your move, Lady Priya," Brielle chided.

Lady Priya quickly selected a card from her hand and tossed it into the center of the picnic rug. It was a perfect spring day with a wisp of wind that would not undo the intricate design of her hair, so upon waking, Brielle had announced the idea of a garden tea party.

The scene was picturesque, sitting by the calm blue lake on the manicured lawn in front of the castle, in view of every courtier to pass by and admire. A servant stood behind her holding a delicate lace-trimmed parasol to shade her fine milky skin from the bite of the sun. The other ladies' skin was of no concern to her. If they became too much kissed by the sun, all the better.

The ladies threw their cards down one by one in quick succession so as not to ire her, but on her turn, Lady Evelyn hesitated. Presented to the King only a month ago, she was the newest and youngest member of Brielle's ladies' court, being only fifteen years old. She was a country girl, coming from an estate in—Brielle did not know or care, to be honest. What was important was that she did not come from noble lineage. Her family had somehow come into a large sum of wealth, and so her presentation at court had been bought. While that made her less desirable, less worthy, and well—less in every way—her wealth did make her notable. At least as notable as a speck on the horizon. Her family could prove important one day, so it was prudent for Brielle to invite her into her inner circle. To bend and fold her into place, like a handkerchief one keeps in a pocket and only pulls out when needed.

"The game takes some thought, Lady Evelyn, but not usually this much," Brielle said sweetly.

Lady Evelyn lifted her eyes to Brielle's sharp gaze and selected a card from her hand. Brielle exhaled a breath of exasperation as Lady Evelyn threw it on top of the pile of cards. Selecting a card from her own hand, Brielle tossed it onto the pile before her attention caught on two approaching noblemen.

"Your Highness." The noblemen both bowed to her with courtly precision. "We were on our way to the castle when we were struck by the most beautiful vision we have ever seen, and we could not pass by without telling you how stunning you look this morning."

Brielle smiled prettily. "Lord Daxton, Lord Waylan."

"Truly, the sight of you and your lovely ladies sitting by the lake is the makings of a famous portrait."

Brielle watched out of the corner of her eye as her ladies soaked in the rich compliment and blushed with appropriate modesty.

"Lady Quinne, what a remarkable necklace," Lord Daxton observed.

Lady Quinne's delicate fingers rose to the ruby necklace that sat flush against her pearl white bosom. Last season her figure had been unremarkable, her breasts no bigger than apples, but this season they had grown as ripe as grapefruit, and the cut of her dress displayed them proudly.

"You are too kind, my lord." Lady Quinne gazed up at Lord Daxton with hopeful eyes, her voice slightly breathless.

"Indeed, you are too kind, Lord Daxton," Brielle said as she frowned. "The piece is quite dull."

"We are very much looking forward to your eighteenth birthday celebration, Your Highness." Lord Waylan attempted to salvage the situation.

"Of course you are. It is the highlight of the year."

The dismissal made clear, the noblemen bowed and took their leave, but not before Lord Daxton slipped a charming smile in Lady Quinne's direction. Her bosom heaved noticeably with her quickened breath.

Brielle took up her playing cards and made a show of studying them. "Lady Priya, what do you think of Lady Quinne's dress?"

Tension fell upon her ladies like a shadow when the sun disappears behind a cloud.

"I-I am not sure, Your Highness," Lady Priya stammered.

"The neckline is quite low, is it not?"

"Immodestly so," Lady Priya eagerly agreed.

Brielle lifted her eyes to find Lady Quinne's face satisfyingly flushed with embarrassment.

"Well?" Brielle pinned her with a look.

Lady Quinne blinked back at her, unsure of what to say or do.

"Go change! I cannot have my ladies' court brought into disrepute by a lady of low"—her eyes slid to her ample bosom—"morals."

"At once, Your Highness." Lady Quinne quickly rose, curtsied, and walked briskly back to the castle.

Brielle watched her as she passed Sienna, who was strolling across the lawn toward them. Sienna exchanged a concerned look with Lady Quinne before turning her attention to Brielle, a knowing look on her face. Brielle returned a sickly sweet smile, confirming that she had indeed publicly admonished Lady Quinne, who was probably now going to go cry in a corner for the next hour and hopefully never wear that dress again.

Brielle waited for Sienna to curtsy before acknowledging her. "Lady Sienna, you are late to my garden tea party."

"My apologies, Your Highness, I was unavoidably detained."

Brielle caught the implication in her words and studied her appearance for a moment; the slight flush in her cheeks, the brightness in her eyes, as if they held a secret. She threw her cards to the ground.

"Lady Sienna, take a turn about the lake with me. I am bored with the current company."

Brielle stood and tucked Sienna's arm into the crook of her elbow. "Someone teach Lady Evelyn how to play the game so that she does not waste my time thinking."

They strolled along the lake in silence for a few moments until they were comfortably out of earshot, save for the servant who followed, shading them with the delicate parasol.

"What did you say to Lady Quinne?" Sienna asked before Brielle could get the first word in.

"Do not change the subject. Were you detained by Lord Jameson?"

Sienna turned her face away and let her eyes drift across the sparkling water. "Our paths crossed, yes."

"How unexpected." Brielle rolled her eyes.

Sienna's lips slipped into a secret smile. "I think he has an affection for me."

"Obviously."

"I think I might be developing an affection for him."

"The second son of a mid-rank noble." Brielle gagged.

"He is kind and educated and attentive."

"And boring and utterly replaceable."

"Brie." Sienna tugged her arm in reproach.

She was the only person allowed to call her that, and only ever in private.

"I should banish you for being late to my garden tea party on account of him."

Sienna threw her a side look, which acknowledged that they both knew she would not.

"Just remember you need the permission of your queen to marry, and since I am going to be your queen, as soon as I find a husband worthy of me, I would try to stay in my favor."

"Speaking of princes, are you excited about Prince Henri's pending arrival? You haven't said a word about it."

Brielle stopped short, aghast. "Who cares about a prince when I have my birthday celebration occurring in a few days?"

"Of course, but—"

"In any case"—she resumed strolling—"he is not a suitor. The Old Treaty prohibits the Kingdom of the North and the Kingdom of the South from uniting through marriage."

"I know, but you always enjoy the attentions of a prince," Sienna mused and gently nudged her side. "I have heard he is quite handsome."

Brielle sighed dramatically. "Fine. Perhaps, at the very least, he will provide some entertainment."

⚬§⚬

Henri leaned his head against the window of the carriage, shutting his eyes to block out the blinding sun. He wished the carriage would stop rocking so violently. It didn't help that he was sitting at the front of the carriage, essentially traveling backward. His stomach roiled and his vision swam.

It was not his choice, of course. His father, the King, sat opposite him, his legs splayed widely enough to take up the entire seat. He was engaged in serious conversation with Lord Keenley, his trusted adviser and commander of his armies, who sat begrudgingly beside Henri. Hence, his seat was cramped. A lesser lord may have tried to take up as little room as possible out of respect for Henri's princehood, but not Lord Keenley. He viewed him much like his father did; at best a disappointment of a prince, at worst a waste of space. And so, Lord Keenley took up as much space as he liked.

Henri's head throbbed. He rubbed his temple subconsciously, trying to drown out the voices of his father and his commander. It was not his choice to ride in a carriage with them. Until today, he had been traveling in his own carriage, sometimes in the company of his friend Nathaniel, sometimes alone with his thoughts and his flask. Today, though, they would arrive at the Southern castle and be presented to the Southern King, and for that they needed to appear united. Hence, father and son, King and heir, exiting from the same carriage.

He had drunk himself into a stupor last night just to take the edge off having to spend an entire day in his father's company, cramped into a small wooden box, sharing the same stale air, listening to his endless talk of war and enemies and taxes. At least by the end of today, the journey would be over and he would be free from the confines of a carriage for a week before they would all bundle in again to make the long journey home to the Northern Kingdom.

The last time he had made the journey south was when he was a boy. He had hated it even more then. He couldn't remember much about the Southern Kingdom, the castle, or the King, but he remembered that he never wanted to go back. And so he hadn't.

Until now.

Diplomatic relations, along with the potential threat of war, demanded that they make the journey. He couldn't think why he would be needed for either. Still, it was only a week and there would be wine and women and entertainment; he would live.

Henri sighed loudly as he shifted uncomfortably in his seat. His rear had gone numb. Again.

"Apologies, are we keeping you from your rest, prince?" the commander sneered.

Henri opened his eyes but ignored the jibe, preferring to stare out the window. They were still traveling on rocky ground. The road would even out as they got closer to the castle.

"You should pay attention. My kingdom will be yours one day and these threats will be yours to face," his father admonished.

Henri ignored him too. Anything he said would not be good enough, had never been good enough, so he remained silent. He could feel his father's disappointed gaze on him, his displeasure thick in the air, before he returned to the conversation with his commander. Henri closed his eyes again.

Hours later, the road had evened out, and the ale induced fog had lifted from his mind. The driver banged on the roof of the carriage, announcing their pending arrival at the castle. Henri felt a wave of relief at the thought of being free of this wooden cage. Besides, he needed to piss.

Moments later, the carriage came to a stop. He could hear flags flapping in the wind, and then the trumpets sounded. His father nailed him with a heavy look, the message clear; do not embarrass me. Henri tightened his lips in return; message received. His father exited the carriage and Henri followed behind him.

They were met by the southern court, all neatly assembled on the manicured grounds in front of the castle, their bodies bowed low in reverence. His eyes skimmed the crowd. Such a posture provided the perfect opportunity to appraise the ladies of the court. He could see many a delectable prospect, but he settled his intentions on the one in the pale blue dress with hair the color of honey. She dared to glance up at him beneath long, dark eyelashes. He would see her hair flowing down her back as she rode him tonight. The thought made his breeches tighten.

"Welcome to the Southern Kingdom," the Southern King said as he held his arms out wide to greet them.

He was a tall man but slender, more suited to the council chamber than the battlefield, it seemed. His eyes looked kind and his smile seemed genuine; the mask of a practiced courtier. Henri's father approached, and both Kings clasped hands in strength, a sign of friendship.

"We are happy to be here."

"Please excuse the Queen's absence, she is not feeling well. Let me introduce my daughter, Princess Brielle." He held his hand out and a young lady stepped forward.

Her curtsy was barely a curtsy at all, more like a slight tilt of her body. His father bristled at the flagrant insult, but she did not seem to notice, or if she did, she did not care. The Southern King did not reprimand her. He was gazing at his daughter with complete adoration. The Princess's eyes were warm brown like a doe's, but they were not soft, they were sharp like an eagle's. She held herself like a queen, her chin high, her movements graceful and deliberate. She was beautiful in the way that all court ladies were beautiful; her skin was soft and unblemished, her long hair fell in perfect waves, her figure was small and becoming, but that was not what made him stare.

"I am sorry that we could not make it for your birthday, Princess. I heard it is quite the event," his father said.

The Southern King laughed indulgently. "Indeed. It lasted four days."

Only Henri could hear the hint of distaste in his father's voice as he replied, "My son appreciates a good party as well."

The invitation was clear, so he stepped forward to present himself, bowing to the Southern King and the Princess.

"The flowers of spring pale in comparison to your beauty, Princess."

An amused smile danced on her lips, as if she would laugh at him but was holding it in.

Her voice was as smooth as silk as she replied, "Welcome to court."

Her court, the words seemed to imply.

His own lips twitched toward a cunning smile as he fixed his eyes on her. She returned his stare boldly, neither of them wanting to be the first to look away. Suddenly, he was glad he came.

Game recognized game.

Under Brielle's relentless supervision, the throne room had been transformed into a festive hall of celebration. Thousands of candles had been placed strategically around the room to provide the hall with a warm, glowing ambience, while elaborate chandeliers were suspended from the ceiling. Long tables overflowed with the season's best food and wine. Musicians played lively tunes on strings and drums and lutes, while courtiers danced across the polished marble floor. Her father's wealth was on display for all to see in every detail. It was a welcome celebration for the King of the North, but also an obvious demonstration of power. The Southern Kingdom was a powerful ally, but could be a dangerous enemy.

At the King's approach, Brielle's ladies curtsied in flawless unison. Brielle bowed her head slightly to her father, who leaned in to kiss her cheek.

"The hall looks splendid, my dear."

"Of course it does, Father," she replied proudly as she kissed his cheek in turn.

"I shudder to think how grand your wedding celebration will be."

"My wedding celebration shall pale in comparison to my coronation day."

Her father laughed and lightly tugged her chin. "And what a beautiful queen you shall be."

Brielle inclined her head in acceptance of the compliment as her father moved on to mingle with his guests. She turned back to her ladies, who were standing in a circle, each one of them dressed as flawless gems in her Crown jewels.

"Did you hear about Lady Taleula?" Lady Priya whispered, and they leaned in closer with anticipation. "She was walking in the court gardens with a suitor today when she fainted and fell face first into a bush! Apparently, her laces were pulled too tight and she couldn't breathe!"

The ladies tittered, except for Sienna, who asked, "Is she all right?"

Lady Priya ignored her. "Unfortunately for Lady Taleula, the bush was overgrown with ivy. It is why she is not in attendance tonight; the rash is rumored to be quite severe."

"Perhaps she should try eating less," Brielle quipped, and her ladies snickered behind their hands.

"Your Highness."

Brielle turned to find Lord Jameson bowing low before her.

"May I have your permission to dance with Lady Sienna?"

Sienna looked to her, her eyes hopeful, and Brielle dipped her chin in approval.

As he rose, Lord Jameson held his hand out in invitation. "Lady Sienna, would you honor me with this dance?"

A smile bloomed on her lips as Sienna placed her hand in Lord Jameson's and let him lead her out onto the dance floor. Brielle watched them as they began the first steps of the dance.

Sienna looked beautiful tonight in a red gown with gold trim, her long blond hair flowing neatly down her back, with two small pearl combs pinning up the sides. Sienna had always been blessed with beauty, even as a child, but it was her easy smile and infectious laugh that drew people to her. She was like the sun: always warm and inviting, never cold or bitter. Lord Jameson was looking at her as if he never wanted to see the moon again. As if the room and everyone in it had disappeared, except for her.

Jealousy seeped into her veins. Of course, her own beauty could not be matched. It was spoken of in kingdoms across the sea. It was the reason princes traveled from far and wide to court her. Her own courtiers complimented her every day. But no one had ever looked at her the way that Lord Jameson was looking at Sienna. And where were those admiring courtiers now? True, she had turned down several requests to dance tonight, content to gossip with her ladies and drink spiced wine, but now that she wished to dance, where were the noblemen?

Brielle surveyed the crowd to find most of the lords dancing or mingling amongst each other. Her eyes caught on Lady Quinne, who was dancing with Lord Daxton, her third dance of the evening. Brielle scowled. It was mystifying how Lady Quinne could garner such interest. She wasn't even that pretty and her dancing lacked poise.

Swallowing the dregs of her wine glass, Brielle walked away from her ladies, her eyes never leaving Lady Quinne and Lord Daxton as they waltzed around the room, oblivious to her scrutiny. She took another glass of wine from a servant holding a silver tray and came to stand at the edge of the dancefloor, away from the crowds of mingling courtiers. She watched as Lord Daxton led Lady Quinne into a spin, making her skirts flair prettily around her ankles.

Brielle felt the heat of a body at her back as someone came to stand silently behind her, closer than any courtier would have dared. Breath kissed the slope of her neck as a male voice said, "I think your scowl might be even more beautiful than your smile."

She didn't turn to acknowledge him, even as she felt his eyes devouring her from behind.

"I see your skill at paying ladies compliments has not improved."

"Perhaps the fault lies with the receiver."

He was trying to bait her. How boring.

"Who is vexing you?" the prince asked as he stepped out to stand beside her.

"Lady Quinne," she replied sourly. "The one in the violet dress."

Lady Quinne was laughing now, her dance partner apparently possessing wit as well as grace.

"Why? You are more beautiful than her."

"Obviously."

"Then how is she tormenting you?"

Brielle clenched her jaw. She would never admit to comparing herself with another lady, let alone feeling envious. Such a thing was unthinkable and completely beneath her.

"Shall I destroy her for you?" His whispered words were like a lover's caress.

She slowly turned to him. His lips were curled into a devilish smile, but his eyes were bright and serious.

"How?"

He took her glass of wine and raised it to his lips.

"Seduction."

Brielle scoffed as he took a sip.

"Lady Quinne has been one of my ladies for three years. Her reputation is as impeccable as her breeding."

"She has never met me."

"Prince or no, you would have better luck with the fillies in the stable."

"What would you give me for it—her reputation?"

Her breath caught at the boldness of his words, even as a thrill snaked down her spine. She appraised him for a moment, as if she were considering it. "Nothing."

He bowed his head. "As you wish."

He handed the glass back to her and she watched him saunter across the room. His long strides quickly closed the distance between himself and Lady Quinne, who was now talking to Lord Daxton, slightly breathless from their dance. Brielle could not hear what was being said between them, but she could see Lady Quinne's eyes darting between her suitors, clearly surprised by the attention. They seemed to brighten as the Prince held his hand out to her in invitation. She took it without hesitation and he led her out onto the dancefloor as if he were showing her off for all the world to see.

Brielle took a deep sip of wine and folded her arms across her chest as she watched them bow and curtsy to each other. Lady Quinne's eyes lowered demurely as a saint. Brielle rolled hers in disdain. The music began. They circled each other, their steps light, and their hands met for the briefest of touches before they parted again. Another circle of steps and their bodies almost brushed before they came to stand apart. They took a step closer, each raising a hand above their heads until he took her fingers lightly in his.

As they moved as one, their eyes fixed on each other, his gaze holding hers as if by command. His steps were confident as he led her across the dancefloor. She seemed so small and delicate cast against his tall, muscled frame. She was clearly giving herself over to him, letting him lead her body as he wished. With a flick of his wrist, he twirled her out away from him and her skirts flared in a perfect arc before he pulled her back into his arms. His hand slid firmly around her waist and a faint blush crept into her cheeks. He pulled her tighter against him in response.

Brielle's breath hitched. She could only imagine what Lady Quinne was feeling right now. The warmth of his body pressed against hers, the strength of his muscled arms beneath her fingertips. He was boyishly handsome, his dark hair flicking over his hazel eyes, his lips full and his smile sensual.

Their steps were faster now, the beat swelling to a climax. Lady Quinne grinned as he began spinning her around and around, faster and faster. She tossed her head back in laughter, enjoying the wild abandonment. The musicians struck their last chord, and the courtiers clapped their hands in admiration, their breaths coming short and sharp to their lungs. The Prince bowed to Lady Quinne, his eyes lingering on her face as he pressed his lips to the back of her hand. Then he walked away.

His strides were long and casual, as if he expected her to follow him. Brielle scoffed at his presumption. Lady Quinne remained standing on the dancefloor, staring after him, as if she could not quite believe what had just happened. Brielle watched as Henri threw a brief glance over his shoulder at her before disappearing through the great doors. Brielle slid her gaze back to Lady Quinne. She looked as if she'd stopped breathing.

"There you are."

Brielle startled as Sienna appeared at her side with Lady Evelyn in tow.

"Why are you standing over here by yourself?"

Brielle tried to return her gaze to Lady Quinne, but she was gone. Clutching Sienna's hand, she pulled her quickly through the crowd, her eyes searching the faces of every courtier, as Lady Evelyn followed closely behind.

"Where are we going?" Sienna asked as they burst through the great doors into the empty hallway.

Brielle strode briskly down the hall, searching the shadows for movement and listening for the slightest of sounds. Surely they could not have gone far. She halted in front of the first set of doors; the royal library. Brielle pushed open the door and marched inside. It was dark. No candles were lit, but moonlight beamed in through the high stained-glass windows.

A whimper echoed within the stone walls, along with a rustling of skirts. Her lips formed a feline smile as she casually strolled around a bookcase to drink in the sight before her: Lady Quinne perched on the edge of a desk, Henri's hand beneath her skirts, which were hitched up around her waist. The front of her dress was pulled down to expose an ample breast, which he was feasting on with desire.

"Lady Quinne!" Brielle exclaimed, scandalized.

Sienna gasped, Lady Evelyn paled, and Lady Quinne shrieked, but the Prince simply lifted his head to smile at Brielle in triumph.

The sharp knock at the door roused Henri from unconsciousness. He opened his bleary eyes to see Nathaniel stepping inside the room.

"The King sent me to remind you that he expects you at the council meeting this morning."

As usual, his friend's expression and tone betrayed no emotion. He didn't appear irritated that Henri was severely hungover and still in bed hours after sun's rise. He didn't seem surprised that Henri was currently pinned to the bed by a soft, naked female. Henri had often admired Nathaniel's talent for being devoid of emotions, especially because his own emotions so often got the better of him.

"Why?" Henri groaned.

Shifting his body out from underneath last night's pleasure, he noted that his mouth was dry as sand and his breath smelled foul. His father did not need him at the council meeting this morning. He would not even let him speak. Any words he spoke would be deemed foolish, those of a boy and not a man. His father and his commander would talk around him, as if he were not there at all.

"You are the heir," Nathaniel said plainly, striding over to the bedside table to pour him a glass of water.

So, he was to be put on display. To show everyone that the King of the North had a son, an heir to the throne, whereas the King of the South did not.

Nathaniel held the glass out to him. Henri reached for a goblet of wine instead and swallowed its contents. His friend's expression did not change in disapproval or admiration. He simply looked past him and said, "It's time to get up, my lady."

The girl did not stir.

"Is she dead?"

"I hope not," Henri returned.

"What did you do to her last night?"

"You say that as if she wasn't a willing participant."

Nathaniel studied the sleeping girl for a moment. "She's not the one who followed you out of the hall last night."

"No, that was just a game. How did you fare last night?"

In all their years of friendship, Henri had never once seen Nathaniel pursue someone. While he was pleasant enough to everyone, and fiercely loyal to Henri, he always seemed to be content with his own company. Sometimes, Henri wondered if he ever experienced sexual urges at all. Perhaps he should have been born a monk instead of the son of a commander.

"We should hurry," Nathaniel reminded him.

Henri tossed the bedcovers back and stood, stretching out his naked limbs. The room swayed a little. A lot. Enough to convince him to drink the glass of water.

"Should I go like this?" He made a sweeping gesture to his naked body.

Nathaniel strolled over to the dresser and retrieved a pair of breeches, a white shirt, and a leather belt. Henri took the pants and pulled them on, trying to balance as best he could while the room swayed around him. A moan drew their attention back to the girl as she attempted to sit up in bed. The girl squinted around the room for a moment as her eyes adjusted. Confusion crossed her face until her gaze caught on him.

"Good morning, Your Highness," she purred through a seductive smile, twisting a strand of her tousled honey hair.

"I have to go."

He yanked on his boots.

"Shall I wait for you to return? Or come back this evening, perhaps?"

Henri knew he was an attractive male, and seducing women had always come easy to him, but he was not so arrogant as to believe that his good looks and charming personality were what drew them to him. A chance to capture his attention, perhaps even win his heart. To be loved by a prince; it could make them queen. Or the king's mistress. Or at the very least, they could have his bastard and perhaps one day he would claim that bastard as his heir. Their son could be king one day. It was worth the risk of ruining their reputation by giving up their maidenhead. And perhaps taking it made him a cad, but he never promised them anything in return.

"I don't think your future husband would approve."

Moments later, they were striding down the hallway, Henri adjusting the buckle on his belt and smoothing down his hair with his hands. Nathaniel pulled a small, round silver box out of his tunic. Clicking it open, he held it out to Henri. Mint leaves. Henri took two for good measure and chewed on them before entering the council chamber.

The room was filled with the Southern Kingdom's councilmen, their chatter climbing over each other for attention, their words strained. His father was standing at the head of the table with his commander, Nathaniel's father, at his side. They raised their eyes briefly to acknowledge his presence before returning to their conversation. The muscle in Henri's jaw feathered, but he tried to appear relaxed, unaffected. This was a performance, after all. None of the councilmen approached him, his father's lack of attention signaling to all that his opinion would not matter and therefore was not worth fighting over.

Henri's gaze wandered to a long wooden table in the middle of the room, large enough to seat at least twenty men and a thing of rare beauty. Crafted from oak, the sides had not been smoothed, their edges left rough and jagged. He moved closer to see that on the surface were carvings detailing the history of the Southern Kingdom: the battles, the heroes, great kings, and even greater victories. In the center, though, lying beneath a sheath of glass set into the table, was a longsword. The cruciform hilt appeared to be made of heavy iron. The straight double-edged blade gleamed in the light.

"The sword of peace," Henri murmured in awe.

"Indeed," said a commanding voice.

Henri startled at the Southern King's presence beside him.

"The sword that ended the battle between our two kingdoms. The sword that our forefathers swore peace on."

"You set it into a table."

"I did." The King smiled, clearly amused at Henri's puzzled expression. "So that each time we come together to decide the future of our kingdom, we are reminded of our oath to yours. That we are allies."

"And so we come to you today," the King of the North interjected loudly, calling all other conversations to cease. "To talk about our alliance in the face of a new threat to both our kingdoms."

His father's words heralded the councilmen to take their seats. The Southern King gave Henri a conspirator's wink before he turned to claim the seat at the far end of the table, directly opposite the King of the North. Henri simply took the seat in front of him, at the center of the table. Nathaniel took the one by his side.

"I have received word that King Heroux has successfully conquered Airedeen," the King of the North announced.

The councilmen murmured amongst each other in disapproval. Some outright swore.

"He will look to our kingdom next. His last three war campaigns have made him a wealthy man. His appetite for land and power knows no bounds. And if the North falls, the South will also fall."

This dramatic revelation did not surprise Henri. His spies had told him as much; that King Heroux now occupied Airedeen and was imparting his rule on the people there. King Heroux had a reputation for imposing harsh laws and even harsher taxes to fund his endless war campaigns.

"A threat to the North is a threat to the South," the Southern King agreed.

"I am told that King Heroux's armies lost significant numbers against Airedeen. If we join our armies and meet him on the Northern border, we will be able to push him back. Show him that this continent is ours and we will not yield to a foreign ruler."

The councilmen banged their hands on the table in agreement. Henri shot a sidelong glance at Nathaniel, but as usual, his friend's face was a mask of neutrality. Henri's spies had also told him that King Heroux's army had suffered heavy losses. A king with a depleted army was not likely to wage open war and chance complete destruction. A smart king would either wait to rebuild his numbers or find another way to conquer the North.

"Do we have any confirmation that King Heroux intends to invade?" The words left his mouth before he could stop them.

The room fell silent. He could feel the weight of everyone's eyes upon him, but none as crushing as his father's.

"As kings, we have both faced enough enemies and fought in enough wars to know when one is coming," his father replied tersely.

Whereas he had not. It was not true. He had marched with his father's armies and fought in several battles as bravely as any soldier. But that did not matter because he was not a king. And nothing he did or could ever do would be enough in his father's eyes. So he returned to silence.

The meeting stretched on for another hour, the councilmen debating the best place to confront King Heroux's armies, how best to run supply lines, their current infantry numbers and resources. When all was said and done, Henri rose from his chair and stalked out into the hallway. He wanted a drink, several in fact, and perhaps something to smoke and someone to—

"Where are you going?" Nathaniel demanded, sprinting to catch up to him.

"I need a distraction."

CHAPTER TWO

B rielle had a book perched on her lap, her gaze fixed on the page of poetry in front of her, but she had not read a single word. She was too busy lapping up the shocked whispers between her ladies. Some sat together embroidering small cushions, some leaned their heads together by the fire, playing cards. Unfortunately, Lady Evelyn was attempting to play the lyre, but even her jilted plucks of the strings could not dampen Brielle's relish at the gossip of Lady Quinne's shameful departure this morning. Of course, she had sent her home to her family estate. Such immoral behavior was unacceptable of any lady, let alone one of her ladies. She had left in disgrace. In tears. In ruins. And Brielle had enjoyed every second of it.

Except now Sienna was giving her a knowing look of disapproval, which Brielle was choosing to ignore. She would not be held responsible for another lady's mistakes. Nor would she forgive them. Ever.

Brielle winced as Lady Evelyn plucked another string. "I thought you said you could play the lyre," she snapped.

"I said poorly, Your Highness, and not for years." Lady Evelyn halted her fingers in the air, unsure if she should continue.

"The Queen's rooms."

Brielle shot to her feet at the intrusion of the Prince and his companion. Her ladies stood as well and hastily curtsied, their embroidery and cards discarded on the floor. The Prince did not appear to notice as he strolled inside to admire the beautiful room, taking in the expensive furnishings and rich tapestries on the walls. He looked somewhat casual for a Prince, his hair slightly unkempt, his shirt not entirely tucked in. His hands were in the front pockets of his breeches as he turned on his heel to face her.

"Aren't you missing a husband?" he asked.

"A technicality."

He returned a wry smile. "Just what every groom wants to hear."

The truth was the Queen, her mother, had not used these rooms in years. She was seldom well enough to leave her bedchamber, and even when she did manage to claw her way out of her pit of never-ending despair, she was never well enough to entertain nobles. Even before she was struck down with her melancholy, her mother had not been the type to hold court. She was plain, uninteresting, and therefore forgettable. The rooms had remained locked for most of Brielle's childhood, but on her thirteenth birthday she claimed them as her own. Her kingdom deserved a beautiful queen, a glittering ladies' court, an unforgettable ruler.

"And who is this?" Brielle gestured to the lord still standing in the doorway. He was as still as a statue, his face strikingly handsome but his expression unnervingly impassive.

"Nathaniel," the Prince said, as if that told her everything she needed to know about the man.

Not that she particularly cared to learn more.

The Prince strolled over to the window and inclined his head to the chess set laid out on the table. "Have you found an opponent worthy of you yet, Princess?"

"Not yet," she replied smoothly, and walked over to join him.

As they sat down at the table, her ladies resumed their places around the room, taking up their cards or embroidery. Their silence was deafening, their ears keen. Brielle gestured to the Prince to make the first move.

"I hear you have not found a prince worthy of you either, despite entertaining many suitors."

Henri moved one of his pawns forward.

Brielle sighed dramatically. "It's true."

"What were their faults? Too ugly? Too simple?"

"Not at all." She moved her pawn to match his. "Though none were as handsome or stimulating as you."

He raised a brow at her choice of words, but accepted the compliment with a dip of his chin. "Then how did they come up short?"

"They all desired to rule my kingdom."

His eyes flicked up to hers and she stared back at him boldly.

"A common pursuit amongst princes," he said carefully.

"The throne is my birthright. My husband may sit beside me as king consort, but I will rule my kingdom."

Henri slowly leaned back in his chair, his attention returning to the board as if he'd only just seen the game.

"And you? Have you found a queen?"

"I have no need of one." He moved his rook.

Brielle arched a perfectly manicured brow. "You intend to rule alone?"

"I don't believe my father will ever give up his throne, not even to death. I'm sure he intends to live forever."

"But he won't," she countered. "One day you will be King of the North."

Henri didn't reply, but his expression hardened as he focused on the game. Her mouth fell open slightly. He was serious. He did not expect to become king. Her mind was so muddled she barely noticed him taking her knight. She frowned.

"You will be my ally, of course," Brielle continued, manoeuvering one of her pieces out of harm's way.

A wicked smile returned to his lips. "Of course."

"We will negotiate fair trade agreements and you will guard my borders."

"I think I will enjoy guarding your borders," he intoned, his voice carnal.

"Then we shall be friends."

"The best." His eyes danced in amusement.

She moved her bishop, taking his piece.

"I may even visit your court one day."

"My father's court," he corrected her. "Not mine."

"You make it sound as if you do not belong there."

"I don't."

"You are a Prince of the North."

"A technicality," he parried, and their eyes met in challenge.

She lowered her voice as she moved her rook. "If you do not belong there, where do you belong?"

He paused to consider the game.

"No one knows, least of all me," he said quietly as he moved his queen.

Brielle furrowed her brows slightly. "I don't believe that. You seem to be quite sure of yourself, and you are undoubtedly well traveled. You must have discovered a place where you feel most like yourself."

Despite being a princess, Brielle had rarely traveled outside of her own castle. She didn't need to, though. She had always known her place was right here; ruling her ladies' court, and one day, her kingdom.

His wary eyes slid to hers.

A triumphant smile spread across her face. "You do have a place!"

"Check."

She peered down at the board, assessed the play, and made a countermove.

"Tell me," she demanded.

He moved his piece to pursue her queen. "Check."

She moved her piece again, if only to buy time.

"It's futile."

"You will tell me."

"Concede defeat."

"A true queen is never defeated and by the end of this week, I will know all your secrets."

"Well then," he said as he knocked over his own king. "It's a good thing we are allies."

Months Later

Brielle narrowed her eyes at the two commoners standing before her as she sat on her father's throne. She had listened to each man rant and rave, hurling insults at each other that made her courtiers gasp at their audacity to say such things in front of a lady, let alone their queen.

And it was all over a couple of sheep.

This was what she had been forced to listen to every day for months since her father's departure for the Northern border. Either she was sitting in meetings listening to her father's councilmen debate the merits of some boring law or she was presiding over the Court of the Common Pleas, listening to the complaints of the common people.

At first, the prospect of it had excited her; hearing tales of sordid behavior, making judgments of fault and passing sentence, relaying the salacious tales to her ladies for them to devour. Instead, she had heard nothing but petty disputes between tenants, accounts of common fraud, unpaid debts, and the theft of livestock. Horses. Sheep. Cows. Goats. The menagerie never ended. Where were the salacious cases of adultery? Or ill-fated plots against the Crown?

Her father's adviser, a wiry man with an impressively large forehead, cleared his throat and leaned down to speak with her. "Mr. Campion appears to be the wronged party here, Your Highness."

She gave him a withering look and he hastily retreated two steps.

"I am the only wronged party here," she declared. "I should fine you both for wasting my time with this frivolous complaint! Now, be grateful for my leniency and get out."

The adviser turned to her, his eyes wide and mouth spluttering. "But, Your Highness—"

"Enough! I have heard enough for today."

She stood and stalked down the center of the throne room, the courtiers hastily parting before her and bowing on either side as she strode past the long line of complainants, which stretched out the door. Courtiers stared after her as she hastened down the corridor, eager to put as much distance between herself and those petulant farmers as possible. She did not care. Let them all know what would happen if they wasted her time with such tedious matters. She was the queen. Or close enough. She did not need to submit herself to such odious tasks.

Brielle scowled as she spotted Sienna leaning into the shadow of a pillar. Lord Jameson stood beside her, lightly stroking her hand with his thumb.

"I cannot stand it a moment longer!"

They jolted apart instantly.

"I cannot be expected to listen to their petty complaints day after day, it is unbearable."

"But, Your Highness, that is what a ruler does," Sienna said.

"Nonsense. A ruler has far more important things to do. I shall appoint someone else to hear their complaints."

"Who?"

"Lord Rivers would be the obvious choice," Lord Jameson suggested.

"Who?" they echoed.

"The King's adviser, Lord Rivers."

"Yes, Lord Rivers. He seemed to have strong opinions on everything." Brielle rolled her eyes.

She latched on to Sienna's arm. "I need to be entertained. To berate someone." She turned to Lord Jameson, her expression puzzled. "What are you still doing here?"

He opened his mouth as if to explain, but thought better of it. He reluctantly bowed and walked away.

"Brie." Sienna's tone was reprimanding.

Brielle ignored it. "Have you anything of interest to tell me? I could be diverted by the smallest piece of gossip."

Sienna sighed. "You received another letter today. From the Prince of Croaza."

They began strolling down the hallway, arm in arm.

"Henri says he's a bore."

Brielle had maintained a dedicated correspondence with Prince Henri ever since he left court several months ago. She routinely informed him of her many prospective suitors and he advised her of what he knew of them.

"He cannot have met every prince in all the kingdoms," Sienna objected.

"He doesn't have to. He has an impressive network of spies."

"Why does he have a network of spies?"

"He doesn't trust his father."

He had not told her that, but it felt true. Perhaps it was the normal friction that every son experienced with his father as he grew into manhood. But she suspected there was more to it than that.

"I think it is wise of him. He will need his own spies when he comes to the throne."

Brielle had her own spies: her ladies. What they didn't know about the nobles of the court was not worth knowing. Brielle steered them in the direction of the gardens, no longer craving the sanctuary of the Queen's rooms.

"He has found fault with every prince who has courted you. Surely they cannot all be bad. Have you considered that he has another motive for not wanting you to pursue any of them?"

Brielle scoffed. "Henri does not desire me."

"You forget I have read his letters."

"We flirt with each other, yes, but only because it is harmless fun. We both know it will never come to anything. The Northern Kingdom and the Southern Kingdom can never unite under the Old Treaty. He is my friend, that is all."

Sienna stopped suddenly and pointed to the grassed lawn.

"He sent you a dozen peacocks for your birthday along with a self-portrait."

Indeed, the peacocks were now strutting across the grass or perched on top of the water fountains, the vivid colors of their feathers gleaming in the sunlight. Brielle smirked. The portrait she had received was as tall as a man and impressively accurate. The artist had captured Henri's handsome face and wicked charm with every stroke. It was hanging on a wall in her bedchamber. She admired it every night before she blew the candles out.

"God willing, your father will return from this war, but one day soon you will need to choose a husband. Perhaps you should lessen your standards a little."

"My standards are that of a queen, and you are being very dramatic. Of course my father will return. It's a border skirmish."

"I think it's a little more serious than that," Sienna said carefully.

"My father has fought in many battles."

"Your prince is there as well. Are you not even a little concerned for his wellbeing?"

Brielle turned to her friend, incredulous. "They could not be enduring anything worse than what I am enduring here."

❦

It was raining.

Again.

It had been months since they'd left the Northern castle to march to the border, weeks since they'd set up camp, and every single day it had rained. Not a light summer shower but a heavy, relentless downpour. The soil beneath their tents had quickly turned to festering mud. It was impossible to keep anything dry; clothes, food, feet. It made everyone miserable, and tempers were running short.

"My scouts tell me King Heroux's army is six days away." The commander leaned over the table to point to a spot on the map just above the northern border.

The Southern King rubbed his chin thoughtfully. "How many men?"

"Five thousand."

"We outnumber them," the Northern King said dismissively.

Henri simply stared into the flames of the small fire burning in a brazier a few meters away. He wished he were closer to it, wished he were in his own tent by his own fire, wished he were anywhere but stuck in this tent day after day, listening to the strategies of old war commanders and the bluster of kings.

"I will honor no terms of war. We will spare no prisoners. If he dares to cross my border, we will show him no mercy," his father declared.

"He will be forced to retreat, but he will not be deterred so easily. He will rebuild his forces and return," the Southern King warned, studying the map they had been staring at for days, as if it had somehow changed overnight.

Henri tuned out their words as the commander provided an update on their intel and resources. He glanced over at Nathaniel, who was standing guard just inside the tent's entrance, no doubt listening to every word but also keeping an ear out for what was occurring in the camp. A couple of fights had broken out in the past few weeks, born out of restlessness and damp discontent. They had been swiftly dealt with, but there was always the chance more would occur. He wished one would occur right now, at least then he would have an excuse to leave.

His thoughts turned to her, as they so often did when he needed distracting. He wondered what she was doing right now, who she was chastising. He had been unable to write her a letter in weeks and he was feeling the absence of her. Her letters were always filled with the latest court gossip, her quick wit and searing judgment providing mindless entertainment. He did not know why, but her letters made him smile.

"Prince?"

The Southern King's voice cut through his thoughts. He blinked at the stern faces now staring at him. The Southern King had clearly asked him a question.

"Apologies for my son," his father interjected. "He has never taken these matters seriously. It seems he cannot even bring himself to pay attention when war is on his border."

Henri's fists clenched at his sides. Perhaps it was the weather that had frayed his last nerve, but he said, "All I have done for days is listen to old men talk in circles. Nothing has changed."

"Then leave," his father spat, his eyes wide with rage. "Go sit in your tent, warm by your fire, and wait for your betters to summon you to fight. Maybe then you might be of use for once. But I doubt it."

Henri glared at his father, his cheeks suddenly warm. He stood and stalked out of the tent into the pouring rain. His boots trudged through the mud on the way to his tent, which was located a spear's throw away from his father's. It was custom to pitch the king's tent in the heart of a camp to ensure that it could be well defended at all times, but he would rather have his tent pitched on the outskirts of the camp than be a breath closer to that man.

Shoving the flap open, he stormed inside his tent. The fire had burned down to embers, but the air inside was still warm, if not damp. He thought about throwing the table across the room, breaking the legs of his chair, smashing glass and screaming his lungs out until he was hoarse. But he had done all that so many times as a boy and it never changed anything. It never helped him feel better. No one even cared. So he slumped into his chair and seethed.

Moments later, Nathaniel stepped inside, his face aggravatingly neutral. Henri knew he wouldn't say anything. He wouldn't try to soothe him or stoke his anger. He never took a side. Sometimes it felt like a betrayal, but Henri understood why. He was the son of the king's commander. His loyalty to Henri as a friend was eclipsed by his loyalty as a son to his father. By the loyalty to his family and their social standing within the court.

Nathaniel poured him a glass of wine, but Henri lifted his hand and shook his head. He must indeed be at the end of his tether if he did not even crave the promise of oblivion. He was tired, he realized, so very tired. And not just because of the months of travel, the miserable rain, and the lack of sleep. He was tired of his life, the endless monotony of it all. He could see it laid out in front of him like a death march: every day like the one before, sitting in silence, waiting, waiting, waiting. For what? His father's death? A throne that he did not want, a court that did not want him? It wasn't worth living for. It wasn't worth dying for. He had tasted moments of freedom. He had glimpsed the possibility of another life in which he was his own man. A man of substance, a man of worth.

Nathaniel shot to his feet, sword in hand, as a boy rushed into the tent. His face was dirty and his chest was heaving as if he had run for several miles. The boy's eyes darted between Nathaniel and Henri, unsure of whether to speak. Normally, Henri would scold the boy for his clumsiness, for bursting into his tent without a care for who else might be inside, without even an alibi to cover his intrusion.

"Go ahead," he sighed, rubbing a temple.

"My prince, there are soldiers coming."

Henri stilled. "King Heroux's army?"

"Just over the hill."

He stood, exchanging a grave look with Nathaniel.

"They're meant to be six days away."

"No, my lord," the boy breathed.

"Go! Sound the alarm!" Henri ordered as he shot out into the downpour.

He was almost at his father's tent when Nathaniel grabbed his arm, stepped into his path, and thrust a firm hand into his chest. Blood sprayed the inside of the King's tent as if someone had tossed paint on a wall. Henri froze in horror as it splattered the fabric again and again, dribbling down in neat lines. Tearing himself from the grip of shock, he reached for his sword, but Nathaniel pressed his hands harder into Henri's chest.

"Run," he said.

The word did not make any sense.

"My father," Henri choked out. *Is dead.* The words stuck in his throat.

Nathaniel suddenly gripped the back of his neck, the movement urgent but tender somehow. "You are the prince."

For the first time, he saw emotion flash in his friend's eyes.

Nathaniel was right. If they had killed both kings, they would come for him next. A horn blared, the warning echoing across the camp and rousing the soldiers from their tents. A battle cry answered as an army washed over the hill, streaming down upon the camp like a tidal wave.

"Run!" Nathaniel shoved him hard, and Henri staggered backward, taking one last look at his friend's grave face before launching into a run.

He needed to find a horse. He needed—

"My prince!" The boy ran up to him, the reins of Henri's stallion gripped in his hand.

He grabbed the boy and swung him into the saddle before hoisting himself up behind him and riding out to flee the battlefield.

Henri's knuckles rapped firmly on the derelict wooden door in a back alleyway. He scanned his surroundings impatiently before glancing down at the boy

standing at his side, wet and shivering. The rain had not abated the entire journey here and both of them were sodden with it. Even his bones felt waterlogged.

In one way, though, he was thankful for the deluge. It meant that the guards
at the gate had not looked at them too hard when they rode into town. They
hadn't even questioned them as to their business here. The streets were also
mercifully empty, with most people sheltering indoors, no doubt by a fire. Even
the stables where he had left his horse were unoccupied. Hopefully this meant
that their arrival in town, and to this particular door, would go unnoticed and
unreported.

The door opened suddenly and a giant of a man peered down at them. He
was the tallest man Henri had ever laid eyes on and he was built like a brick wall.
Combined with his skin as dark as night and his large eyes the color of obsidian,
the man was intimidating. It was why Henri had hired him.

"Master Delphine," the man frowned in concern and quickly stepped aside
to allow them to enter.

Henri ushered the boy inside first and then followed. He almost groaned in
relief to be out of the rain and enveloped by warmth.

"Thank you, Omar," he said.

They were standing in a crowded room backstage, which was almost stuffy
with heat. Through the sides of a heavy, cherry red curtain he could see scantily
dressed women dancing provocatively on stage. Beyond them, the room was full
of men drinking, gambling, groping, and enjoying the performance.

Naked women rushed past Henri and the boy, fixing their hair and make-
up, and changing into extravagant, brightly colored costumes. Some of them
stopped at the sight of Henri and their expressions changed from surprised to
worried. For his part, the boy did not gape at their naked bodies or breath-taking
beauty. Either he was too wet and miserable to be aroused or he had seen such
flesh before.

"Go get Madame Fleur," Omar instructed one of the girls before turning to
the others. "You fetch some towels and dry clothes. You get some water and hot
broth."

They scampered off and Omar turned back to him, his face grim. "Are you in danger, master?"

"Both kings are dead," Henri replied wearily. "Our scout told us that King Heroux's army was six days away, but they were just over the hill. An assassin must have slipped inside the king's tent. I tried to get to him but—"

He couldn't bring himself to admit it out loud; how he had fled the battlefield rather than avenge his father's death or fight beside his men.

Bleak understanding settled in Omar's eyes. "They would have killed you."

"There is no way we could have won that battle. We had the numbers, but they had the element of surprise. They caught us off-guard. It would have been a slaughter."

"So we have a new king," came a stern female voice.

Henri turned to Fleur and offered a bitter smile in greeting. She was dressed like the other girls, in fishnet stockings and a lace corset that showed off a figure she still retained after all these years. But unlike the other girls, she had an air of authority about her, and a sharp temperament that brokered no argument from patrons. No doubt it was honed from years of experience in the flesh business.

"And you have lost your kingdom." Her eyes shifted as her mind calculated the ramifications of this news. "King Heroux will be looking for you."

Henri nodded. "I don't think anyone recognized me on the way in. The rain was too heavy to see much of anything. If you will permit me to stay here the night, I will leave in the morning."

"Leave," she spat the word out as if it was offensive. "Where will you go?"

"I will find a boat and cross the sea."

"Don't be stupid."

Henri laughed despite himself. It was still a novelty that someone would have the audacity to speak to him in such a way, despite his princehood. During the many times he had been a patron of this place, Fleur had treated him with the utmost respect, befitting of his station as a prince and the fact that he was their best customer. But when he secretly became owner of this establishment, he had impressed upon her that he did not want to be treated like a prince. He had created the persona of Master Delphine, a businessman.

"You will stay here," she insisted. "This is your home now. This is where you belong."

Ironically, the Sodisce had always been the one place where he had felt like he did belong. Within these ruby curtained walls he had found escapism and pleasure unlike any other. It made him feel—human. Like he was simply a man.

It was actually Brielle's words that had prompted him to consider buying the place. Months ago, over a game of chess, she had asked him if he had a place where he felt most like himself. He had known the answer instantly and from that moment on he could not get it out of his head. So he had asked Nathaniel to help him purchase the place in secret. His father would have lost his mind if he knew his son, the prince of the North, preferred owning a brothel to ruling a kingdom.

Henri had come to an arrangement with Fleur, who had been working at the Sodisce for most of her life; he would fund this place and visit when he could, but she would manage it in his absence. They were partners of a sort. Over time, though, they had become friends.

"It is too dangerous," Henri protested. "King Heroux will scour this entire continent looking for me. Anyone harboring me would be considered a traitor to the Crown."

"It is too dangerous for you to leave. Besides, we know how to keep a secret."

Indeed, they did. All the men and women in his employ knew who he was and yet his identity had remained confidential. The rampant changes he immediately made to the business had secured their loyalty. Anyone working at the Sodisce now did so out of their own free will. Men like Omar protected the girls and everyone was paid a fair wage.

"And who is the young lad?" Fleur asked as she studied the boy.

Henri placed a hand on the boy's sodden shoulder. "This is Ele, one of my spies at court. He spotted King Heroux's army over the hill and ran to warn me."

"Brave boy." Omar's voice held a hint of admiration and gratitude.

The girls appeared again, their arms weighed down with various items, including dry clothes. Ele's eyes hungrily latched on to the bowls of broth and bread that were set down on a nearby table.

"Go on lad," Henri encouraged.

He took off in a sprint and began slurping the broth greedily, barely taking breaths in between mouthfuls. Fleur held a towel and shirt out to Henri who obediently peeled off his soaked shirt and dried his skin before pulling the fresh linen over his head. As she held pants out to him, he hesitated.

"You haven't got anything us girls haven't seen a hundred times over," Fleur quipped, and the girls giggled. "Haven't you got customers to attend to?" she tossed over her shoulder at them.

The girls reluctantly dispersed and Henri cast Fleur a wry grin as he stripped off his wet pants. When he was dry and dressed, he joined Ele at the able of food. The boy had already consumed his bowl of broth and was now nibbling on a chunk of bread. Henri felt his insides twist at what he was about to ask the boy to do, but he had little choice. There was no time for the boy to rest or wait for the weather to improve. It might already be too late.

"Ele, once you have finished eating, I have a task for you."

The boy swallowed, but his features turned serious.

"I need you to deliver a message for me, to the Southern Princess. You will deliver the note to one of the maidservants of her most trusted lady, Lady Sienna. She will ensure that only the princess reads it."

Ele nodded without complaint.

"After you have completed that task, you are free to return home, though I would ask you to keep my whereabouts a secret. I will pay you for your silence."

The boy's features crumpled in anxiety. "Oh, please my prince, let me stay and serve you. I will do whatever you ask of me. Just please don't send me home."

Henri frowned. "You will be risking your life if you stay by my side."

"Yes," he agreed eagerly.

"The boy probably does not have much of a home to return to," Fleur suggested gently. "A mother, several siblings perhaps, all living in a hovel, all desperate to eat. He would not be welcome back there. He would probably starve by the month's end. The boy should remain here in your employ. Besides, we always have a use for brave friends we can trust."

Fleur was right, the boy had already proven his loyalty. He had seen an army of thousands marching for his sovereign and he had not fled. He had risked his life to warn Henri, even when the odds of survival seemed impossible. That was more loyalty than most people had ever shown Henri. He owed the boy his life.

Henri slid his gaze back to Ele whose face lit up in hope. "Very well then. In that case, I have another task for you. Once you have delivered the note to the Southern Princess, you will travel to the Northern castle. I need to find out if Lord Nathaniel survived the battle."

"Yes, my prince."

"It's Master Delphine now."

Ele's lips stretched to a conspirator's grin. "Yes, master."

CHAPTER THREE

“**B**rielle, wake up.”

Sienna’s panicked voice startled Brielle awake. She raised her head just enough to see her friend hurriedly lighting candles around the room.

“You need to get up right now.”

“Why? What has happened?” Brielle reluctantly sat up against her pillows.

“Your father … “ Sienna hesitated. “He is dead. God keep him.”

Brielle stared at her blankly. Sienna was wearing a white cotton nightgown underneath a heavy fur-lined cloak and her hair was bound into its usual long braid, which was tossed over one shoulder, but her eyes were wild and frantic.

“King Heroux’s army defeated them.”

Sienna approached and held a folded piece of paper out to her, the seal already broken. Henri’s seal.

“A boy passed this to one of my maidservants. He said that it was urgent.”

Brielle unfolded the note carefully, fingers trembling. It was Henri’s hand writing, hurried but distinct. She read the words through blurry tear-filled eyes before returning her gaze to Sienna’s.

Sienna’s face crumpled in sympathy, but she said, “There’s no time. We have to hurry.”

She turned to the nearest dresser and yanked open the drawers. Holding up a purse, she emptied the contents of a jewelry box like a thief.

“We have to wake the councilmen. If my father is … “ The words died on her lips. She could not bear to say them out loud. It wasn’t possible. She swallowed hard against the lump in her throat. “Then I am queen.”

“Your mother still lives,” Sienna reminded her.

"She is incapable of being queen." Brielle tried to compose herself, wiping the tears from her cheeks and taking control of her thoughts. "We need to make preparations to defend the city."

"Brie, the Prince said to get to safety. He would not say that unless it was not safe for you to be here."

She tossed a green velvet cloak on the bed. "There's no time to change clothes, put that on."

"Of course it is safe here," Brielle countered as she slipped out from underneath the thick, warm covers.

Sienna was relieved to find her legs did not wobble beneath her. She was strong. She could do this. She was born to do this.

"Your father was betrayed! King Heroux's men may already be inside the castle walls!"

"I will not abandon my kingdom when it is under threat."

Sienna stepped within inches of her face and grasped both of her cheeks in her hands. "They will kill you."

Her fingers were ice cold, her grip uncomfortably firm.

"King Heroux's men, your father's councilmen. They would never allow a woman to rule. You are a fool to believe otherwise."

Brielle stilled, frozen in place by shock and confusion. Sienna removed her hands and the action stirred Brielle from her suspended state.

"The councilmen are loyal to me," she insisted.

"No. They were loyal to your father, the King. You are all that stands in their way of claiming the throne for themselves and you are unprotected."

"But I am their queen."

"You are a woman!" Sienna said, exasperated. "Only a woman."

She left Brielle standing in bewildered silence as she moved about the room. It couldn't be true. The throne was hers by right. She had been raised to rule. Her father had never told her otherwise. The councilmen had respected her authority these past months, had treated her like their sovereign. They had, at times, looked vexed by her, but that was to be expected. They were not used to her. She would establish her rule over the kingdom and the councilmen, just as she had established her rule over her ladies.

But what if she was wrong?

What if they had only respected her authority because they believed her father would return? What if they had indulged her, like a child, making her think she was playing the game, but really they had no intention of letting her play the game at all? Perhaps it was better to watch events unfold from a safe distance. Let it be known that she escaped the castle unharmed, and hope that the councilmen would unite and fight in her name. If they did not, she would know the truth.

She felt a cloak being hastily wrapped around her shoulders.

"We do not have much time. Where are your shoes? These will do."

Slippers were thrown at her feet. She dutifully slid them on.

"Where are we going?"

"To claim sanctuary." Sienna tucked things away into the pockets of her cloak and gripped Brielle's hand firmly in hers. "We trust no one."

Brielle nodded and squeezed her hand in return. They slipped into the adjoining room, Sienna's room, to avoid the guards at her door. Sienna led the way out through a series of corridors and passageways, her movements silent and swift, as if she knew exactly where each guard was posted and which shadows were deep enough to disappear into. As if she had done this before. They moved along the hallways until they halted outside a door.

"What are we doing?" Brielle whispered.

"We cannot leave the Queen."

Brielle's eyes widened as she followed her friend through a door into the bedroom of her mother's companion. They padded silently across the carpet, eyes fixed on the body snoring in the bed, before easing open the door that joined to her mother's bedchamber.

Brielle's heart beat wildly in her chest. She had not seen her mother in years. When she was a girl, she would visit her every couple of months, out of hope or love or desperation. She didn't know. But every visit was the same; she found her hopeless and helpless, a wounded animal lying on the floor, soaked in its own misery. She began to detest her. Her weakness, her frailty, her plainness. So she had stopped visiting. Her father, the king, never visited his wife. He hardly spoke of her, except in formalities. It was easy to forget she still lived.

"Your Majesty," Sienna whispered into the darkness.

Brielle hovered by the door.

Sienna leaned over the four-post bed in the middle of the room, placing a hand on the lump that lay there under the blankets. A muffled sound made Brielle shiver.

"Your Majesty, you must come with us. It is not safe for you here."

"Who are you?" a voice croaked.

It was familiar, but Brielle did not want to remember it.

"My name is Sienna. I am a friend of your daughter."

"Brielle." The voice hitched, more alert now. "Is she here?"

"Yes, Your Majesty." Sienna looked over to her and even in the dark, Brielle knew her eyes were pleading for her to come closer.

She didn't.

"The King's enemies are coming, we must get you to safety."

"Where is Maude?"

Her lady's companion, Brielle presumed.

"We cannot trust anyone, Your Majesty."

"I cannot go."

"You must."

"No, no, I can't," she wailed and Brielle shifted nervously on her feet. She was going to wake everyone up.

"Please, Your Majesty," Sienna begged.

Her mother began howling as she sat up in her bed, sobbing words Brielle could not understand. In the beam of moonlight that stretched across the sheets, she could see her. Her body was small and frail, her face drawn and lined with age, her hair a tangled halo around her head. She did not stop sobbing as her vacant eyes stared back at Brielle with only the faintest of recognition.

Sienna's hand gripped Brielle's. "We have to go."

Brielle didn't breathe again until they disappeared back into the shadows.

The cathedral was hundreds of years old, no doubt built by the hands of her forefathers, or at least under their instruction and funded by their coin. Now her ancestors rested beneath it. Brielle had attended this church every year of her life, had been baptized in its holy waters, would be married underneath its marbled archway, but she had never once been down the steep winding staircase to the crypt below.

When the bishop had led them here, she had been horrified. She had demanded their best room, preferably their best two rooms, but the bishop had blustered that the order of the brotherhood could not be defiled by the presence of women. Not even their Queen. Sienna had reasoned that the fewer people who knew they were here, the safer they would be. The custom of honoring sanctuary for those on holy ground had been in place for generations, but some soldiers had been known to violate it. So Brielle had reluctantly descended the stairs into darkness.

The air down here was thin. The oil from the lamps filled the tomb with a foul odor and lined her nostrils with grease. Dozens of crypts rested on the ground in neat rows, the likeness of kings and queens carved into the stone. And it was quiet. So very quiet. As if no world existed outside. As if everyone else was dead.

They had been down here for three days now, sitting in the dirt amongst the dead, waiting. Every few hours Sienna climbed the narrow stone stairs to speak to the bishop and ask for news. The first time she went, Brielle had given her a list of things to return with. New clothes to replace her filthy nightgown, hot water to bathe in, cold water to drink, food, rugs to spread across the dusty floor, blankets, a bed so she could rest comfortably, some playing cards, perhaps, for entertainment—she was terribly bored. Sienna had returned with nothing, the ruby ring on her finger noticeably absent.

Brielle was enraged. Her father's generosity had kept the church fantastically wealthy. The bishops in particular had been well cared for, and this was how they treated their queen?

The next time, Sienna returned with water and a small package of food; bread, some cheese, and fruits. That was it. They had consumed it with a ravenous fever, even though the bread was not fresh or warm, and the fruit was bruised and sour.

Since then, her thoughts had been consumed with all the ways she would make them pay when she returned to her throne. She would strip the church of its wealth and send the bishops to some far away monastery for the rest of their miserable lives. But first she would take a bath. And eat real food. And snort a bushel of herbs to remove the smell of grease that she feared was permanently lodged in her nostrils.

The sound of Sienna's steps on the stairs had Brielle launching to her feet.

"Well?" she snapped as her friend appeared.

"King Heroux's men are in the city," she replied, somewhat breathless from the small flight of stairs.

"They have taken the castle?"

"They did not need to." Sienna winced. "The councilmen welcomed them."

"Traitors!"

Part of her did not want to believe it. The very thought made her stomach turn to acid at her father's memory. Her father had made these men great, lavished them with wealth and property, praised them for their intelligence and loyalty, and they had not even raised a banner to defend his kingdom. His legacy. Her birthright.

"But I do have good news. We make our escape tonight."

"Escape? Escape to where?"

"Outside the city." Sienna passed her a small package, presumably of food. "From there, I am not sure."

Brielle unwrapped the cloth as they both sat in the dirt. She longed to wash her hands—in fact, she longed to wash her entire body—but there was limited water and she had learned that it was better to save it for drinking as there was no guarantee when they would be offered more.

"How?" she asked warily, passing some bread to her friend.

They both tore into it, gobbling it down like savages. She wasn't sure how much longer she could live like this. She needed a hot meal: rich meats soaked in gravy, buttered herb potatoes, snappy green beans. Her mouth watered even as she filled it with stale dough.

"There is a door," Sienna replied after swallowing, "further down the catacomb that leads out onto the river. A boat will be waiting for us there at midnight."

"Who will be waiting for us?"

"Lord Jameson."

"Lord Jameson! What happened to trust no one?"

Sienna stiffened. "I trust him with my life."

"Obviously. With mine as well."

There was no choice, she realized. The alternative was to stay here, buried in a tomb where they would surely die of starvation. Or boredom. Or worse, be dragged out by King Heroux's men and publicly executed. Perhaps they would not even bother with ceremony and would simply cut their throats on the steps of the cathedral.

The hours passed slowly, but eventually midnight came. Sienna led them deeper into the catacombs, and just as she'd been told, there was a door. She jerked the rusted lock back and shoved the door open. A small block of concrete allowed them to step one foot outside before it fell away to the water, where a boat was waiting. The figure in the boat pushed back his hood, and they both sighed with audible relief.

Lord Jameson steadied himself to stand in the boat before reaching a hand out to Sienna. He helped her step down into it, and they caught each other in a fierce embrace. The boat was small, only large enough to seat four people, but it would do. He helped Sienna to her seat and reached back for Brielle. She stumbled into the boat and took a seat beside her friend. Lord Jameson pulled his hood back up, resumed his seat, and took up the oars.

Their pace was slow as he rowed them out into the middle of the lake. The night was cold, but mercifully there was no wind to add to the chill. The sound of the oars slapping against the water filled her ears like a steady heartbeat. Lake Evren ran parallel to the city and could be seen from the castle gates. They would be visible to the guards, but there was no reason to suspect that they were anything more than poor fishermen or perhaps a small passenger ferry. At least she hoped so.

No one said a word. They hardly dared to breathe as the boat moved steadily along the water. Brielle looked out at the city. Her kingdom. Did her people mourn their fallen king? Did they whisper of their missing princess and pray for her safety? Or had they also welcomed King Heroux with open arms?

She had only ever visited the city during times of celebration. Festival days mostly, when she would parade through the town square on her snow-white horse, never joining the people or meeting them, but displaying her beauty for all to admire. The people were always overjoyed to see her. They cheered, they threw flowers, they lifted their children onto their shoulders for a better view. It was hard to think of those same people cheering for a man who had slaughtered their king.

It was strange to see the castle like this. She had never seen it at night, quiet and shrouded in darkness, as if it were sleeping. It felt like she was dreaming. She thought she saw a flutter of white as something fell from a window in the high tower, but her eyes were misty with tears and the darkness was probably playing tricks on her. Brielle turned away and wiped her damp cheek with the heel of her hand.

Sienna suddenly lurched forward and threw up over the side of the boat.

"Sienna." Lord Jameson stilled the oars and leaned forward, rubbing circles into her back.

"I'm fine. Just a little sea-sick," she managed before hurling her guts again.

"Sea-sick? We're hardly moving," Brielle admonished, but she felt slightly nauseous too. Had felt sick and uneasy and scared and angry and tired and hungry for days.

After an hour, the lights of the city had almost disappeared in the distance behind them. They sailed along the river with only the moon to guide them, but no one removed their hood or spoke a word, so Brielle remained solemnly silent. Even her thoughts quieted. In truth, she was just relieved to breathe fresh air again, though the smell of the oil lamps was still slick on her skin.

In the hours before dawn, Lord Jameson rowed for shore. He stepped out onto a narrow wooden pier that looked as if no one had used it in years. Reaching back for Sienna, he lifted her out of the boat. They both walked ahead to the edge of the bank, talking together in shallow whispers.

"Lord Jameson." Brielle tried to stand, bracing herself against both sides of the boat. It rocked perilously beneath her. "A hand," she called out.

It looked like they were arguing now, though their voices were still too faint to hear. Brielle surveyed their surroundings. Thick oak trees lined the riverbank and two horses stood saddled and ready nearby.

Two.

She reached out to grip the pier and winced as splinters pierced her fingers. Pulling the boat closer, she managed to grasp the pier with both hands before hauling herself up, quite without grace or dignity, onto the wooden planks. She crawled for a moment on her hands and knees before standing up on stiff legs, her temper flaring.

"Lord Jameson," she commanded, and they both turned to take in the sight of her fury as she approached. "What kind of escape is this? Why have you only two horses?"

Sienna exchanged a nervous look with Lord Jameson.

Before she could get a word in, Brielle said, "Never mind, you two can ride together. We need to get to Clontarf."

She stalked off in the direction of the horses. She yanked the reins free of their tether before her eyes widened in horror. "Where is the side saddle?"

"What is in Clontarf?" Sienna asked as she came up behind her.

"A tavern."

"Why do we need to go to a tavern in Clontarf?" Lord Jameson begrudgingly grabbed the reins of the other horse.

"I have a plan. Clearly, you do not. You cannot even be trusted to get three horses. So you will take us to Clontarf and I will not answer any questions until you do. Now help me into this saddle."

She had never ridden a horse with one leg on either side before. The very idea was unthinkable, but she would do it. To reclaim her kingdom, she would do it.

Sienna exchanged another look with Lord Jameson before he took a knee before his queen.

They had been traveling for less than an hour, but it felt like an eternity. Brielle was not used to the feel of a saddle between her thighs, the relentless rocking of a horse beneath her. Her back ached from sitting rod straight and the muscles in her legs throbbed. She was a skilled rider, as all royals were, but she had never ridden a horse on a long journey before. When she rode her snow-white mare, it was always for short periods of time and for the sake of public appearances.

Shifting her attention to focus ahead rather than on her myriad of discomfort, her eyes widened in horror at the woodland looming in front of them. Brielle yanked on the reins, pulling her horse to a firm halt.

"Where do you think you are leading us?" she demanded.

"We need to stay off the King's Road," Lord Jameson tossed over his shoulder.

Brielle's lips parted in disbelief. "You cannot honestly mean to take us into the Red Wood?"

The Red Wood stretched for miles across both the Northern and Southern Kingdoms, but no one ever entered it. It was cursed. Rumored to be filled with vengeful spirits, lost souls and blood magic. Everyone knew the stories, each one telling a dark, terrible tale. Those desperate enough to chance entering the wood had never come out again.

"We have no choice." Lord Jameson turned his horse around to face her. "King Heroux has taken the Northern Kingdom and sent his men to claim the Southern Kingdom. He has effectively taken the entire continent in one battle.

Every road, every town in both kingdoms, is now occupied by King Heroux's men. And you are a traitor to the Crown with a bounty on your head. We cannot afford to be seen."

Brielle's gaze flicked to Sienna who stared back at her with fear. She didn't know if her friend's fear was due to the threat of King Heroux or the prospect of entering the Red Wood. Either way, Sienna remained silent. Her arms tightened around Lord Jameson's waist as if it brought her some measure of comfort.

"But no one goes into the Red Wood," Brielle protested weakly.

"They are only stories. Told to children to keep them out of the woods and minding their manners. Besides, we won't go too far in. Just far enough not to be seen from the road."

Lord Jameson resumed leading the way. She had heard many stories of the Red Wood throughout her life, and none had been told in jest or as a light warning to wayward children. The stories were enough to keep even the bravest of men out of the woods.

Reluctantly, Brielle spurred her horse onwards. She couldn't believe she had been forced to spend several nights in a crypt with the dead and now she had no choice but to enter the Red Wood. King Heroux would pay dearly for making her endure this.

As they crossed the threshold into the woodland, Brielle's eyes scanned the trees warily. It looked like any other wood; dense with foliage, the palette a mixture of greens and browns. The floor was covered in what looked like a soft, spongy moss and the air smelled clean and fresh and cool. It was unnervingly silent apart from the dried leaves being crushed beneath their horse's hooves. Even so, Brielle thought she could hear—something. A sound as light as the wind rustling through branches or the echo of a breath being released. Like the hum of silence in a crowded room when all eyes were upon her. Brielle glanced around them nervously, feeling a cold shiver snake up her spine. It was as if the trees were whispering to each other as they passed them by. Like they were being lured in by the promise of peaceful serenity, and it was only a matter of time before their surroundings turned dark and sinister.

And they did. Turn dark at least.

When the sun finally descended for the day, Lord Jameson announced they would make camp. He helped Sienna down from their horse before assisting Brielle to dismount from hers. As her feet touched the ground, her legs wobbled beneath her, bowed by sitting astride for hours. She winced as she brushed the dust from her skirts, though that was rather pointless considering the dirt covering her hands. She took several painful, humiliating steps only to lean against a nearby tree. Sienna looked exhausted as well, but she still managed a sweet smile for Lord Jameson.

"I'll go collect firewood," he offered.

"Would you like some help?" Sienna asked.

"No, you rest. I'll be back soon."

Brielle tried not to bristle as she noticed Sienna's eyes following him as he walked off deeper into the woods, as if she would miss his presence beside her. She had been sitting behind him, pressed up against his back all day. Surely she should be sick of his company by now.

"How are we even meant to bathe?" she grumbled.

She could still detect the faint scent of the oil lamps on her skin and now she smelled like leather and horse sweat. She hadn't bathed in days and her skin was becoming itchy.

"Hopefully we will find a river along the way."

Brielle's eyes shot to Sienna in revulsion. "I am not bathing in a river."

"We can't risk staying at an inn."

She ground her teeth in frustration at the indignity of it all.

"At least we are safe," Sienna reminded her.

An owl suddenly cooed loudly and they both shrieked in fright. Brielle searched the trees for the offensive animal, afraid it might swoop down at her.

"Safe in a cursed wood," she muttered.

"It's just a normal wood, Brie." Though Sienna's voice betrayed that she was not so convinced.

Brielle startled as Lord Jameson appeared from the shadows. He was carrying a load of branches and sticks in both arms.

"I'll get a fire going," he said as he settled the pile on the ground and began arranging it.

Moments later, a small fire was crackling, but Brielle still couldn't bring herself to sit down. Her posterior was far too numb. She felt like walking the ache out of her muscles, but she knew how much it would hurt, not to mention how embarrassing it would be, so she continued to hover by the tree.

"Once you erect the tents I should like to eat. I'm rather hungry," Brielle said to Lord Jameson.

In truth, she was starving. They hadn't eaten since leaving sanctuary last night.

Lord Jameson exchanged a nervous glance with Sienna. "We don't have any tents."

"What do you mean we don't have any tents?" Brielle shot back angrily. "What kind of escape plan is this? First, you only bring two horses. Then you don't bring tents. Where are we meant to sleep?"

"The ground." The words almost sounded like a question.

She stared at him, equal parts enraged and dumbfounded. "The ground. Out in the open. Together."

He looked to Sienna who promptly changed the subject. "What do we have for food?"

Lord Jameson strolled over to his saddlebag and retrieved a few small packages wrapped in cloth. He handed them out and Brielle unwrapped hers eagerly to find a small piece of honey cake and some dried fruit.

She narrowed her eyes at him from beneath furrowed brows. "This is it?"

"There are some villages along the way to Clontarf. I will stop in and buy more," Lord Jameson replied. "Though they may not have much food to sell."

"Why not?" Brielle asked tersely.

"There have been poor yields. Every year has been worse than the one before; foul weather, plant diseases, pests. Entire estates have fallen into ruin because of it, the farmers and workers forced to move off the land. Food is scarce in most of the small villages."

Brielle frowned. She was surprised to learn of it. She had not heard anything about poor harvests. Not that she was likely to hear such things at court; the palace always had an abundance of food. Brielle ate her meal begrudgingly, savoring every tiny morsel. It was not enough to satisfy her hunger, but it was more than enough to fuel her desire for revenge.

After finishing her meager supper, she tried to find a patch of ground to lie down on that was soft and free of rocks and twigs and crawling bugs. The fire provided a kindle of warmth, but she was grateful when Sienna laid down beside her, pulling her body in close to hers and letting her head rest on her shoulder. Brielle glanced up at her and saw reassurance in her kind eyes. They would get through this together, they would survive it. Not even the Red Wood could keep her from reclaiming her kingdom.

He watched them from the shadows as they slept beside the pitiful fire. From the moment they entered his wood, he had felt them; the knowledge seizing his senses and alerting him to the potential danger. He and his blood brothers had moved swiftly to get here, for the woodland stretched for long distances across the land and could take weeks to travel the entire length of it. Fortunately, they had not been too far away when the wood warned him of the outsiders.

Once upon a time, the woodland would not have reacted so vigilantly to trespassers, but history had not been kind. Its memory was long, as long as the roots buried deep beneath the soil. It had learned the hard way to be wary of strangers. And these people were indeed strangers.

He did not know yet if they posed a threat to the woodland or not. Most people would never dare enter it, which meant these travelers were desperate, and desperation often created the most dangerous people.

He sensed his blood brother beside him silently pulling the knife from its sheath in preparation. He was right. They could kill them now, be done with it. Stalk over to them on hushed steps and slit their throats. The souls wouldn't even wake. He could leave their bodies to disintegrate into the earth. The insects would happily feast on their flesh until there was nothing left but bones, and eventually their corpses would become wildflowers. The woodland would absorb them just like it had thousands of bodies over time, both friends and enemies.

And yet there was something that made him hesitate. His blood brothers watched him closely in the darkness, waiting for his decision, for the signal to move in and kill them. Perhaps it was the fact that the wood was calm, despite their intrusion, that made him question the decision to spill blood tonight. Perhaps it was that he suspected these people were not ordinary folk. Nor were they the outcasts or outsiders that sometimes sought refuge in the last place anyone would ever want to go.

He would watch them, he decided. Perhaps they would leave the woods in a day or two. Which was a risk in and of itself; letting trespassers live to tell the tale of their forbidden night in the Red Wood. The stories would lose their power if he started being merciful. But even so, he would wait and watch them. Ultimately, the woodland would decide if they lived or died. After the traumas it had endured, the wood had every right to pass judgement on those who entered it.

CHAPTER FOUR

A knock on the door almost sent the inked quill in Henri's hand scratching across the parchment. It had been weeks since he turned up at the back door of the Sodisce and in that time he had managed to stay hidden, but it still startled him whenever anyone knocked on his office door.

"Come in," he called out, since the rhythm of the knock proved it was Fleur.

When she opened the door, she gave him a knowing look before announcing, "You have a visitor."

Ele stepped inside and Henri shot to his feet. He was equal parts relieved to see the boy and anxious for the news he brought.

"Master," Ele tipped his head respectfully and Fleur shut the door behind him.

She stood in front of it, arms crossed. It seemed he was not the only one keen for news.

"I delivered the note as you said," Ele began. "The word on the street is that the princess escaped the castle."

Henri's shoulders sagged in relief. He wasn't sure whether Brielle would heed his warning or not. It was why he had sent the note to Sienna, knowing she would read it and urge Brielle to take it seriously.

"She has likely taken a boat across the sea," he speculated aloud. "She would have distant relatives somewhere."

"What other news?" Fleur prompted.

Ele hesitated and the tension returned to Henri's body.

Nathaniel.

"He is dead, then?" His heart seized in his chest.

"No master. Lord Nathaniel is alive. He returned to court shortly after the battle."

Henri sat down before his legs could give way beneath him and drew in a deep, calming breath. It was a miracle. He had not thought it possible that his friend would survive the slaughter, but a small part of him had clung to a fool's hope.

"How did he survive?" The suspicion in Fleur's tone caught Henri's attention.

Ele fidgeted nervously. "They say his father, the commander, betrayed the king."

"What?" Henri sputtered.

"They say Lord Nathaniel knew of the betrayal."

Henri sat in stunned silence. It couldn't be true. His mind replayed the events of that day, dissecting them like the remains of a carcass. The commander was the only other person in the king's tent that day. The commander's scout had been the one to report that King Heroux's army was six days away when, in fact, it had been waiting just over the hill. Henri had assumed an assassin had found his way into the king's tent, but the truth had been far simpler, far worse.

How long had the commander been in alliance with King Heroux? His motives were plain enough: more money, more land, more power and influence. The king had kept tight control over his kingdom, leaving scraps for a favored few to live off. The commander had been one of those favored few. Evidently, it had not been enough.

Nathaniel had known about his father's betrayal, and that pain was worse. The realization gutted him like a fish. It had been fortuitous that Henri had stormed out of the tent that day, but it was not concern for his friend that had made Nathaniel follow him. Henri remembered it all so differently now. The way his friend had offered him wine, poisoned perhaps, or in an effort to get him drunk so he could slit his throat without resistance. The way Nathaniel's hand flew to his sword when Ele had burst into the tent. He would have needed to kill the boy, of course. He could not afford any witnesses to his betrayal.

But the rest of it did not make sense. Nathaniel had stopped him from running into the tent where the commander's blade was carving up the bowels of kings. He had stopped him. And told him to run.

Henri ran a hand over his stubbled chin as his mind churned over the consequences of this bitter truth. Nathaniel knew about the Sodisce. He had helped Henri to purchase it in secret. He would know that Henri would likely seek refuge here, if only temporarily. Yet Nathaniel had not informed his father or his new king. If he wanted power and influence, all he had to do was reveal Henri's secret.

"What will you do?" Fleur asked.

Because he should do something. He should want revenge for such a betrayal. He should want to avenge his father's death and reclaim what had been stolen from him.

Henri's attention landed on Ele and then slid to Fleur behind him. "Nothing."

Nathaniel's betrayal ripped his heart out, but it didn't change anything. His father was dead, his kingdom conquered, and he had started a new life for himself. A life that he had only ever lived in stolen private moments. He could be happy here, running this business, leaving his old life behind. He had never wanted to be king. Fate, it seemed, had a sense of irony.

Clontarf was apparently on the other side of the world. Or at least it felt like that after several weeks of traveling. Brielle had hardly slept that first night in the Red Wood. Not only was the ground beneath her hard and uncomfortable, but the sounds echoing through the trees kept her from drifting off to sleep. She startled with every rustle of leaves, every shadow that seemed to shift in the moonlight. Lord Jameson had assured her that no wild creatures roamed the wood, but she was almost certain he was lying. She felt something. A presence. A knowing.

Whenever they came close to a village or a farmhouse, Brielle and Sienna would remain hidden in the Red Wood while Lord Jameson went to purchase supplies. They were always painfully low on food and water. At least it felt that way to Brielle as she was used to having both on hand whenever she felt like them. They ate two meals a day: porridge in the morning, and bread and cheese for dinner. If they were lucky, they could buy dried strips of meat or root vegetables. She had never eaten a potato whole before. Just a potato. No butter, no salt, no pepper, no seasoned herbs. Just plain, crumbly starch. The food filled her stomach, but she was still hungry; hungry for flavor and heady aromas and the satisfaction of a delicious meal.

In addition to the lack of food, their traveling pace was also frustratingly slow. Not only because they were navigating through dense woodland, but also because it was unbearable to be stuck in the saddle for hours on end. Her backside had become permanently numb, the skin of the insides of her thighs had been rubbed raw, and her back muscles were as stiff as the trees she passed. She could hardly walk. Or lie down. And she certainly could not sit.

Sienna had to be feeling the same unrelenting torture, but somehow she endured it without complaint. Sometimes she would fall asleep, slumped forward against Lord Jameson's back as they rode together through the wood, her arms entwined around his waist. His hand would rest on her interlaced fingers, as if he needed to be assured that she was still with him. Brielle tried not to notice, tried not to feel the sting of jealousy, but she did. She felt it every time he helped Sienna down from their horse, his hands firm but gentle around her waist. She felt it whenever he glanced over at her in the dark as they lay in front of the campfire to sleep.

"A town," Sienna called out, stretching her neck to peer over Lord Jameson's shoulder.

"Clontarf," Lord Jameson replied.

Brielle slouched in relief. Tonight she would sleep in a bed and eat real food and drink wine and have a bath.

Lord Jameson looked over at her. "Now will you tell us who we are to meet at the tavern?"

"A friend."

Trust no one seemed to be her new motto in life.

"I'll need more than that if I'm going to find them."

"I'll find them."

Jameson's features tightened in concern. "You're both staying here. We can't risk you being seen."

"We are in the Northern Kingdom. I have never been to the Northern Kingdom. No one will recognize me."

In truth, they were only in the Northern Kingdom by a few miles, quite near the border between kingdoms, but still.

"We can't risk it."

Brielle kicked her heels and her horse lurched forward, surging into a swift gallop as if it was sick of the snail's pace of the past few days and was dying to run the stiffness from its legs. She could hear Lord Jameson yelling at her as she dashed out onto the dirt road, racing for the town. It was exhilarating. She was finally breaking free of that horrid wood and barreling toward civilization.

She only slowed to a canter as she approached the gates. Sitting high in the saddle, her back straight, she rode past the guards. They eyed her disheveled appearance, her ragged attire and destroyed slippers, but they did not stop her.

The town was bustling with activity. It felt odd to be surrounded by people again after spending weeks in limited company, even if the people were only commoners. She had never been to a town outside her city before. The sights and smells and sounds were overwhelming. Especially the smells. Brielle lifted her delicate fingers to her nose, but that did nothing to prevent her from breathing them in. A combination of animal manure, unwashed bodies, sweat, and rotten food. Nevertheless, it was exciting. A welcome change from the monotonous solitude of the Red Wood.

"Brielle," Lord Jameson hissed from behind.

She turned in the saddle, her expression incredulous. "How dare you address me so informally!"

He grabbed the reins of her horse and jerked it closer to his. "No titles while we're here, just names."

She opened her mouth to protest but Sienna shot her a loaded look.

"We don't want to draw any more attention to ourselves than you already have."

She closed her mouth sullenly and let him lead her horse alongside his own as they made their way through the crowded streets.

He exhaled a long-suffering sigh. "What is the name of this tavern we're looking for?"

"The Sodisce."

It did not take long to find it. They had dismounted their horses, paid for their keep in a nearby stable, and were now standing across the street from a three-story stone building. It was adorned with bright paper lanterns, and a distinct sign hung atop the door with the picture of a dancing lady. The sun was already sinking in the sky and patrons were pouring in.

"I don't think that's a tavern." Sienna frowned.

Brielle ignored her and made to cross the road, but Lord Jameson—just Jameson—stepped in her path.

"You can't go in there."

"Yes, I can."

"They won't let you in."

"I know the owner." She swiftly stepped around him and crossed the road before he could stop her from bursting through the doors.

Inside was like nothing she had ever seen before. The room was expansive, with plush lounges and mahogany tables peppered across the polished wooden floor. Heavy curtains hung from the ceiling, dyed a dark shade of red. More curtains closed off smaller spaces at the edges of the hall and framed the stage at the very end, upon which several scantily dressed women danced. The room was packed with patrons, in some corners shoulder to shoulder, drinking and laughing and gambling and groping. Brielle frowned at the sight, but then again, these people were commoners. Their morals were not the morals of nobles.

The air was filled with the sickly scent of sweet perfume, stale liquor, and something else she did not recognize. The whole place was an assault on the senses, a feast for the eyes, like a fantastical dream. Yet something about it felt inherently dangerous. The feeling crept up her spine like a spider, setting the hairs on the back of her neck on end.

"Good evening, sir."

Brielle blinked at the woman who suddenly appeared in front of her. She was addressing Jameson, who Brielle hadn't noticed was standing beside her. Sienna stood at his side, her mouth slightly parted in awe as she took in her surroundings.

"I'm afraid your lady friends will have to wait outside."

The woman was in her forties perhaps, but her face was still reasonably attractive. Her auburn hair was twisted up into an intricate design of curls, and around her neck was an impressive set of jewels. Fake, Brielle thought. They had to be. The woman's dress was positively scandalous, the neckline so low it was a miracle her breasts did not fall out. And her accent was strange, foreign and guttural.

"My apologies, madame," Jameson offered somewhat awkwardly. "My friends and I wish to meet with the owner of this fine establishment."

"Master Delphine?" the woman asked, eyeing them carefully.

"Henri," Brielle corrected her.

The woman locked eyes on her, calculating, until she finally said, "I know no one by that name and the owner is not here tonight. You may come back tomorrow if you wish."

Brielle snatched her arm in a vise grip. "I have traveled for weeks on horseback, slept in the dirt, bathed in disgusting rivers, and been feasted on by hundreds of tiny insects. If I were you, I would not underestimate my wrath!"

"Get your hand off me." The woman tried to jerk her arm back, but Brielle only dug her nails in deeper.

"Henri!" Brielle shouted.

Several men appeared from nowhere, and Sienna shrieked as they seized her. Jameson punched one in the face as Brielle called out again before suddenly, he was there. Henri's eyes were wild. He looked older than Brielle remembered. His hair was styled differently and his jaw was lined with stubble. He looked rugged instead of polished, the boyish looks replaced by those of a man.

"Henri," Brielle breathed.

"Not here," he ordered as he ushered them through the crowd to disappear behind a heavy curtain and into a small room.

The room was simply furnished with a desk and a few chairs. Behind the desk was a low-lying latticework cabinet, a tray of decanted liquors displayed on top. A boy was perched on the corner of the desk, assessing them all with keen eyes. The woman with the protruding bosoms walked over to stand beside him.

Henri rounded on Brielle, his tone furious. "What the hell are you doing here?"

She blinked dumbly. "Looking for you."

"I told you to get to safety. That meant flee the continent. Don't you have some distant relatives across the sea?"

"And leave my kingdom to my enemy? Never!"

She frowned as his lips parted in aggravated astonishment.

"I thought you would be happy to see me." She hated that her voice wavered slightly.

"Well, I'm not." He turned from her and flipped his coat up to rest his hands on his hips.

Brielle stood in silence, equal parts confused and angry. She didn't know why he was so furious. He was acting as if he hadn't expected her at all.

"You own this establishment?" Jameson asked tentatively.

Henri turned to him, his eyes blazing. "Who are you?"

"My apologies, Lord Jameson." He fumbled forward slightly, unsure whether to bow or not.

Henri simply thrust out his hand. "Henri."

"Jameson," he said as he shook it.

Brielle's mouth fell open. He was acting like a common merchant.

"Well, this has been a reunion I would rather forget," she said bitterly. "We can discuss your plan for reclaiming our kingdoms tomorrow." Brielle pivoted to the middle-aged woman standing beside the boy. "Have someone prepare rooms for me and my companions. We will need hot water for baths, and the best food and wine you have. We will also need clean clothes."

"This is not a boarding house, my lady," the woman protested.

"No, it is a tavern and taverns have rooms."

This might have been her first night in a city, but she was not a simpleton.

"This is not a tavern," the woman said, her tone murderous.

"Then what is it?"

"A gentleman's club," Sienna interjected as the woman replied, "A whore-house."

Henri paced the length of his office, which was difficult given how small the room was. He was beyond furious. He had hoped Brielle would be smart enough to board the next ship to safety.

But she was not smart.

She was shockingly, frustratingly, stupid.

"Who was that, then?"

The steely look on Fleur's face told him she already knew but wanted him to confirm it out loud.

"The Southern Princess."

He rubbed his stubbled chin in thought and resumed pacing.

"She shouted your name so loud it will be a miracle if you are not discovered by sun's rise."

He knew it. For weeks, he had managed to stay hidden, overseeing the business but not taking any unnecessary risks. He didn't have to. Fleur ran the business well enough without him. Tonight, though, his name had been shouted to the rafters. And he'd been seen. There was no telling who was in his establishment tonight. Soldiers, definitely. Bounty hunters, perhaps. Men desperate enough to sell their own kin for coin, certainly.

"Ele." He turned to the boy perched on the edge of the table.

The boy's serious expression told him he had been patiently waiting to be assigned a task.

"Send your friends to the streets to listen for any word of soldiers coming here."

Ele tipped his chin and scampered out.

"Tell the girls to do the same," Henri instructed Fleur. "Pillows talk."

Fleur nodded, the lines around her eyes deepening with concern. Her arms were crossed firmly in front of her chest, but he reached for her hand anyway.

"It'll be all right. No matter what happens, everything will be all right."

"I'm not worried about myself."

He gave her a knowing smile. "Harboring a fugitive of the Crown is no small thing."

"No one here would ever betray you," she insisted fiercely. "They can torture me if they want to. I would never give those bastards anything."

"It won't come to that. You will deny any knowledge of who I am, and you will take the money and keep this place running, just as you always have."

She averted her gaze but nodded once in acceptance, the movement tight.

"Have a man guard their doors. I don't want anyone wandering into their rooms by mistake."

⌁

The wooden bathtub was narrow and short, so much so that she could only just sit in it, but the water was luxuriously hot. Brielle squeezed a washcloth between her shoulders, savoring the feeling of the water running down her back. Sienna was scrubbing days of travel out of Brielle's hair and combing it out over the side of the tub.

Back home, her copper bathtub was large enough to disappear in, the sides lined with soft linen sheets, the water scented with rose oil and fresh petals from the royal garden. She would soak for as long as she pleased, having her muscles massaged by her ladies, her nails buffed and polished to perfection. But she had never appreciated it quite as much as this bath.

The only thing that ruined her complete contentment was the sour, churning pit in her stomach. Not from hunger. They had already gorged themselves on food and wine, so much so that Sienna had almost thrown up. No, her stomach was soured with disappointment. She had been holding on to the hope of seeing him again. She thought he would be waiting for her, his note surely a message to come find him. She had imagined him sleepless from worry, desperate for news of her, but he had acted as if he never expected to see her again. As if he did not *want* to see her again. As if he had already forgotten about her.

Henri had told her about the Sodisce in his letters. Not outright, of course, and certainly not that it was a gentleman's club. He had claimed it was a tavern. Nevertheless, in every word she could hear how much he loved the place. He told her how he had visited it several times throughout his travels and admired it for what it was; a place of pure escape, he said. The one place where he felt most like himself. The way he spoke about it prompted her to remind him that he was not a man without means, and if he wanted something, he could simply buy it. Weeks later, Nathaniel helped him purchase the Sodisce in secret and he had been managing the place ever since.

It had made sense to her at the time; it was a tavern and Henri enjoyed a good party. But now she had a sinking feeling that there was more to it. He had become a businessman. A man who owned something, who built something. Something his father did not know about and could not take away from him. But now that his father was dead, he would need to give this place up and fight for his destiny; to become King of the North.

"Why do the men here get to be called gentlemen when the women are called whores?" Brielle griped.

"It's a brothel, Brie," Sienna said, as if that explained anything. She pulled a wooden comb steadily through her hair as she added, "Though I suppose the same could be said for life in general."

A brothel. Who could have predicted that she would ever set foot inside a brothel, let alone sleep in one?

"I cannot believe the Prince of the North owns a brothel," Sienna remarked, coming around the tub to sit on a stool in front of her. A towel rested in her hands for when Brielle was ready to come out of the water. "And I can't believe he told you about this place."

"We used to tell each other everything," she said softly.

They would write to each other about the latest news from their kingdoms, her endless suitors, his travels, and they would flirt with each other because it was fun and harmless. She recognized his loneliness as if she were looking into a mirror. But now she did not recognize him at all. Gone was the arrogant swagger, the careless attitude, the seductive smile. He had grown older and serious. And apparently couldn't care less about her.

Brielle stood suddenly, the water running down her body in tiny rivers. She stepped out of the tub into the waiting towel that Sienna was holding out for her. Sienna was yet to bathe. They would share the water, apparently.

"He has been through a lot, Brie," Sienna said gently. "His father was murdered, his kingdom stolen from him."

"So was mine," she shot back angrily.

"I know. All I am saying is that these things change a person."

"I am not so changed."

Despite her words, she did feel like a different person, but only because she had been forced to live like a peasant for the past few weeks. She had not changed at her core.

"He is still your friend. We would not be here if he wasn't."

"I'm tired," Brielle said, dismissing the conversation.

She pulled on a clean nightdress, courtesy of the voluptuous madame, and crawled into the bed with a sigh, letting Sienna wash and dress in peace. The bed was small, the mattress lumpy, and the sheets thin, but it was a bed. After sleeping on the hard ground for weeks, she would have accepted a bed of straw.

Brielle welcomed the heat of Sienna's body when she slipped in beside her. Silence fell over them like a warm blanket. Sienna had changed as well, Brielle thought. Not completely. She was still the friend Brielle had known and loved since childhood, but something about her had changed.

"You love him, don't you?" Brielle asked after a few moments, her words barely a whisper.

"Yes."

Brielle inhaled a deep breath.

Moans started echoing through the wall, followed swiftly by the banging of a headboard. Brielle lifted her cheek from the pillow, narrowing her eyes at the wall behind them. She slammed her palm against it several times and ordered them to be quiet. Honestly, people could be so inconsiderate.

⬥⬥⬥

Henri leaned back in his chair, an ankle crossed over a knee, the top two buttons of his white shirt undone. He had hardly slept last night, and the fog of fatigue was starting to roll in. Brielle, on the other hand, looked transformed. She was not primped to the extent of refined royal elegance, but she had bathed and washed her hair and was no longer carrying a stench.

Her eyes were hard as they fixed on him across the desk. It reminded him of the day they met. Both of them recognizing something in the other, neither of them wanting to be the one to look away first. Though his small office was cramped with company, no one dared break the silence between them.

"Where is your friend?" Brielle finally asked, her tone laced with poisoned sweetness.

"Who?"

"Lord Nathaniel."

"Back at court." Henri tried to keep the bite from his voice.

"This is your new friend, then?" Brielle raised a mocking eyebrow at Ele. "Is he not a bit young to be your drinking companion?"

Henri ignored the provocation. She was angry at him and trying to rile him. Brielle pulled at the fabric of her dress, the material obviously chafing against her skin.

"Is something wrong with the dress?" Fleur asked tightly, her watchful eyes never missing a thing.

The dress was plain wool, dyed gray, with long sleeves and a neat tie at the back. It was the simple dress of a kitchen maid. It did not suit her.

"I can fetch you one that the girls wear if you like," Fleur said a little too sweetly.

Brielle's eyes widened at the implication before she glared at her. "Leave."

"Brielle." His tone was a warning.

"And take the boy with you. We need to speak in private."

"Anything you want to say can be said in front of them," Henri countered.

"It's fine, we'll go." Fleur gestured for Ele to join her.

The boy slid off the side of the desk, and Henri gave Fleur an imperceptible nod as they left. Brielle watched them go before sliding her gaze back to him. Sitting up straighter, she clasped her hands in her lap, evidently resolved to stop pulling at her clothes. Even if it killed her.

"So, let's hear it."

"Hear what?"

"Your grand plan to reclaim our kingdoms."

"I don't have one."

Her expression darkened. "What? You've had weeks to think about it. What have you been doing this whole time?"

He lifted both arms out. "Running a business."

"Do not play games with me."

"This is not a game. It is my life now, my livelihood. Everything I have, everything I care about."

She scoffed. "You cannot be serious. A born prince content to spend the rest of his life managing a brothel? I knew you were depraved, but I did not know you were simple."

He stared back at her, unmoved.

She cocked her head to the side. "Or are you a coward?"

"I do not want my father's kingdom, I never have."

"Well, I want mine!"

The words felt like a slap. As if he were to blame for taking it away from her.

"Brielle," he said gently, "it's over. You have no army. No allies."

"Then I will buy one."

"With what?"

"With this." Sienna stepped forward and retrieved a string purse from inside her cloak, emptying its contents out onto the table.

Brielle's breath hitched, her eyes wide with surprise. "You took my jewels?"

"I thought you would have need of them."

Henri studied the haul, running his fingers over each piece. Diamonds. Emeralds. Rubies. Gold.

"You could buy an army with this," he agreed. "Mercenaries. But they will need someone to lead them, to keep them in line."

"I will," Brielle replied.

"You don't know the first thing about war."

"I do not need to. I have an army and I have an enemy."

"You'll be dead before you even reach your enemy. Your army will turn on you."

"Then help me," she demanded.

She was desperate, all talk and false bravado. He felt for her. He knew what it was like to lose everything. To somehow reforge himself and rebuild his life. It was why he would not risk losing what he had.

He pushed the jewels across the table. "I'm sorry."

She scoffed again, her face incredulous.

"I can organize safe passage for you across the sea, but that's the best I can do."

"You are a coward. You're just going to give up?"

"I'm going to let go," he returned coldly. "I made a choice. To live. To build a life for myself. And not just for myself. I am responsible for the lives of everyone who works here."

Fleur, the girls, his men, Ele; they had all been born on the streets, poor, abused, neglected and yet they had accepted him. Shown him kindness, trusted his vision for this place, believed in him. They knew who he was; any one of them could have betrayed him, then as well as now, but they hadn't. They were loyal to him because he respected them, took care of them, protected them.

It must have been written all over his face because Brielle's expression fell. "You would choose them over me."

He shook his head slightly. "It's not even a choice."

He watched her heart break as the truth finally settled on her. He had no words of comfort to offer. There was nothing more he could do for her.

"Master." Ele burst into the room, Fleur behind him, her face white as death. "Soldiers are coming."

Henri shot to his feet. "You both know what to do. Ele, bring the horses around just in case."

"What? W-why are soldiers here?" Brielle stammered.

"You led them straight to him," Fleur hissed at her before disappearing behind the curtain.

"What do we do?" Jameson asked.

"The jewels," Henri said urgently and Sienna quickly swept them off the table back into her purse. "There's a panel in the wall there. It opens to a hidden room."

Jameson began feeling the wall for the panel as Henri retrieved his sword from the cabinet, fixing his belt around his waist. Jameson clicked the panel open and ushered the girls inside as Henri yanked open the desk drawers. He concealed a knife in his coat and a dagger in his boot before he slipped behind the panel and clicked it back into place.

Silence filled the hidden space, save for the sound of blood rushing in his ears. The room was dark and musty, like an old wine cellar, but there was a sliver of light between panels that allowed him to peer into his office. Several heartbeats passed before he heard Fleur's voice as she led the soldiers inside.

"I told you, Master Delphine is not here today. He left last night after some trouble broke out with a patron. He didn't say where he was going."

Two of the soldiers spread out across the room, rummaging through drawers, tossing papers to the floor. One of them strolled over to the silver tray on the cabinet, lifted the lid on the decanter, and poured a knuckle of whiskey into a glass. He raised it to his lips and poured it down his throat as if it wasn't the finest whiskey in the land.

At a flick of his wrist, a soldier was bending Fleur over the desk, a knife to her throat. Henri jerked, his muscles tensing, but a hand gripped his shoulder, steadying him. He couldn't see Jameson in the dark, but he didn't have to. He knew the lord had already decided that Fleur was not worth it, but to Henri she was. If it were just him, he would not have hesitated, but it was not just him.

"I'll ask one more time, whore. Where is the prince?"

Fleur spat in his face. The soldier's movement was as clean as a knife slicing an envelope open. Blood spurted from her throat, spraying the desk, the curtain.

Henri's heart fell out of his chest.

"That's how I like my whores," the soldier purred. "Dead."

The other soldier poured another knuckle of whiskey. "Search the premises. Kill whoever you need to. Take whatever you want."

Henri pinched his eyes closed and clenched his jaw, his breaths coming in hard and fast.

He would kill them.

He would kill them all.

A hand tugged his, small and soft. He couldn't see Brielle, but he knew it was her. They were waiting for him, depending on him, to lead them to safety. He grabbed her hand firmly and began moving down the hidden passageway and around a corner until they came to a small door. It opened up into the back of a stable, where Ele was waiting with two saddled horses.

"Why are there only ever two horses?"

Henri ignored Brielle as he furrowed his brows at Ele in a silent question.

"I can serve you better here, master," Ele explained, handing him the reins.

Henri hesitated as Jameson helped Sienna into the saddle before giving Brielle a boost onto the other horse. His instincts were roaring at him not to leave the boy, but there were no more horses and perhaps Ele was right. Fleeing with them did not guarantee the boy's safety. He would have a better chance here.

"Stay hidden until they leave," Henri ordered.

The boy nodded firmly. "I'll take care of it for you."

Henri hauled himself up into the saddle and Brielle's arms locked around his waist as they took off at speed, knowing that the moment they cleared the stable the soldiers would see them. They were right. The soldiers had surrounded the building and were now shouting amongst each other and mounting their horses in pursuit.

The streets of the town were narrow and winding, but Henri knew them well and Jameson seemed to be a decent horse master, able to keep up with him despite the sudden twists and turns. Henri had planned this route the moment he arrived here. It was the most difficult to navigate by horse, but the quickest path to the gates. He only hoped they hadn't closed them.

Henri could hear the soldiers behind them shouting orders and cursing people for getting in the way. He knew that some of them had probably taken another route, trying to cut them off at the pass, but they would be faster. Dust flew as the horses barreled down the laneways and finally broke out into the square.

The gates were still open, merchants passing through with their wagons, the guards barely checking their goods. Henri spurred his horse on, feeling Brielle's arms tighten around his waist as they shot out of the town and onto the road, heading straight for the Red Wood.

CHAPTER FIVE

B rielle clung to Henri, burying her face into his muscled back. She was going to die. Either by falling from this horse at neck-breaking speed or by a soldier plunging a sword into her back. She could hear them shouting, the pounding of their horses so close she could almost smell their sweat. She cringed as they shot into the Red Wood, leaping over a fallen tree, tossing up soil as they banked a hard right. This damn wood. She could not believe she was back here.

The sound of scraping steel stole her attention as Henri unsheathed his sword. The wood was slowing them down, she realized. Dodging trees and sliding on uneven ground was bringing the soldiers closer. Part of her was surprised they had dared to follow them into the Red Wood, but of course the prize was too great to lose. The true heirs of the North and South presented to King Heroux for public execution would instantly amount to wealth and reputation.

They kept going, barreling deeper into the wood, which seemed to be un-naturally aware of their presence. The wood had gone silent. Still. The air was noticeably colder under the canopy of trees. And the soldiers—after a moment she could no longer hear them.

"Stop!" She tugged on Henri's waist and he slowed their horse, turning to look behind them.

Jameson stopped as well and looked to them in question, his chest heaving with exertion. Sienna's face was pale as she gripped her hands around his waist.

"I can't hear the soldiers anymore," Brielle said as her eyes searched the trees.

As if in answer, a thin mist rose in the distance from where they came, shrouding the trees and blanketing the rocks. A mournful cry echoed around them. An animalistic sound. Almost like the howl of a wolf, but softer, more tortured. Like a wounded ghost.

"We keep going," Henri ordered, and spurred his horse.

The deeper they went, the more the woodland changed around them. The trees became narrow and malformed, their bases stretched out along the ground, their trunks curving into a half-moon shape and then shooting up only to curve the other way, as if someone had twisted them. A thick green vegetation carpeted the woodland floor, not grass, almost like moss but denser. It seemed to glitter in the spots where sunlight touched it.

"Henri," Jameson called out as he tried to steer his horse to curb Henri's. Both horses jerked and whinnied, skittish in these eerie surroundings. "I think we have gone far enough. These woods are cursed."

"We can't go back."

"You are pushing the limits of my hospitality," said a lilting male voice.

Jameson's horse reared at the sight of a stranger ahead of them, and Sienna was thrown to the ground. Brielle screamed in horror as Henri tried to soothe the startled horse beneath them.

"Sienna!" Jameson scrambled down from his horse and rushed to her side.

"Is she all right?" Brielle asked.

Jameson hauled her up, inspecting her head, her neck, her body.

"I-I'm fine," Sienna stammered, pushing herself into a seated position.

When Jameson was finally satisfied nothing was broken, he whirled around, pulling his sword from its sheath and pointing it directly at the stranger. The man was lounging along the arc of a deformed tree, his leg dangling over the side. Jameson did not make it one step before several men appeared from behind the trees to surround them, their longbows trained on them.

The stranger's lips curled into an amused smile. His copper hair was long and unruly, falling just past his shoulders in waves. Dark stubble lined his mouth and chin, while a hideous white scar ran down his left cheek. His eyes, however, were the most striking blue.

"I allow you to camp in my wood for weeks, uncompensated, when I could have killed you in your sleep, and you draw your sword on me?"

Brielle's lips parted in shock as the horse stirred beneath her. *His* wood. Was he truly claiming that he lived in the Red Wood? With these men? She had never seen any sign of anyone else in these woods. But perhaps that would explain the strange feeling she had felt every day they traveled in the Red Wood. She hadn't mentioned it to the others because she could hardly put it into words. It was different from the feeling of being watched, though clearly this stranger had been watching them. It did not feel like eyes were on her, it was more like a presence. A sentience.

"I think it is time to reassess this situation," the stranger said as he pushed off from the tree.

He was tall, and his skin was darkened from the sun. His clothes appeared to be made of a combination of black cotton and tan leather, fashioned almost like armor with a leather breastplate and pauldrons. A silver amulet hung around his neck.

"We were just leaving." Brielle was surprised to find her voice steady and commanding.

"Is that so? The land beyond my wood will be crawling with the King's Guard. Less the dozen we just killed, of course." He grinned, bearing straight white teeth. "We don't take kindly to trespassers."

"Then let us come to a business arrangement," Henri suggested. "Let us stay for a while in these woods and you will be compensated."

The man clasped his hands behind his back and paced a few steps, considering. "Or I could just kill you."

"If you were going to kill us, you would have done it already." Jameson narrowed his eyes curiously.

The man cocked his head and shrugged. He was playing with them.

"Who are you?" Brielle demanded.

His gaze switched to her, those eyes so intense, like water trapped under ice.

"The Vogel," Henri offered, irritably.

"The what?"

"Vogel. It's a bird," the man explained.

"He's an outlaw, a wanted criminal," Henri said. "They call him the Vogel."

A criminal. Brielle blinked. "And what are your crimes?"

"He's a common thief."

"Thief, yes. Common, no," the man said.

"He robs travelers on the road."

"Only the wealthy ones," he countered.

Brielle studied the man. He did not look like a common thief. He looked strong and cunning. He had seen violence—that much was clear by the scar on his face—and the way he held himself made it seem as if he was confident nothing could ever touch him again.

"So we'll pay you compensation and you'll let us stay." Sienna's voice was hopeful.

She had managed to stand and take a few steps toward Jameson, who was still holding his sword in a defensive stance. The Vogel turned his back on them to consider for a moment. His men did not move, they only awaited his orders, their arrows locked on their quarry. He turned back to them and his eyes pinned Brielle with an assessing stare.

"Answer me one question truthfully and I'll let you stay."

Brielle swallowed hard as her heart tripped over itself.

"Why do the King's Guard want you so badly?"

His tone sounded curious, innocent, but she knew better. Her expression tightened. She was done playing this game.

"You know why."

If he had been watching them for weeks, he had heard every word she'd said; her complaining and lamenting and scheming.

"I am Queen of the Southern Kingdom," she announced, lifting her chin.

His lips slowly unfurled into a cunning smile before he bent into a swift, mocking bow. "I am Citric."

They were blindfolded before Citric's men led them deeper into the Red Wood. The material smelled foul. Brielle did not want to know where it came from.

The wood was silent as they moved through it, save for the occasional call of an animal or trickle of water from a nearby stream. It felt like they had been traveling for hours when they finally stopped.

"You can take the blindfolds off," Citric said.

Brielle yanked the material down from her eyes. In the distance ahead of them was an old stone ruin. She could see that many years ago it had stood several stories high, but now it was mostly rubble, the walls collapsed, the roof missing. The remaining walls and foundation were overgrown with wild vegetation, as if the woodland was reclaiming the land as its own. In front of the ruin stood dozens of large round white tents.

Brielle was so captivated by the sight in front of her she did not notice the others had dismounted their horses and Henri was holding his hands out to assist her. She swung her leg over and braced her hands on his shoulders. She tried not to wince as her feet touched the ground. Everything hurt: her thighs, her back, her neck, her arms. She returned her attention to the sight in front of her. People were milling about, performing various tasks as children played freely amongst the trees. It was a community. In the Red Wood. People actually lived here.

"What is this place?" Brielle breathed, her voice filled with wonder.

"Alkhiem" Citric replied. "City of tents. A refuge for outlaws, outcasts, and outsiders."

"And the ruins?"

She couldn't quite believe it; not only that people lived here now, but also that people had lived here a long time ago.

"It was a grand house once. We are restoring it."

Indeed, she could see men working on the far side of the ruin, wooden scaffolds set against the stone wall.

A sharp gasp drew her attention as Sienna bent forward, clutching her stomach. Jameson rushed to her side and put an arm around her waist to support her. Their heads bent together as she murmured reassurances to him. Perhaps she had hurt herself when she fell from the horse. But as Brielle approached, she noticed both of their hands were resting protectively on her stomach. She stilled, even as her heart stumbled in disbelief.

"You are pregnant."

Sienna's eyes caught hers, panicked and pleading.

Brielle shook her head. "How could you? How could you be so reckless?" She narrowed her eyes at Jameson with lethal focus. "And you! You will marry her," she demanded.

"We are married," he shot back angrily.

"What!"

"Handfast."

"What does that mean?"

"It's a pagan ritual where two people make a solemn oath to each other," Citric interrupted, amusement dancing across his face.

"In front of a priest?"

"No."

Brielle whirled back to Jameson. "Then you are not married."

Sienna opened her mouth to speak, but Brielle cut her off. "How could you be so foolish?"

Jameson stepped in front of Sienna as if to shield her from Brielle's wrath. "We would have married in front of a priest but we needed your permission, and you never would have given it because you never would have let Sienna go until you got married yourself, which never would have happened because you're a spoiled, selfish brat!"

Brielle recoiled, slightly shocked, but her anger rose up fast and hot. "If you think so little of me, then why did you save me?"

Jameson looked at her, stunned. Her stomach hollowed out at the realization. He hadn't saved her. He had only wanted to save Sienna. Two horses. For them to return to court, to his family. To get married and share a life together. That is what they had been arguing about on the riverbank.

Brielle stumbled back a few steps, the taste of betrayal bitter on her tongue. Her closest friend had considered abandoning her. Henri had not come for her or even waited for her. She had been betrayed by the two people she trusted most in this world.

"We have a priest," Citric offered.

⊰≈⊱

Henri kneeled at the entrance of the tent he had been given. Unlike the other white dome tents, which were large enough to house a family, his tent was triangular and only large enough to fit a single bedroll. That was all he had, and it wasn't even his. From sundown to sun's rise, he had gone from being the wealthy owner of a fine establishment to nothing and no one.

Fleur was dead. How many of the others had been murdered? Roused from their beds to be questioned, tortured, and put to the slaughter. He prayed Ele had stayed hidden. The boy was brave, but he was not stupid. He would have waited for the soldiers to leave before searching the Sodisce for survivors. Surely they would not have killed everyone. But even if they lived, how would they survive without him? Without Fleur?

His fist flew to his mouth as he choked on a sob. She had died protecting him. He never thought it would come to that. He had been so very careful. Rage burned through him like wildfire at the memory of Brielle shouting his name to the rafters. Her stupidity, her selfishness, had cost him everything. It had cost Fleur her life.

He ran a shaking hand through his hair and forced himself to take a steadying breath. Of course, it was so easy to blame her, but deep down he knew who was truly at fault. He never should have gone there after fleeing the battlefield, by doing so he had put them all at risk. They were his responsibility, his people to protect, and instead he led the wolves to their door. Fleur was dead because of him.

Henri lifted his eyes to the sky as tears threatened to spill over. He had lost everything. Everything he had ever cared about. He needed a drink. He needed oblivion.

He turned to survey the camp, searching for any sign of what he needed. His attention caught on a few young men playing dice on the head of a wine barrel. He plastered his best courtly smile to his face as he approached them, but even so, the young men shifted warily in his presence.

"Care for another player?"

The young men exchanged glances with each other, but conceded some space for him to join them.

"This would be more fun if it were a drinking game," he suggested cheerfully. "Loser takes a drink. Whiskey, perhaps?"

The young men seemed to consider for a moment before one of them replied, "We don't have any whiskey, but we have a still and make our own brew. I'm not sure what you'd call it, but it's strong."

Henri returned a vacant smile. "The stronger the better."

⚜

Brielle stared at the space she had been given. Once it had been a room in a grand house with four walls and a roof and a hearth. But now it had three crumbling walls, a dirt floor, and the open sky overhead. Part of her was thankful that she did not have to sleep cramped inside a tent, but at least a tent had a roof. And privacy.

A bedroll had been dumped unceremoniously in the corner. That was it. The hearth was filled with soil and leaves. She was going to freeze tonight. She wouldn't even have Sienna's body lying next to her for warmth. Sienna had said nothing after the argument, but she also hadn't resisted when Jameson led her away into the camp. Brielle knew she would stay with him tonight and probably every night after. Married or not, there was no point in pretending anymore.

Pregnant.

She was still reeling from the revelation, along with all the other realizations, but she did not want to think about them anymore. She couldn't. Hot tears sprang to her eyes, but she blinked them away as she stepped back out into the empty expanse of the crumbling ruin.

She did not know where she was walking, only that she did not want to be still. Brielle wandered about the ruin, exploring its beauty and devastation. It had once been majestic, this house. Some of the archways still stood, along with some of the grand pillars. There were stone staircases that no longer led anywhere and hollowed-out windows that had once held glass between their frames. Some of the walls featured colorful murals, which had faded over the years. Sweeping vines now crawled over them, hiding the images from view. Moss filled the cracks.

In some areas, the floor was gone and her feet met dirt and soil, but in other areas it was stone. In one particularly large room, the floor was made up of thousands of tiny tiles, no bigger than the palm of her hand. An intricate pattern seemed to merge into a larger pattern, but she could not quite make it out. The room was too large and some of the tiles were broken or missing.

Brielle wondered who had lived here long ago. Obviously someone wealthy enough to build a grand house, but why choose to build one in the Red Wood? She could not think why anyone would want to live alone in the middle of a woodland, miles from the nearest town, let alone a woodland that was cursed. And what had happened to these people? Had they abandoned their home after realizing their folly? Or had something sinister happened to them?

The tantalizing aroma of meat roasting over a coal fire wafted to her nostrils, and her stomach gave an involuntary growl. Looking up at the sky, she saw that it had changed color to hues of pink and orange as the sun began its descent. She had not realized how long she had been wandering about, but now dusk was here and she was suddenly fiercely hungry. She recalled she hadn't eaten since breakfast.

Brielle made her way out of the ruins and into the camp, following the aroma to an open area where women were tending to several large cauldrons and a boar was being turned on a spit. People were starting to gather there, sitting around weathered wooden tables or felled logs with woven rugs on top to eat their meal. The women were dishing out the food to whoever approached them and there seemed to be a table where people could help themselves to bread and fruit. The food was in abundance.

Brielle hovered for a minute, unsure what the proper protocol was, but her growling stomach urged her forward. She gingerly grabbed a wooden plate and approached one of the women. They served her without question, dishing out vegetables and succulent cuts of meat. She fetched a warm bread roll and searched for a quiet space to sit. Perching herself on a rug that had been placed over a log for comfort, she balanced the plate on her knees and looked around at this strange community. Everyone was talking and laughing amongst each other. No one was paying any attention to her at all.

The food smelled amazing. It took all her willpower to restrain herself from tearing into it like a starving beast. When she finally glanced up from her plate, she noticed Sienna and Jameson sitting on the other side of the fire pit. Empty plates were discarded on the ground at their feet and Sienna was resting her head on Jameson's shoulder, her eyes closed, their arms intertwined.

How had she ever been so blind? She had known they had feelings for each other, perhaps had even shared a stolen kiss or two, but never would she have ever believed they had gone behind her back and made promises to each other. Jameson's accusation echoed in her ears. He was right, of course; if they had approached her and asked permission to marry, she would have denied them without a second thought, and probably would have stewed for a day at their insolence in even asking.

Sienna was *her* friend, the only real friend she had ever had. She had proven that time and time again when she had kept Brielle's secrets and comforted her during times of distress, while the other ladies had only feigned empathy and then savagely ripped her apart behind her back. Sienna was loyal, but she was also just—good. Brielle had never heard Sienna say a bad word about anyone, and while she sometimes chided Brielle when she thought she was being too harsh, Sienna also understood what it was like to be a girl at court. Where civility was a mask to hide envy and hatred, and information was a currency to be sold to the highest bidder. Wealth and beauty were the only forms of protection a girl could have, and even then, sometimes they attracted the worst kinds of predators. Sienna understood and yet she did not let it change her kind heart.

Brielle watched as Jameson pressed his lips to Sienna's hair. He obviously loved her and he was a good man. Perhaps he deserved her. She could not think of any other nobleman who would have risked his life and that of his family's by aiding an enemy of the Crown. Even if he only did so out of deference to the woman he loved.

"Are you in love with her or him?"

Citric's words cut through her thoughts as he sat down beside her.

"What?" She blinked.

"Or do you desire them both? I'm not judging, just curious."

Her mouth fell open, but there were no words.

"Or are you simply lonely? You appear to be losing all your friends."

"I-I am not," she stammered.

He cocked his head and she turned her gaze away from him, infuriated. Her attention caught on the sight of Henri walking along the outskirts of the open area. Before she could think better of it, she stood up and marched over to him. It was only when she got closer that she noticed his gait was unsteady and his cheeks were flushed.

"Where have you been?" She forced her tone to be cheerful, but even she could hear the reprimand in it.

He did not acknowledge her, he just kept stumbling forward.

"There's food. Do you want something to eat?"

His eyes darted around, as if he was disoriented. He was probably looking for his tent.

"Henri."

"Leave me alone."

"You should eat something. I can get a plate for you if you like."

She had never waited on anyone her entire life, but she could feel Citric watching them and if Henri told her to go away again, she would die.

He suddenly turned on her, his face inches away from hers as he snarled, "I don't want anything from you!"

Brielle froze. That was so much worse.

"You couldn't just leave it be, could you? You had to come find me and ruin everything. You couldn't just let it go." He planted his feet in the ground as if he were getting ready to take on an opponent. "Do you even realize what you've done? Do you even care about all the people that died today? For *you*?"

He spat the word as if it were distasteful. As if she were the lowest creature on earth.

She tried to compose herself. "You are drunk."

"Do you even remember her name?"

"Who?"

His eyes turned deadly, and his features tightened with barely restrained wrath.

"I wish it had been you."

The words were like a curse. They sucked the very air from her lungs.

"I wish it had been me," he said softly as he turned away.

Brielle watched him stumble through the city of tents as her heart thundered in her chest and hot, angry tears stung her eyes. She wiped them away before she stalked off, seeking the sanctuary of the ruin, to the single bedroll in a room with three crumbling walls.

⚜

Brielle did not sleep well. She had curled up into a ball, trying to find some kindle of warmth, but it hadn't helped. She had lain there frozen all night, her teeth chattering loudly in her skull. Just before sun's rise she finally managed to fall asleep, but the sounds of the camp soon woke her. Irritated, frozen, and exhausted, she sat up on her bedroll. She was still wearing the same dress as yesterday, the only dress she had. It no longer made her skin itch, but it was beginning to smell like sweat and smoke. She wondered where everyone bathed.

Brielle ran her hands through her tangled hair and smoothed down her skirts before venturing out into the camp. It seemed like everyone had woken hours ago and was already engaged in various duties. The women were gathered near several large oak barrels and wooden tables. The men were nowhere to be seen, save for those who were working to restore the ruin. That had been the hammering sound that had woken her.

Brielle wandered over to the women, hoping Sienna would be among them. She desperately needed to talk to her. She had never gone so long without speaking to her, without having her comforting presence beside her. She was starting to feel the absence of her, as if she had lost a limb. But Sienna was not among the women.

"There's some porridge still left in the pot," an old woman offered, and waved her meaty arm at a large black cauldron sitting on a smoking pile of coals.

Porridge. Again. She had never eaten it in her life before fleeing the castle, but now it felt like she could not escape it. After retrieving a bowl, Brielle helped herself to several scoops of slop before joining the women at one of the long tables.

The women were preparing various fruits and vegetables; cleaning them, peeling them, cutting them, crushing them. The produce looked impressive; large and juicy, skins bright and unblemished. She hadn't seen food like that since she fled the Southern Court. Certainly everywhere Jameson stopped for supplies the food had been scarce, the quality poor.

More women were standing around a large oak barrel, which was big enough to bathe in and full of soapy water. Some plunged garments beneath the surface using a wooden paddle, while some scrubbed the garments against a ribbed wooden frame. They were washing clothes, she realized. Brielle suddenly had an urge to strip off her dress and hand it to them to clean, but she was keenly aware of having nothing else to change into. Behind the women were several lines of rope strung up high between trees. Once the garments were drenched and scrubbed ferociously, the women tossed them over the ropes, letting water drip down to the soil below.

Children played nearby, running in and out of the trees, howling as they chased each other with sticks. The women watched them casually, and every now and then the children would come by the tables to snatch a berry or piece of honeyed bread. Brielle had never seen children play like this before. At court, children were confined to their nurseries under the supervision of their nursemaids and only trotted out on special occasions when they were old enough to behave. She had certainly never been allowed to run about like that. The very sight was strange. The children looked wild but happy.

"When you're done eating, you can help Willow peel the potatoes," the woman called out over her shoulder.

It took Brielle a few moments to comprehend that the words were meant for her. She glanced between the women at the table, who were all watching her expectantly. Did they not know who she was? She assumed that word would have spread around the camp as soon as they arrived, but clearly Citric had ordered his men to keep quiet. She was not sure what that meant. Perhaps he thought someone might betray them, or more concerning still, perhaps he thought they would not be safe if people knew. Whatever the reason, Brielle decided it was probably best not to reveal herself.

"I do not know how to peel a potato," she explained politely, hoping that would put the issue to rest.

"Like this." A girl about her age—Willow, she presumed from the pile of potatoes in front of her—held up a small blade and deftly sliced the skin from the potato. The ribbon of skin fell into a bowl before she placed the potato into another bowl.

"The men use the skins for their still to make brew."

Brielle didn't know what that meant. "I can't do that, I would cut myself."

The women giggled and murmured amongst each other.

"You can help with the washing, then," the old woman persisted, putting an end to the chatter. "There's a spare washboard here."

"I have never washed clothes before."

"Well, now's a good time to learn, then, isn't it?"

Brielle watched the women viciously scrubbing the garments against the wooden board. Their sleeves were rolled up to their elbows and their forearms were gleaming with soapy water. The women were strong and muscular, clearly built for hard labor, whereas she most certainly was not.

"I do not think I'm well suited to that."

"Well suited?" The woman scoffed, and the others burst out into raucous laughter.

Brielle's cheeks burned.

"Now you listen to me. Everyone here works. There are no servants and no masters here, just good folk trying to live as best we can. You want to live here? You want to eat? You've got to earn it."

Brielle narrowed her eyes at the woman. How dare she speak to her like that! Besides, she was paying compensation for staying here. Not that any of these fools would know that.

"Here." A young woman placed two large bowls in front of her, one of them filled to the brim with corn. "You can shuck these."

"Shuck?"

"Peel the husk back," the woman explained, and provided a demonstration before returning to her seat at the opposite end of the table.

Brielle considered her options. The corn seemed like the least offensive one.

"Fine."

She took a corncob from the top of the pile, grabbed the top of the husk, and tried to yank it back. It did not budge. It took a few attempts to figure out how to best pull the husk back. After the first few corn husks, the skin on her palms had turned pink and raw and her arms hurt from the effort. Brielle wanted to get up and abandon the task, but it was clear that if she did, they would never forgive her for it. She did not know how long they would have to stay here, so it was better to try to win these women over. She could do that. She had created one of the most beautiful ladies' courts in all the kingdoms and ruled over it for years. She could win over this haggard lot.

After a while of chatting amongst themselves and then falling into a comfortable working silence, the women began to sing. At first it was just one young girl, her voice clear as a bell, but then others joined in, adding their voices to the chorus. Brielle did not know any of the songs they sang, but everyone else seemed to know them well enough. Some songs were lively and filled with joy, while some were sad and beautiful. Some spoke of trials and battles, some of grief and lost love, others of the land and the harvest and spirits. The woodland seemed to stir as the women sang, as if the trees themselves were listening intently.

It seemed to make the time pass quickly because soon her bowl was empty and the task was done. Brielle felt an odd sense of satisfaction, as if she had proved everyone wrong, but then she was horrified at the sight of her roughened hands and broken nails.

"Would you like to learn how to make bread?" a woman offered from down the end of the table.

The others turned to Brielle expectantly.

She recognized this moment for the opportunity it was. She flexed her fingers. "I'd like to learn how to peel potatoes."

They cheered in approval, and Willow shoved a bowl of potatoes toward her with a grin. It was the last thing Brielle wanted to do, but she knew it would buy her some acceptance. She forced an uneasy smile as Willow handed her a small knife. Brielle watched closely as Willow gave her careful instructions.

"Did you get that from peeling a potato?" Brielle indicated to the nasty red scar across Willow's palm.

"No," Willow replied simply, and returned to her seat.

Brielle began to slowly peel the skin from the flesh of the potato. It did not come off in smooth, neat ribbons like Willow. It was more like deep gouges of flesh, which left the potato looking like it had been violently assaulted.

Brielle was halfway through the bowl when she heard their voices. She turned to see a dozen men striding through the woodland toward the camp, carrying heavy sacks over their shoulders. Some of the women left the table to greet them, but most stayed, content to continue working.

"Where did they go?" Brielle asked, keeping her tone light but curious.

"Raiding travelers," Willow replied. "The rest of the men are tending to the crops, or running the still, or hunting, or out on patrol."

Citric was leading the group, laughing at something the others were saying. He had an easy smile, she observed. His eyes caught hers before she could look away and she saw something flicker across his face. She supposed it surprised him to see her at the table working with the other women. Or perhaps he was surprised to see her making friends.

He veered off from his men and began walking in her direction. Brielle squirmed uncomfortably. No doubt her hair was a tangled mess and she probably had shadows under her eyes from the lack of sleep. Not to mention she smelled like a mixture of old worn clothes, soil, smoke, and sweat. She grimaced inwardly, but there was nothing to be done about it. She was still a queen, she reminded herself, and lifted her chin slightly.

"Looks like you had a good morning," the older woman called out to him as he approached, her face beaming with a wide grin.

"I have something for you, Aelis."

Citric reached into his sack and unfurled a beautiful dress. It was the color of fresh cream with a lilac silk sash and flowers woven into the bodice. Pearl buttons featured at the wrists.

Aelis laughed heartily while the other girls snickered.

"I don't think I'll be attending a ball anytime soon."

"You could wear it for me." The corner of his lips lifted seductively.

"Twenty years ago, perhaps." She chuckled. "There's no way that's fitting me now."

Citric sighed, as if her rejection had wounded him.

"What will you do with it?" The words left Brielle's lips before she could stop them.

He turned to her, his eyes knowing. She wanted the dress. There was no point in hiding it.

"Sell it. Like everything else."

Brielle clenched her jaw. He knew she wanted it and he was not going to let her have it.

"And what do you do with the money? Give it to the poor?" Her tone was mocking.

"I am an outlaw, not a philanthropist."

She returned a sour look.

"I see you are contributing to society for once."

"So you keep the money for yourself, then." She ignored his barb, determined to land a blow of her own.

"The money is used to look after my people. Everything I do is for them. Can you say the same?"

The women were silent as they watched their verbal sparring. She did not want to undo the acceptance she had just worked so hard to win, but she couldn't help herself.

"What makes these people yours? Have you named yourself King of the Red Wood?"

Citric dropped his sack to the ground at his feet. "I am no one's king, nor do I desire to be. These people choose to live here, this way, as I do. We are bound to this land. Our dream is to build a home, to live our lives free of fear and persecution from the Crown."

Brielle did not know how to respond to that.

"What makes your people yours?" he returned fire, his eyes dancing with challenge.

She hesitated a moment, unsure how much to reveal but not wanting to back down from his blatant provocation.

"My name. My birthright."

"Ah." He clasped his hands behind his back and shifted his weight. "You know, some say your family was not the first to rule this land."

Her blood heated in her veins. So they knew. They had been playing her for a fool this entire time, laughing behind her back at the queen who had been brought so low as to peel potatoes.

"They lie," she seethed.

He shrugged, unaffected. "History is written by the victors. I doubt your name will be recorded."

CHAPTER SIX

H enri leaned back against the base of a gnarled tree, his legs sprawled out in front of him, a cup of brew in his hand. He still didn't know what to make of it. It was unlike any liquor he had ever tasted. It was not pleasant. It burned his throat like fire and numbed his lips as if they had been swollen from a thousand bee stings, but it also numbed everything else and that was the point. His thoughts became sluggish until he no longer remembered to think about anything at all.

Some of the young men from last night had collected him from his tent this morning, keen to show him around the camp. He had insisted that they show him the still first. He had been wretched, his head splitting with pain and his stomach roiling with regret, but he had been all too happy to follow them. The still was a reasonable distance from the camp and was tended to every day by a few of the men. They had shown him the workings of it, clearly proud of their invention, and he had lavished them with enough praise that they did not mind when he had poured himself a cup, even though it was barely past sun's rise.

He couldn't remember what happened after that. He didn't know where they had gone or how he had ended up at the base of this tree, or even really where he was. But he also didn't care. If he died here and now, it would not matter. His life was worth nothing. He no longer had a purpose or a future. No one depended on him or even needed him. And if this was all he had, he would gladly give it up and watch it fade away on the wind.

Brielle ate alone that night, watching the flames dance in the firepit. No one spoke to her or came to sit beside her. It was clear she had been the source of amusement for the day and any inroads she thought she had made with the women were a farce. She felt six years old again, surrounded by the wolves at court. It had been a long time since she was on the outside of a group. The topic of whispered conversations. The target of searing judgments. The unwitting punchline to a joke.

There was no sign of Sienna or Jameson at dinner. Brielle had wandered about the camp in the afternoon searching for them, but she did not find them, and she did not have the courage to ask anyone if they knew their whereabouts.

A sinking thought had dawned on her; maybe they had abandoned her after all, taken the horses and returned to Jameson's family estate. At first the thought filled her with a fiery, indignant rage, but after a while her anger dissipated and all that was left was the ashes of hurt.

After the hurt dissolved, she began to understand why they would want to leave. They were not enemies of the Crown, no one knew they had assisted her to escape. She doubted anyone would have recognized them at the Sodisce. They could return to his family's estate, get married, and live their lives in peace and comfort. Their new king would welcome them at court. They could look to the future and that of their unborn child. To stay here, living in a tent in a cursed woodland with wanted outlaws and enemies of the Crown, was just senseless.

And yet she hoped she was wrong.

She hoped her friendship meant more to Sienna than logic and self-preservation. Perhaps that made her the spoiled, selfish brat Jameson had claimed her to be. She should not want her friend to be in danger, to put her life at risk on her account. But she did not want to do this alone.

There was no sign of Henri at dinner either, but Brielle had no urge to go looking for him. He had made it clear last night that he blamed her for everything that had happened, and although that was entirely unfair and none of this was her fault at all, she did not know what to say to convince him otherwise. She had only done what she thought was right. She did not start any of this. She had only survived it, and barely. What else was she supposed to do when her kingdom was taken from her? She had thought he would understand, but he didn't. He had expected her to run away, to accept things as they were dealt to her by the hands of men, to start a new life elsewhere without complaint.

It was like he did not know her at all.

Perhaps he didn't. Perhaps she had never really known him. She had expected him to wait for her, to fight with her, to reclaim their kingdoms together, but he had walked away from everything as if it meant nothing to him. As if *she* meant nothing to him.

The way he had looked at her last night, she didn't think she would ever be able to forget it; the pure hatred in his eyes. People had disliked her before, of course—ladies of the court, servants, her father's councillors—but none of them had ever hated her. She was not sure how to even approach him after last night, how to begin repairing their friendship, or even if it could be repaired. Perhaps Citric was right. She was losing all her friends. Or worse still, perhaps she never really had them to begin with.

No, that was not true. Henri had written to her the moment he fled to safety, warning her of the danger she was in. He did not have to do that. If anyone had intercepted that note, it would have put him in grave danger and yet he had done it. Sienna had also risked her life to save her that night. She could have ignored the note and left the castle in silence, leaving Brielle to her fate. She would never have fled on her own, so convinced was she that her father's councilmen would protect her. She would be dead right now if it wasn't for both of them. But then things had changed. They had both betrayed her.

After finishing her meal, Brielle wandered silently back to the ruin, her thoughts haunting her like her shadow. She startled at the sight of Citric leaning against a crumbled wall outside her room, his arms folded across his chest, his foot crossed over an ankle.

"What do you want?" she snapped. She was in no mood for his taunts.

"You didn't light a fire last night. You would have been freezing."

She furrowed her brow at the thought that he would even notice such a thing. Or care.

"The hearth is full of soil and leaves," Brielle explained.

"You have two hands."

Brielle recoiled, affronted.

"I watched you, you know, every night that you camped in my woods. You never once collected firewood. But now there is no one to collect firewood for you. And if you don't have a fire at night, you will freeze."

She felt her anger rise again. He had come here just to torment her.

"It doesn't matter because even if I had firewood, I do not know how to light a fire."

"Your companion lit a campfire every night. You did not think to watch him and learn how it was done?"

Of course she had watched him, but she hadn't really noticed what he was doing. There was no reason to pay attention. It was unthinkable that one day she would need to light her own fire.

Citric pushed off the wall and began to walk away. "You're going to freeze tonight."

⋄⟨⟩⋄

Henri was frozen. It was so cold he was surprised to find he was still alive. His name was echoing in his ears as if someone was calling to him, but the sound was distant and muffled, as if his head was underwater. Perhaps he had fallen into a river. But then he would be dead. He felt a crack of pain against his solid cheek. On the second crack, his eyes burst open and his limbs stirred.

"He's alive."

Henri blinked up at the people standing over him; Sienna and another young man he did not recognize. Jameson was kneeling in front of him and was obviously the one who had slapped him awake.

"Here we go."

Jameson hauled him up beneath his armpits to sit him upright against the tree. He must have slouched to the ground at some point. The world spun uncontrollably, and Henri fought the urge to spill the contents of his stomach onto the ground, though he suspected there was no contents to spill. He pinched his eyes closed, wincing at the effort.

"Henri, what are you doing out here?" Sienna's kind voice was heavy with concern.

"He's been drinking," Jameson muttered.

"Guilty," he managed, his eyes still closed.

"All night? You could have died out here!"

He did not have the strength for more words.

"Is he hurt?" the other male asked.

Henri opened his eyes just enough to see the unfamiliar man lean in closer to him, his eyes scanning his body for injury.

He must have had a confused expression on his face because Sienna explained, "This is Father Bastien."

A priest. He recalled Citric mentioning he had one.

"Father, could you give me a hand, please? We're going to have to help him back to camp."

Henri didn't have time to protest before Jameson and Father Bastien hauled him up between them. He lurched forward, his arms swung around their necks, his feet unsteady on the ground. They were slow going, stumbling forward one step at a time, navigating over rocks and through trees. Sienna walked behind them, or so he assumed. He didn't have enough energy to lift his head.

He could hear the sounds of the camp as they entered it, the conversations that died as they passed. He knew he must be a sorry sight, but he was beyond caring what people thought of him. At long last, they found his tent and ungraciously dumped him onto his bedroll. He hit the ground with a violent thud, but despite the pain, he welcomed its solid form underneath his body. Sleep called to him, dragging him below its depths.

"What should we do?" Sienna's voice was laced with concern.

"Leave him here to sleep it off," Jameson replied.

"I'll get some more blankets," Father Bastien offered. "He's half frozen."

"I should tell Brielle," Sienna said.

"No. You heard him the other night. He doesn't want anything to do with her," Jameson countered.

"He didn't mean that. She cares about him."

"Sienna, she almost got him killed. She put us all in danger. She only cares about herself."

If Sienna protested, Henri didn't hear it. Their words faded, drowning under water again. He hoped he would drown as well.

The night had not been kind. It had been even more frigid than the night before, which Brielle had not thought was possible, but she was barely living proof. Her bones brittle, her teeth rattling, she had shivered through every painful minute of it. She would not survive another frozen, sleepless night, of that she was sure. She had no choice; tonight she would have to have a fire, even if it killed her.

At dawn, Brielle forced her frozen limbs from their atrophy and stared across the room into the hearth clogged with soil, as if it were her enemy to slay. She would need something to help her dig the soil out, so she went into the woods to forage for a suitable tool. Exhaustion settled over her like a heavy cloak, making her shoulders slump and her feet stumble, but eventually she spotted a short, thick stick. Returning to her room, she set about digging the soil from the hearth. Within moments, her hands were black and dirt was wedged underneath her fingernails, but she no longer cared.

After she dug the soil out of the hearth and wiped the stone surface clean with her bare hands, Brielle stood up, ready to complete the next task: finding firewood. The camp had well and truly woken by then and although she was hungry, she did not stop for breakfast. Partly because she was determined to see this task through, but mostly because she did not want to see the smirking faces of the women who had played her for a fool yesterday. She was sure they would find it hilarious to know that she could not even light a fire and had almost frozen to death these past two nights.

The woods were littered with sticks and rotting branches and split bark. Brielle had no idea what kind of wood to look for, so she began picking up everything in sight. It did not take long for her arms to fill. She wasn't sure how much wood was needed to sustain a fire, but she would rather have too much than not enough. It would take several trips, she realized miserably.

Brielle trudged back to the ruin and dumped the sticks into the hearth. A large black beetle scuttled out from underneath the pile and she shrieked, immediately retreating to the back of the room.

"It's a wood beetle," Sienna said, standing in what would have once been the doorway. "They are harmless."

"It just frightened me half to death! I would not call it harmless."

"You're collecting firewood."

Brielle scowled at the surprise in her tone. "It's freezing without one."

"I can help you if you like."

They held each other's eyes for a moment, but Brielle did not reply. She simply walked out and let Sienna fall into step beside her. Together, they wandered out into the woods and began silently collecting firewood.

Sienna seemed to know exactly what she was doing as she scanned the ground and discriminated between sticks. She had helped Jameson collect firewood every night that they had camped in these wretched woods. Brielle had not thought much of it at the time, had not thought to be impressed by her resourcefulness. She wondered if they had resented her for not helping them. The truth was, it never occurred to her to help. Did that make her a spoiled, selfish brat like Jameson claimed? It was the kind of accusation one would level at a child. She was a queen. She was never meant to learn how to collect firewood or light a fire or peel a potato. Surely that did not make her a bad person.

Brielle glanced over at Sienna, who had already collected an armful of firewood, while she had only managed to pick up a few measly twigs. There was so much she wanted to say to her, from furious accusations to a groveling apology to feigning complete indifference. But she didn't say a word until their arms were full and they were walking back to the ruin.

"I thought you left," Brielle admitted, her words tentative and quiet. "Returned to court."

"I would never leave you!"

Brielle released a breath she didn't realize she'd been holding.

"I would understand if you did."

Understand but not forgive.

"Jameson just needs some time. It has been hard for him. He worries for me."

"And you are his now."

That was the truth that was crushing her chest, splitting her heart like a grape. Sienna had always been hers, but now she was his.

"I am his wife, yes, but I will always be your friend, Brie."

"But it will never be like it was before."

Her eyes saddened. "Nothing is like what it was before."

Sienna dumped the firewood to the floor in front of the hearth. Brielle tossed her wood on top. Kneeling down, Sienna began sorting through the pile, putting the larger pieces aside.

"We are getting married," Sienna said, looking up at her with a shy smile. "By a priest this time."

Brielle raised her eyebrows. "So there really is a priest here."

Sienna nodded. "We would love for you to be our witness."

Brielle was fairly sure Jameson would prefer her to not attend the wedding at all. At her silence, Sienna returned her attention to sorting the pile of wood.

"I am happy for you," Brielle offered, and it was true. She was. Even though her heart was breaking.

Sienna smiled up at her, gentle and sweet. Her friend, but no longer hers.

"Will you teach me?" Brielle indicated to the hearth.

"Of course. Then we can go bathe in the river. If we go during the day, there is a chance we will get some privacy. Most people bathe early in the morning or late at night."

The idea of bathing sounded wonderful, even in the murky waters of a river with questionable privacy.

Brielle frowned suddenly. "I don't have another dress to change into."

"I have been helping the weaving women. I am sure we can find you something."

It was midafternoon by the time Henri woke. His body was warm, weighed down by several blankets, but his clothes were damp with sweat. He smelled atrocious. His head was hazy but no longer splitting, and his stomach was raw, but he felt hungry. He was alive, and that was disappointing.

Reluctantly, Henri hauled himself to his feet and stumbled out of the tent. Surveying the camp through blood-shot eyes, he wandered around looking for the familiar faces of the young men he had been drinking with last night. Yesterday. Some day. He couldn't remember. They were nowhere to be found. He searched his vague memories for which direction the still was in, but the only thing he could remember was that it was some distance from the camp. He could take a gamble and just start walking, but he would probably end up lost again.

The distant clash of metal pricked his ears. His heart kicked and adrenaline surged through his veins, alerting his senses to danger, but there were no sounds of terror and screaming. The women weren't even bothered by it. Curious, he followed the sounds of battle until he finally stepped out into an open area.

The men were training. Swords, bows, knives, hand-to-hand combat. Henri's stomach lurched, and he leaned against a tree, unsure if he was about to hurl his guts up or pass out. He couldn't recall the last time he ate something. Perhaps two days ago, perhaps longer. There was plenty of food in the camp, he knew, but still he lingered by the tree, watching the men. They were not soldiers, that much was clear. They did not form lines or practice moving and fighting as one unit, but they were not amateurs. Their bodies were strong, their moves skillful and sharp and agile.

His father had insisted that he train from a young age, with a personal tutor at first and then with the other soldiers when he was old enough not to embarrass himself or his father. His father had tried to hone him into the perfect soldier, a warrior king. As a boy, Henri had been excited by the idea of learning how to fight and had enjoyed his lessons immensely. They took him out of the classroom and boring council meetings and let his blood and body run wild. But when he realized what the lessons meant to his father, and that he was being molded into something he did not want to be, he resented them. He would truant or turn up drunk. It pissed off the commander to no end, but there was nothing he could do about it. Henri was a prince.

That was how Henri met Nathaniel. The commander had paired his son with Henri in the training ring, hoping they would form a friendship that would last long enough to one day give him an advantage at court. They did become friends, but Henri did not become a perfect soldier or a warrior king. And in the end, the advantage did not matter because the commander murdered his father and Nathaniel betrayed him.

Henri sensed someone watching him and lifted his gaze to find Citric's eyes fixed on him, despite the fact that he was across the field sparring with an opponent. His stare felt like a hot iron brand, but Henri met it without flinching. He did not know what to make of the man known as the Vogel. That day in the woods, he had dismissed him as a common thief, but the man had avoided capture for years despite his father's best efforts to hunt him down. He was clever. And dangerous. Watching him now, it was clear that he was well trained. Every move he made was controlled, calculated, and lethal. Despite his discipline, though, there was a wildness about him. An unpredictability.

Growing tired of his scrutiny, Henri moved to leave, but Citric called out to him. "If you're looking for your new friends, I'm afraid they are out on patrol."

Henri didn't reply. He would find them tonight. Until then, he would eat some food, perhaps wash this stench away in the river.

"I told them not to give you any more from our still. This is not a tavern, nor a brothel. You abuse my hospitality." His tone was even, but the warning was clear.

"Relax, I had a few drinks. No harm was done."

Citric exchanged a look with his sparring partner before he began strolling over to Henri, his strides long and casual. He did not stop until he was an inch away from his face. Henri stilled, not from fear but from meeting the blatant challenge. He would have liked to be steadier on his feet, and he was all too aware of his foul odor, but still, he would not allow himself to be intimidated.

"I do not accept drunkards into my home."

"Only thieves and murderers?"

The corner of Citric's lips twitched, the cunning smile of a snake.

"I heard the rumors that the Prince of the North had escaped the slaughter on the battlefield. It is hard to believe that both Kings were murdered and yet you escaped."

A muscle in Henri's jaw feathered. "What are you implying?"

"Perhaps you joined in the slaughter. And then fled like a coward."

His fists flew before his mind knew what he was doing, but Citric blocked the blows easily, so Henri grabbed a fistful of his tunic and shoved him backward. Citric let him, dancing back a few steps, his smile growing wider.

"I did not kill my father," Henri spat.

"But you are a coward."

He shook his head as his heart pounded riotously in his chest. He swayed on his feet, suddenly dizzy. "No," he breathed as he leaned against the tree, waiting for the world to stop spinning. "I am nothing."

"She does not seem to think so."

Henri frowned, confused, until he caught his meaning; Brielle. He had not seen her since he tore into her that night, blaming her for everything he had lost. He felt shame at the hazy memory, but it had been easier to target her with his fury than to face his own guilt. No matter how much he drank, though, it was still there, waiting for him. Like an endless pit of darkness filled with every wrong choice he had ever made, every life lost because of him, all of it pointless because in the end he was worth nothing.

"She risked her life to find you."

"She thought I would have a plan to reclaim our kingdoms. I don't. All I wanted was to disappear, to start a new life, but she can't comprehend that it's over. She cannot imagine a world where she is not queen."

"A Prince of the North was content to hide in a brothel for the rest of his life?" Citric furrowed his brows. "You are a coward."

Henri glowered at him. "I remember you, you know. Demonstrating your bowman skills at one of my father's military parades. I was fifteen years old. You wouldn't have been much older than me, but they said you were the best bowman in the army. How does one go from a skilled soldier to a wanted outlaw?"

"War," he replied simply. "You watch hundreds of men die for one man's pride. You face your own mortality every day, knowing your life means less than nothing."

"So you become a criminal. Robbing innocent people for your own personal gain and creating a reputation for yourself so you feel important. Is that it?"

"I remember you too, Prince. Sitting next to your father on the dais, watching the parade from the comfort of your cushioned arse. Were you drunk that day as well?"

Probably.

"A boy who lives in the shadow of his father cannot grow to be a man. But when the father is gone and the boy still fails to grow, who's at fault then?"

Henri felt his blood heat and tensed his muscles to lash out, but hesitated when he caught sight of Brielle. She was walking with Sienna around the edges of the clearing, arm in arm, as if they were promenading in the court gardens. Citric turned his head in their direction and his amusement faded. As they got closer, Brielle's features morphed into the cool court mask she wore so well. It wounded Henri to see it, to know that she was putting on armor because of him, because of what he had said to her.

"The women missed you this morning," Citric called out to her, "though I think the potatoes were relieved."

Henri didn't understand the reference and if Brielle did, she was clearly ignoring it, preferring to cast her eyes out over the men who were training rather than acknowledge either of them. That was fair. He had no right to expect her forgiveness, especially when he had not asked for it. In truth, he was not sure how to ask for it or whether there was any point in trying. Brielle was not the type to forgive or forget. He knew she let very few people get close to her. He was the same, so he knew how deep the wounds went when someone betrayed that trust.

"Care to learn?" Citric inclined his head toward the men.

Brielle's eyes widened in horror at the suggestion that she would ever go anywhere near a weapon.

"No, thank you." Her voice was clipped and regal.

They watched her walk on, arm in arm with Sienna, who threw them an apologetic smile over her shoulder.

Citric did not take his eyes from them as he said to Henri, "You should train with us. It is a better outlet for the anger you have, trust me."

Henri and Jameson wandered out into the open area where some of the men were already training despite the early hour. The men watched them with wary eyes, but didn't say anything as they walked over to claim a vacant space.

After returning to camp yesterday, Henri couldn't stop thinking about the conversation with Citric. He was right. Henri couldn't keep drinking himself into oblivion. It gave him a temporary reprieve from the chokehold of his guilt and anger and loss, but they were always waiting for him when he sobered. He needed to face what had happened, accept it, and decide what he was going to do with his life now. He owned nothing but his choices, and he did not want his choices to be the reason that Citric rescinded his hospitality to them. If he did, they would be in immediate danger. They would have nowhere else to go.

So he had approached Jameson and asked him to train with him. He needed an outlet for the war of emotions raging inside of him. He needed to keep moving, to exhaust his body and stop thinking. Or at least think about things other than Fleur's mutilated body. His failure to protect them. His failure to protect anyone or anything he had ever cared about.

"They're well trained."

Henri blinked, refocusing on the scene in front of him. Jameson was watching the men fight; some with swords, some with nothing but their bare hands and brute strength.

"Yes, they are, for a group of outlaws."

"I think you know these people are more than that," Jameson countered.

Henri knew what he meant. Despite the tents and the rudimentary lifestyle, Alkhiem was not a disorganized camp of misfits and vagrants. It was an established community with leadership and structure and culture. Everyone had a role, a way in which to contribute to greater good. The women took care of domestic duties and minded the children, while the men tended to the crops and livestock, and ensured the camp's safety. The people here lacked for nothing. In fact, food and water and shelter were in abundance. The Red Wood was surprisingly fertile, in a way that the Northern and Southern Kingdoms hadn't been for years. Everyone worked together without complaint so that the community could thrive.

"It makes you wonder just how long they've been here for," Jameson said. "And what desperate situation made them risk coming here."

He had a point. Despite the scarcity of food and other general hardships, most people would not risk entering a cursed wood in the hopes of finding salvation. Everyone knew the stories of the Red Wood. They were the seeds of nightmares and cautionary tales. The type of stories parents told their children to encourage them to behave.

"Did you come here to talk like women or fight like men?" a rough voice said.

Henri and Jameson turned their attention to the man who had called out to them. The men around them stopped sparring and were watching them, grinning with amusement.

"We came to see if there were any worthy opponents among you, but alas, we're disappointed," Jameson returned.

"Is that so?" The man approached, jerking the sword from its sheath in one swift motion.

"We came to train." Henri stepped between them, holding his hands out in a gesture of peace. "Not to fight. We meant no disrespect."

Henri's gaze caught on Citric as he entered the training ground with a few of his men. Upon seeing him, Citric dipped his chin in acknowledgment, but said nothing as he wandered over to the far side of the field. The men reluctantly resumed their training, though the threat of violence still hung heavy in the air.

Henri turned back to Jameson and loosed a breath. He was pretty sure starting a fight would result in Citric rescinding his hospitality. Henri unsheathed his sword and took up a defensive stance, but Jameson didn't follow suit. He continued to watch Citric as he tightened the string of his longbow.

"Have you noticed their hands?"

"What?" Henri relaxed his stance.

"All the men have scars on their right palms. Some have them on both palms."

Henri furrowed his eyebrows. He hadn't noticed. He'd been too busy obliterating himself to notice much of anything lately.

"Sienna said some of the women have them too, on their left palms."

"Has she asked them about it?"

"No. She said she doesn't want to pry."

Henri considered for a moment. "Tell her to ask them about it."

They exchanged a meaningful look, and Jameson nodded in resolution. Henri resumed his defensive stance and this time, Jameson matched him.

CHAPTER SEVEN

C itric stood on the far side of the training field next to a table with various weapons laid out on it; a battle axe, a bec de corbin, a flail, and a flanged mace. Nearby was a rack holding several swords and quarterstaffs. His longbow was strapped to his back, having already been stringed and tightened, and his arrows in his quiver were oiled. Still, he swung his longbow from his back and pretended to tighten the string. He could feel their eyes on him, the prince and his companion. They were watching him cautiously.

Moments ago, Citric had felt the sudden rise in tension from his blood brothers tugging at his awareness. It had spurred him to enter the training ground under the guise of practice so that he could investigate the cause of such enmity and ensure that no violence resulted from it. It had not surprised him to find that the cause was the prince and his companion. But it had surprised him to witness Leif's outburst toward them. It was uncharacteristic of him and only provided further evidence for what Citric already knew; the men were growing restless. They had had enough of hosting an entitled princess and a drunken prince.

Leif stalked toward him from across the field, his hands clenched into fists at his sides. Citric did not need the blood bond to know how enraged his friend was feeling, but he felt it anyway, as if the emotions were his own. The vicious anger pumped through his friend's body, pulling his muscles as tight as a bowstring. Leif wanted to tear the prince and his companion to pieces. The rest of the men felt the same way. Their wrath almost overwhelmed Citric's senses, coating his tongue in a bitter taste of copper. They were like a pack of hungry wolves. If

Leif had drawn blood, they would have gladly circled their prey and joined in the slaughter.

Citric understood what his men were feeling because he felt it too. Their presence in this place was wrong. It was disrespectful to the spirits. They did not belong here, among his people. In truth, he had been struggling to leash his own inner beast and had almost lashed out yesterday when the prince stumbled onto the training ground, hungover and searching for his next drink. But Citric had been playing this game for too long to let his emotions get the better of him. Hidden and patient, calm and calculating. That was how he had lived his life and that was how he would protect his people. Like holding a burning iron against severed flesh, their presence here was excruciating but necessary.

"What was that about?" Citric asked casually as Leif came to stand at his side.

His hands were on his hips now and his words came out in a fevered rush. "They were talking about Alkhiem. Speculating how long we've been here for and what drove us to live here."

"They are curious. It's to be expected."

"They are suspicious. They were counting our numbers, observing our skills." Leif shook his head, crushing his lower lip between his teeth. "I don't like it. They shouldn't be here."

"They are here for a reason," he pointed out calmly. "Besides, they won't be here for much longer."

Citric speared his gaze across the field to see the prince and his companion sparring with each other. They moved like well-trained soldiers, competent but predictable. Used to the reassurance of an army at their back and the protection of armor around their organs. He would bet gold they had never been involved in a scrappy fight for their lives. Broken knuckles and splintered bones, blood, sweat, and bile. They would have never learned how to take like a poor man.

Take a beating.

Take a stand.

Take a life.

His blood started to heat in his veins, but he willed it to simmer.

"Did you get what I asked for?" Citric's words held an edge that was not there before.

Leif moved to brush by his side, the sleight of hand putting the object into Citric's tunic. He tilted his head in thanks, but his friend only returned a hard look, his disapproval clear. Citric understood, but he did not need to explain or justify his decisions to anyone. He had dedicated his life to protecting his people and he would do whatever was necessary to ensure their survival.

Yesterday had been wonderful. Sienna had taught her how to build a fire, and then they had gone to the river to bathe and wash the dirt from their hair. She had been given a new dress to wear, still scratchy and plain and unflattering but clean, and then they had spent the day walking and talking like they used to. Sienna had even sat with her at dinner, forcing Jameson to join them and tolerate her company by default. It felt good to laugh again, to not feel like she was on the outside.

This morning Brielle had woken up feeling refreshed, thanks to the fire, which had burned steadily all night. She strolled up to the breakfast table as if she owned it, helping herself to a generous bowl of porridge and a shiny red apple. The women eyed her warily, but she did not care. They could say whatever they wanted. She did not need them anymore. She had barely finished breakfast when Sienna rushed up to her, her eyes wild with panic.

"It's gone."

"What?" Brielle frowned, confused.

"Your jewels. They're gone."

"What!"

"They were hidden in the folds of my cloak and this morning when I went to check on them, they were not there. They would not have fallen out, someone must have taken them."

Brielle's expression tightened in anger. She glanced around to find that the women had paused in their duties and were watching her closely, waiting to see what she would do. She pressed her lips into a hard line and stalked off in the direction of the clearing where she could hear the men training. Citric was on the far side, sparring with one of his men. She marched as close as she could get to him without being in range of his swinging sword.

"One of your people is a thief!" she accused loudly.

It was not until the words left her mouth that she realized the stupidity of what she'd said. Still, she stood her ground. The men stopped sparring, all except for Citric and his opponent. It surprised her to see that Henri and Jameson were among the men. Henri had looked awful yesterday, weak and hungover and smelling like a common beggar, but today his clothes were clean and though stubble lined his chin, his eyes were bright. Right now they fixed on her, uneasy.

"If you want to make accusations, you had better have proof," Citric said, refusing to take his eyes off his rival.

Brielle suddenly became aware that the women had followed her and were now gathered behind her to watch the confrontation. She was used to being the center of attention, but not like this.

Brielle squared her shoulders. "My proof is that my jewels are missing."

Citric ceased training. Sweat trickled down his neck as he reached into his tunic and held something up in his hand.

"You mean this?"

A purse. *Her* purse.

Brielle's eyes flashed with anger. "You took it."

"Compensation, remember?"

"What! That's a fortune!"

He shrugged, pocketing the purse back into his tunic.

"I thought you only stole from the wealthy."

"You just said you have a fortune."

"But I need it."

"A boat across the sea does not cost as much."

She gritted her teeth. "I need it to pay for an army to reclaim my kingdom."

"Your kingdom is lost." He said the words as if she were a simpleton.

"But it's mine!" She hated the way her voice sounded. Like a child demanding the return of a favorite toy.

"This is how the world works, is it not? Men become kings because they take what they want. They take it even if it is not rightfully theirs. If you want it back, you have to fight for it. So fight me."

Brielle stared at him, shocked. He could not be serious. But he looked serious.

"I will not fight you."

"You expect others to fight for your kingdom, but you will not fight for it yourself?"

Brielle could feel the crowd swelling behind her, tense as they watched and waited for her response. Would she be reckless enough to try to fight him? Or would she accept defeat and walk away? Either way, she would be publicly humiliated.

She couldn't win.

That was the point.

Her cheeks flushed as she narrowed her eyes at him in a death stare. He met it boldly, unfazed, the challenge laid bare for everyone to see.

"I will fight for her."

Henri stepped forward, the hilt of his sword gripped tight in his hand. Citric glanced back at Brielle, who barely had time to nod her concession before he swung his sword at Henri's neck. Henri stumbled backward but regained his balance before the next strike.

Citric was relentless, attacking him with a speed and ferocity Brielle had never seen before. Henri was barely keeping up. Each blow was stronger and deadlier than the last, forcing Henri to retreat and defend until he was down on one knee, holding his sword above with both hands to block a savage overhead attack. Citric punched him in the face, sending his sword scattering across the yard.

Brielle gasped as Citric discarded his own sword and allowed Henri to get to his feet before attacking him with his fists. Henri blocked several blows and managed to land a few of his own, but Citric was too fast. Henri rammed into his middle, trying to tackle him to the ground, but Citric held firm as if his legs were rooted into the soil. He clasped his fists together to form a hammer and brought them down on Henri's back. Henri's legs gave way and Citric brought his knee up to smash into his face. A crack reverberated across the field as Henri flew backward to the ground. Both of them were bleeding now, the fight clearly won, but even with Henri sprawled on the ground at his feet, Citric was not done. He laid into him with a fury that defied belief.

"Stop!" Brielle launched herself at Citric, trying to pull him away, but she might as well have been a fly buzzing at a bear. No one moved to help. No one even said a word. Desperate, she spotted the dagger at Citric's side, freed it from its sheath and pressed the blade to his throat.

"Enough!"

Citric stopped, his arms hanging limp at his sides, his chest heaving from exertion. Brielle's heart pounded wildly as if it would break free from her rib cage. Citric's eyes took in the damage he had done to Henri's body, his broken, bloodied face, but he showed no signs of remorse. Brielle tried to hold the blade steady against his skin, but her hands were shaking, and hot tears were threatening to spill over. She willed herself to not cry in front of them. In front of him.

Citric stood, staring down at Henri for a moment, before switching his cold gaze to her. She knew he could see the tears in her eyes. Her fear. Her shock. Her utter humiliation. Shame rose inside her like bile.

"Kings must be willing to let their people die for them. To be a king is to risk the lives of the people you care about the most. Are you prepared to do that?"

The crowd stirred behind her, murmuring amongst themselves.

Citric made to turn away from her when Brielle said, "I am not a king."

Henri sat with his back against the cold stone wall, tilting his head up to the open sky in an effort to stop the torrent of blood that was gushing from his nose. Everything hurt. His ribs felt like they had been shattered, his nose was most definitely broken, his arms throbbed from bearing the force of repeated sword strikes, his face was bruised and bloody and swollen and his lip was split.

He hadn't taken a beating like that since—he couldn't remember ever taking a beating quite that bad. Maybe because he was the prince, and no one had dared to really lay into him. But also because he had never seen anyone fight with the relentless anger and lethal hatred that Citric had. Whether he was the source of that hatred or merely the target of its fury, he did not know. He had felt it, though. He was feeling it now.

"Here." Brielle held a damp cloth out to him and he pressed it firmly to his nostrils to staunch the flow.

After the fight, Jameson had pulled him to his feet and helped him hobble into the ruin, while Sienna had fetched a bowl of clean water and torn several clean strips of linen for bandages. They had both hovered over him before Brielle had ordered them out of her room. Jameson had given him a curt nod of respect before clutching Sienna's hand and leading her away. Henri didn't know why Brielle did not want them to stay. He would have expected Sienna to be cleaning his wounds while Brielle paced the room, ranting with rage and plotting her revenge. Instead, she was silently tending to his wounds, unaware or unconcerned with the blood soaking into her dress.

Brielle pressed a rag to his split lip, and he hissed as the touch seared his skin.

"Sorry. I have never done this before."

"It's all right," he mumbled through his swollen lips. "It looks worse than it feels."

Her deadpan expression told him she did not believe that for one second.

"I've had worse," he insisted.

He was trying to ease the guilt on her face. He couldn't stand to see it. It made her look vulnerable, and he had never seen her like that before. She was always so sure of herself, marching head first into any situation, demanding the world bend to her whims.

Now she wouldn't meet his eyes as she said, "You did not have to defend me, you know."

"I know," he breathed. His lungs expanded, and he winced against the sharp pain.

"I thought you hated me." Her words were tentative, pained.

"I never said that."

"You said you wished it had been me."

He shook his head, regretful. "I didn't mean it."

"You said you wished it had been you. Did you mean that?"

He didn't know what to say. His silence said it all.

Seeing the fear and hurt in her eyes, he said, "I will always defend you."

He did not know the truth of those words until he said them out loud, but he felt it now, as sure as the sun's rising. He would always defend her. From those who sought to humiliate or hurt her. Because she was all that mattered now, all that he had left. And because some things were worth fighting for.

She was worth fighting for.

Her gaze flicked up to his, and his breath caught. She was so beautiful, her eyes soft and warm brown like a doe's. He had seen them dance with mischief, light with rage, and turn cold as ice, but he had never seen them look at anyone the way they were looking at him right now. As if her soul had been stripped bare for him to see. Only him. It made everything seem so simple. Her fingers brushed his cheek as she dabbed the rag lightly against his lip. He watched her throat bob as she swallowed nervously. He was making her feel nervous. He smiled at the thought, though the movement caused him pain.

"Let's leave this place," he said, reaching up to take her hand in his. "Go across the sea, anywhere you want. Start a new life."

She furrowed her brows slightly. "But my kingdom—"

"Is lost, Brielle."

"No." She shook her head stubbornly.

"You have no army and no means to finance one."

"I will get my jewels back. I will take back what is mine."

"How?" he said, exasperated, his hand falling to his lap.

Her features hardened in determination. "I will find a way."

⚜

Brielle hid behind a tree, watching the men in the clearing train. She had left Henri to rest on her bedroll. He had barely had enough strength to lie down. Citric would pay for what he did to him. She did not know how, but she would make him pay. First, though, she would get her jewels back. She didn't know exactly what her plan was. She couldn't threaten him and she couldn't fight him, but perhaps she could outsmart him. So she stayed hidden and watched, waiting for the right time to strike.

It surprised her that he still had the energy to train after what he did to Henri. He had been depleted and breathless, she had seen it, but perhaps the fight had only stirred more restless energy or bloodlust. It made her shudder to think of the fire that fueled such murderous violence. She had only ever seen Citric calm and composed, humorous and unaffected. It was like watching a beast escape from its cage. His men had not seemed shocked by it. Perhaps they had seen it before. It was little wonder the King's Guard had never caught him. Most soldiers would never stand a chance against him.

Sudden movement caught her attention. Citric was leaving, heading back toward the camp. Brielle followed him at a parallel line, maintaining a fair distance between them. Careful to keep her feet soft, she tried not to rustle leaves or snap a twig. She did not know how he came to live this life, but she knew that he could probably sense when someone was tracking him. She needed to be so very careful.

Brielle watched as he made his way to a small white dome tent and disappeared inside. There was nothing unusual about the tent. That was what was so strange about it. He was the leader of this rebellious rabble, and yet his tent was the same size as everyone else's. It was also on the outskirts of the camp, not in the center. If the camp was ever attacked, he would be the first line of defense. Or the first to die.

Citric emerged with clothes tucked under his arm and walked back into the woodland. Brielle's heart tripped over itself in panic. Should she follow him or search his tent? Perhaps he had hidden her jewels somewhere inside. Without a second thought, she dashed as quietly as she could through the trees. Quickly glancing around to make sure no one was watching her, she slipped inside the tent.

It was disappointingly basic. A bedroll, a small oil lamp, the makings of a small armory, and some clothes. She searched the bedroll, then his clothes, running her hands along the seams of the fabric, feeling for hidden pockets. Nothing. The purse wasn't here. Perhaps he had hidden it with all the other loot he stole. She had no idea where he stored that. She had seen the men returning from raids, showing off their haul, but then it always seemed to disappear. Perhaps he was heading to the secret location right now.

Brielle opened the tent flap and gingerly peered outside. Satisfied no one was watching, she shot out into the woods. He had been heading north, so she ran that way, hoping he had not veered off in a different direction. When she eventually spotted the river ahead, she slowed her pace and lingered amongst the trees. Perhaps he had been heading to the river to bathe. Her eyes scanned the river, but she could not see him. Suddenly the wind picked up, surging north, scattering leaves in its wake. Unsure of what else to do, she began making her way upstream.

After a while, though, she began to doubt herself. He could have gone downstream or somewhere else entirely. She was wasting her time. She was about to give up when she spotted him. He was submerged in the river with his muscled back to her, running his hands through his long copper hair, which slapped wet against his skin. Brielle froze. What was she meant to do now? She wished she had a bow. She wished she knew how to use a bow. If she did, she could stay on the safety of the riverbank while aiming it at his heart and demanding to know where her jewels were. He would have no choice but to tell her. Perhaps she would still let the arrow fly afterward.

Brielle scanned the riverbank to find his clothes discarded under a nearby tree. Her jewels could still be in his tunic. The irony almost made her laugh out loud. The great Vogel having his own haul stolen right out from underneath him while he bathed. She would need to be deathly quiet. One small sound and he would know she was there.

Brielle crept closer ever so slowly, darting from tree to tree, quieting her breath and softening her footfalls. When she was finally behind the tree, his clothes within arm's reach, she dared a look out into the river. His back was still turned to her, his arms gliding calmly through the water as if he were caressing it. She reached out and silently grabbed his clothes, pulling them back behind the tree. Crouching down, she rummaged through his tunic. It smelled of sweat and the scent that all men had, but her purse was not there. She searched his pants. Nothing. There was nothing else to search, only his belt and dagger.

Brielle resisted the urge to scream in frustration. He must have hidden her jewels with the rest of his loot. She would need to wait for the men to return from another raid and then follow them. Her gaze lingered on the dagger. She had clenched it in her palm this morning, held it against his throat, but she hadn't really taken notice of it. It was a plain weapon. The hilt was made of wood, and strange crude markings had been carved into it. It looked old, personal. Maybe it was a family heirloom. Perhaps she should steal it and barter it in exchange for her jewels.

"Have you come to fight me for them?"

Brielle shot to her feet, the dagger erect in her hand. She didn't know why she had darted further behind the tree. He had clearly seen her. Or sensed her. Reluctantly, she stepped out into the open.

Citric was standing waist-deep in the river, watching her calmly, like a predator. His chest was broad and his abdomen lined with muscles glistening from the water. They tensed as he stood there. She could see deep scars along his shoulder and rib cage, as if someone had stabbed him several times. Her eyes drifted lower to the snail trail of hair beneath his belly button, which disappeared under the water. If he took one more step out of the river, she would see all of him. The thought made her blood thrum in her veins.

"Or have you come for something else?" The corner of his lips tugged in amusement.

"You will give them back to me." It thrilled her to hear the conviction in her voice.

"Make me."

How she hated him, that smug expression and arrogant tone. She didn't care that she couldn't fight. There was no one here to embarrass herself in front of, save for Citric, and she couldn't care less what he thought of her. She gripped the dagger in her hand and stalked into the water, watching him with precision, anticipating any move he might make. But he didn't. He simply waited for her.

Without warning, she slashed the knife at his chest, but he side-stepped her easily. She lunged again to stab him in the gut, but he grabbed her wrist, spun her around, and bent it back so viciously that she screamed and dropped the dagger into the water. He let her go, and she stumbled backward, deeper into the water, cradling her wrist in her other hand.

"Tell me, can princesses swim?"

Brielle's heart stopped. He was standing between her and the riverbank, and she was already waist-deep in water. He advanced a step, and she instinctively took a step backward.

Deeper.

The water was lapping at her breasts now. Of course she could not swim, there was no need for her to learn how to swim. She should have never been forced to swim in disgusting rivers or fight wanted criminals or build her own fire. He took another step toward her, but she resisted the urge to retreat. If she retreated any farther, the water would be up to her shoulders. She needed to be quick. She could try to dash around him, but he would anticipate that, and she knew she would not be fast enough.

Citric advanced another step, but she planted her feet in the muddy soil and refused to yield. He took another predatory step, and she steeled herself as he came so close they were sharing the same breath. Every inch of her body went rigid in alarm. She was all too aware of his naked body almost touching hers. He could try to drown her, but she would fight him with her bare hands, gouge his eyes out with her fingernails if she had to.

His ice-blue eyes descended between them to where the water was skimming the top of her milky white breasts. Brielle's breath hitched as a pool of heat kindled inside her body. No one had ever been so bold as to look at her like that—with animalistic desire. How dare he. She hated him. She had never hated anyone so much in her life. She wanted him to pay for everything he had done to her, to Henri. She wanted—

He dipped his head closer, and her gaze fell to his lips. They were full and sensual. Suddenly, she wanted so badly to feel them against hers. There was nothing she wanted more in the world. His eyes searched hers. He was hesitating, she realized, waiting for her to close the breath of distance between them. But she didn't. Couldn't. Even though every cell in her body was electrified by him, she could not seem to move.

His expression changed, swift as the wind, and he lifted his head before turning his back on her. Brielle blinked, confused, as if released from a spell. Her eyes caught on the blade glinting beneath the water and she dived for it before lunging to wrap her arm around his throat.

"My jewels. Tell me where they are."

He stilled. "We both know you won't do it."

She gripped him tighter, pressing the blade to the skin beneath his jaw. He didn't move. But he didn't relent either. Could she kill him? If she had to? To reclaim her kingdom? She forced the blade to pierce his skin.

He didn't flinch.

Didn't whimper.

Because they both knew he was right. She could never kill him. She could never kill anyone. He moved slowly out from underneath her grip and she lowered her arms in defeat as he turned to face her.

"Your jewels are mine," he said plainly. "But I know someone who might be interested in funding your campaign."

⚜

Brielle laid awake that night watching the stars overhead, unable to sleep. Her mind was a whirlwind of thoughts and nervous energy. Citric had told her he knew someone who wanted to lead a rebellion against the Crown. Someone who saw the injustices that the common people faced every day and who was determined to fight back. Someone wealthy and highly placed at court. Perhaps one of her father's councilmen. Perhaps when everything had happened he could not risk revealing his true loyalties, but now he was ready to fight and put her back on her rightful throne.

Citric had said that if she wanted to meet with them, he would send word, but it would take several days for them to arrive. In the meantime, he had warned her not to tell anyone about it. She had no choice but to agree to his terms. She had no other options available to her. Upon returning to camp, she had gone about the rest of the day as if nothing had happened. She hadn't almost kissed a notorious outlaw. She hadn't tried to kill a man—twice. She hadn't agreed to a secret meeting with a court spy to plot a rebellion against the Crown. She was a naïve girl, a fallen princess who had been publicly humiliated and defeated, wasn't she? A devious smile crept across her lips.

"Can't sleep?" Henri croaked.

He was lying beside her on her bedroll. He could hardly move from his injuries, so it had made sense that he would spend the night with her instead of being carried to his tent. Jameson had been kind enough to retrieve his bedroll, which Brielle was now lying on. Weeks ago, she would have balked at the idea of sleeping next to a man or even being in the same room as one unchaperoned, but now it did not seem so scandalous. Besides, it was only Henri. She welcomed his company. And his body heat.

"Would you like some water?" Brielle turned on her side to collect the cup and tilted it against his lips.

He took a generous sip. "Thank you."

She set the cup back down and resumed her position lying down, staring up at the stars. The fire cracked and popped in the hearth. She was getting good at building fires. She had enjoyed the shock on Henri's face when he watched her light it earlier. She had pretended not to notice. She preferred him to believe that she had always been this capable.

"What are you thinking about?"

Revenge. My kingdom. That almost kiss. Revenge.

"Nothing important."

She could feel his eyes on her, contemplating. She sensed him hesitate, weighing up his words.

"I know it's hard to accept, but perhaps it's for the best. Paying for a mercenary army to reclaim your kingdom was never a solid plan."

After she returned to camp, she had told him she failed to retrieve her jewels. He had not looked surprised; in fact, he looked relieved. Part of her wanted to tell him everything, to share her sliver of hope so that it might grow and feel like something tangible in her hands, but she didn't. He would only destroy it by pointing out the obvious dangers and trying to talk her out of it.

"You are right. I need a better one."

Henri sighed pointedly. Brielle tried to ignore him, but his apathy toward the loss of his kingdom was unfathomable to her. And even if he was somehow justified in letting go of his birthright, which he wasn't, he could at least have the common decency to not expect her to do the same.

"Do you really think you could live like them?" Brielle asked. "Perform hard labor every day, find a wife, have children, eventually die in some hovel?"

Henri paused. "It's not such a bad life. To work hard to build something, to be surrounded by people who love you. I would rather that than live my life caged by a crown, every day facing unknown threats, fearing betrayal from everyone around me, knowing that everyone I love could be taken away from me at any moment."

Brielle turned her head to stare across at him. "It wouldn't be like that."

"Yes, it would. When you have something that everyone else wants, you have to fight every day to keep it. Do you think you could live like that? Is that really the life you want?"

Brielle sighed, turned her head back, and fixed her attention firmly on the stars. "I want what is mine."

CHAPTER EIGHT

This was a terrible idea. Brielle shifted nervously on her feet as she took in her surroundings. She was standing in what could have once been a narrow, deep river that had dried up over the years, except that to her right, the land sloped upward to form a natural bridge. And a dead end. The only way in or out of this ditch was to her left, and Citric was blocking it. She could not climb out. The walls were too steep, high enough that she could not see over the edge and narrow enough that two people could not stand shoulder to shoulder.

It was a trap.

She was a fool.

She had believed him so blindly that she hadn't told anyone about a secret meeting with an alleged rebel benefactor. She hadn't told anyone where she was going or who she was going with, that she was leaving the camp at all. Citric had betrayed her to the King's Guard. She knew it. They would arrive any moment now and take her away to be publicly executed. He would pocket the handsome reward and never think of her again.

Bastard.

Brielle slid her gaze to him. He was casually leaning against a wall of soil covered in moss. He flicked his eyes to her, and she quickly looked away. She should have told Henri. He would have seen this for what it really was. She had to think. She had to escape, but she had no weapons. She chided herself for not carrying at least a dagger. It was becoming more and more necessary these days.

Brielle barely noticed the soft birdcall until a loud mournful cry echoed in response. She turned to Citric, wide-eyed. She had heard that cry before, when they fled into these woods with the King's Guard in pursuit. It had echoed through the trees like a tortured, wounded ghost. But it was no ghost. Citric had made that sound. A birdcall.

Her heart plummeted as she heard a horse approaching. She was out of time. She threw a panicked look to Citric, who simply stared back at her with hard eyes. There was no way she would get past him. Perhaps she could tackle him to the ground, wrestle his dagger away from him. At least then she would have a weapon. But even with a weapon, she would not stand a chance against the King's Guard.

"You have got to be joking."

Brielle looked up to see a horse's head peering down into the ditch, along with a cloaked rider. To her surprise, the voice was young, female. The rider tossed back her hood and Brielle's mouth fell open.

"Lady Evelyn?"

The young girl looked down at her with blatant contempt. "It's Eve."

Brielle stared back at her, speechless. She recalled the day the girl had been presented to her father at court; she had been fifteen years old, small and unremarkable. Now she looked older and markedly different, though barely a year had passed. She certainly did not look like a lady of the court. She was wearing men's clothes. Pants. They clung to her legs, highlighting her slim figure. It was scandalous. The clothes looked familiar. They were exactly like the clothes Citric's men wore; a mix of dark cotton and thick brown leather fashioned like armor. Eve's long wispy hair fell down to her waist, with the sides braided back tight against her skull. She looked as if she had been riding for days and sleeping rough, but she also looked—fierce.

"You called me away for *her*?" She speared the accusation at Citric.

He shrugged, unaffected. "You said you needed allies."

"Allies, yes. Not more enemies."

Brielle furrowed her brows. "I am not your enemy. I am your queen."

Eve scoffed. "You're not my queen. You're queen of nothing. Without your title, your lands, your money, your ladies, you are nothing. Worse than nothing. You're ordinary."

Brielle winced at the word as if she'd been struck. Eve grinned at the sight of it.

"You have a common cause, a common enemy," Citric reminded her.

"So? Why do I need her? She can't fight, she has no army. She's useless."

Brielle opened her mouth to protest, but Citric cut her off.

"She has a claim to the throne, a recognized claim. People need a figure to follow, to fight for."

"Everyone hates her."

"That's not true!" Brielle objected.

"Oh, but it is." Eve smiled down at her as if she'd tasted a fine wine. "You were just another self-centered royal who happened to look pretty in a silk dress. Your ladies couldn't stand you, the rest of the court loathed you, and your people cursed your name."

"My people love me!"

"Please," she sneered. "You had no idea what your people were suffering through every day, you still don't, because you don't care."

"I do," Brielle insisted, even though she had no idea what the girl was talking about.

"I bet you don't even know what happened to your own mother."

Brielle's spine stiffened. She had not thought of her mother since they left her that night, weeping and wailing in her room like a frightened child. A foreboding chill crawled over her skin as she forced the words out of her mouth. "What happened to my mother?"

Eve's expression was unfeeling as she said, "She threw herself from her tower window."

A vague memory stirred in the back of her mind; sitting in the cramped boat as Jameson rowed them silently downstream, a flutter of white falling from a window in the high tower.

"Or perhaps she was pushed. It doesn't really matter. She's dead."

Brielle blinked numbly.

"Oh, don't pretend you care. You never could stand her. You took her rooms and title before she was even dead in her grave."

Citric pinched the bridge of his nose. "This isn't helping."

"It's true! She doesn't care for anyone but herself."

"You both want the same thing, to bring down the King. That's all that matters. Everything else can be negotiated another time."

Citric wandered out of the ditch and moments later, appeared at Eve's side.

"You've come all this way, you might as well stay with us for a few days."

Eve threw a spiteful look down at Brielle before she rolled her eyes and disappeared. Still somewhat dazed, Brielle stumbled out of the ditch and mounted her horse to follow them back to the camp. A heavy silence settled between them, stretched taut with tension, but Brielle was grateful for it. There were no words for what she was feeling right now. She could not get the image out of her head. It replayed in her mind's eye over and over again. That flutter of white falling from a high tower.

Her mother.

When they finally approached the camp, she was vaguely aware of Henri standing with Sienna and Jameson, his expression strained. He ran to her the moment he saw her.

"Where the hell have you been? We've been searching everywhere for you."

"Seriously?" Eve drawled as she led her horse past him. "This just keeps getting worse."

Henri frowned at the girl, confused. Henri helped Brielle down from her horse as the others dismounted.

"You might remember Lady Evelyn," Brielle said.

"Eve," she corrected her. "And I doubt it. He had his hand up Lady Quinne's skirt, not mine."

Eve stalked off into the camp, where she was immediately greeted by everyone, as if they already knew her. Even the children ran up to her, chanting her name with glee. Then, to Brielle's surprise, Sienna ran over to her. They embraced each other in a tight hug, their faces bright with joy at seeing one another.

Brielle bristled at the sight of it. She had not realized they were friends. Close friends, by the looks of it. Eve pulled away and looked down at the small bump now protruding from Sienna's skirts. She threw her arms around her neck with renewed excitement, congratulating her.

Had Brielle congratulated her? She had been too shocked and scandalized and hurt to even think of it. In fact, now that she thought about it, they hadn't talked about the baby once. Brielle had not felt her small bump or asked how she was feeling. She had been so caught up in everything else that she had not thought about her friend at all.

"What is she doing here?" Henri asked, his tone wary.

"Citric told me he knew someone at court who might be willing to fund my campaign."

"You left camp to meet a court spy and you didn't tell anyone?" he raged.

"A decision I regret."

He clenched his jaw and inhaled a long-suffering breath. "Eve?"

"She is wealthy. New money."

"Why would she want to bring down the King?"

"I do not know, but it does not matter. She is my only chance. Except she hates me."

"She was one of your ladies."

"You say that like they all hated me. Envy is not the same as hate."

"How does she know Citric?"

Brielle noted the verbal sidestep with irritation.

"I do not know."

They exchanged a meaningful look.

"We need to find out," Henri said.

Henri had watched Eve all day from a casual distance as she spoke with everyone in the camp and caught up on all the news. She had remarked at how much older the children were and had held the new babies that had been born in her absence. Clearly she knew these people or had lived here once, which was odd for a lady of high breeding, let alone a lady of the queen's court. In the afternoon,

Eve sat with the women and helped them prepare food. She took to the tasks as if she performed them every day. She joined the conversation as if she had been there from the beginning.

Henri tried to remember her from when he visited the Southern Kingdom, but he couldn't. Brielle had so many ladies at her court and his attention had been solely focused on her. He could hardly remember meeting anyone else.

Even if their paths had crossed, she would not have been memorable. She was not beautiful in the way that most court ladies were. Her features were still quite young, though her manner was as confident as a woman fully grown. He could not imagine her in a dress, dancing gracefully with a courtier, lowering her gaze demurely to any lord who paid her a compliment. She wore the clothes of a man and somehow moved like one; confident, arrogant. And though her eyes were small and narrow, they always seemed to be watching everything.

As dusk fell, the people gathered and the women began serving food. The hunting party had caught a stag, and the meat had been roasting all afternoon, tender and pink, the smoky aroma of spiced flesh wafting on the breeze. Finally alone, Eve sat near the campfire, eagerly consuming the food on her plate with a cup of brew at her feet. She looked too young to drink liquor so potent, but she did so as if it were water.

Henri thanked the women piling food on his plate before he turned and made his way over to her.

She didn't even look up as she said, "So you've finally decided to stop watching me."

He inclined his head to the spot next to her. "May I?"

She lifted her face to him, her murderous expression daring him to sit.

So he did.

She looked away, equal parts furious and unimpressed, but despite himself, he could not help being impressed by her. For someone so young, she seemed completely self-assured. It was in the way she carried herself, the way she spoke so forthrightly. As if she knew exactly who she was and what she believed in, and nothing and no one in the world could sway her. It was admirable. And strangely alluring. She turned her attention back to him and cocked an eyebrow before he realized he'd been staring.

"Is this her doing? Has she sent you to seduce me for information?"

"Would it work?"

Her expression deadpanned.

"I didn't think so."

He let a tactical silence expand between them as he ate his food. The tension grew thick like smoke until he could almost taste it in the air. After a few moments, she shifted slightly, and he smiled inwardly at her discomfort. She turned to him, sensing his smug victory.

Her eyes fixed on him, no doubt trying to unnerve him.

"What happened to you?"

He furrowed his brows, surprised at the question. Her gaze traced the lingering shadows of bruises beneath his skin. It had been over a week since the fight. He had healed enough to walk unaided and had returned to sleeping in his own tent, but his body was still tender to the touch and his ribs hurt every time he inhaled. He doubted his nose would ever heal properly.

"Citric," he replied, trying to sound dismissive.

Her lips split into a beaming smile. "That was a long time coming."

"Why do you say that?"

"Ask him."

"I'm asking you."

She did not reply. She simply turned her attention to the campfire, a ghost of a smile on her lips.

"You seem to know each other quite well. Odd for a lady to be so well acquainted with a notorious outlaw."

She shrugged her slender shoulders. "I know all sorts of people. In fact, I have been getting very well acquainted with an old friend of yours. Lord Nathaniel. He's stationed at the Southern Kingdom now."

Henri straightened at the mention of his friend. Her tone was implying, but he couldn't quite decipher the meaning behind her words. Nathaniel had never shown an interest in anyone, friend or lover, except for him, and that was only at the insistence of his father, and purely for the purposes of political gain. Nathaniel was like a fortress; heavily guarded, impenetrable. Even after a decade of friendship, Henri had often felt as if he knew nothing personal about him. It had never bothered him much because Nathaniel had always been a constant by his side, loyal.

Until he betrayed him.

"You really have no clue do you," she bit out, her tone suddenly angry. She shook her head in disbelief and shot to her feet. Before walking away, she tossed over her shoulder, "You two deserve each other."

⁂

Citric was leaning against a tree, watching the interaction between Eve and the prince from a distance, when suddenly she stood up and stormed off. He pushed away from the tree and cut through the camp so that their paths would cross. She must have caught sight of him out of the corner of her eye because she stopped to confront him.

"Why did you call me back here? Both of them are as ignorant and useless as each other. How are they supposed to help me?"

"I told you." He kept his voice calm and reassuring. "Both of them have a recognized claim. The people will fight for them. And the princess is determined to reclaim her kingdom. She may be ignorant, but she does not lack resolve."

"Resolve only gets you so far."

"You need them."

"I doubt it," she shot back tersely.

A grin tugged at the corner of his lips, but he tried to keep it at bay. It would only inflame her fury if she saw it. Eve was an extraordinary young woman, but she always felt everything so intensely. Grief. Love. Anger. It led her to be impulsive at times and quick to draw judgment. Her convictions and readiness to act were useful qualities in a spy, but she needed to learn to manage her emotions. He hoped it would come with experience and maturity.

"How did they even get here?" she asked.

"They fled into the wood trying to escape the King's Guard."

"You should have let them die."

"Perhaps. But I didn't."

Eve scowled and released an exasperated breath. "How exactly do you see this playing out?"

"I have merely set the board and brought the players together. Now it's between all of you to figure out who makes the first move."

She stared back at him for a moment, her shrewd eyes calculating. Finally, she said, "I saw the remains of what you did to the prince."

A flash of regret passed over his features before they tightened into a neutral expression. "I shouldn't have let it happen. It hasn't been easy having them here."

"You don't need to justify yourself to me. I would have killed them, remember?"

Citric smiled a little as he regarded her; this girl who had grown into a strong young woman.

"Do you want to know how I would play it?"

"How?" she asked curiously.

"Let her come to you."

⟡

Despite the warmth of the fire in the hearth, Brielle did not sleep well that night. Every time she closed her eyes, she saw the fluttering white figure fall from the highest tower. Her mother. Surely if she had been pushed, she would have screamed.

She had not screamed.

Brielle tossed and turned on her bedroll. She tried to distract her mind with other thoughts, but it was no use. The hours crept by like thieves in the night and the memory still haunted her, chasing sleep away. Her mother was dead. She did not cry, though. She should cry. The woman had been her mother, after all. She should feel something, and she did, but whatever it was, it did not feel right. It certainly wasn't enough to make her cry. Perhaps Eve was right, she only cared about herself.

In the early hours of the morning, just before sun's rise, Brielle finally relented. She wrapped a shawl around her shoulders, courtesy of Sienna's friendship with the weaving women, and silently slipped out of the ruin.

The woods were dark and quiet, with only a shadow of silver light from the moon. It was barely enough light to see one foot in front of her, but she would not be wandering far. She just needed to walk. Anywhere would do.

The moonlight cast the trees in shades of black, the space between them in hues of gray. The air was heavy with the scent of morning dew. As she walked, a light mist snaked along the floor of the woodland, enveloping her feet so that she could barely see past her ankles. The sight was eerie at first because the mist seemed to appear out of nowhere and move so quickly she thought it might seize her by the feet and drag her down. But it didn't. Of course it didn't. The light mist danced around her ankles, making it look like she was walking through clouds.

As the sun spilled over the horizon, the woodland became the most beautiful view she had ever seen. Soft warm light beamed through the trees as if God himself was casting it. Dew droplets glistened as if the woodland floor were a sea of diamonds. Brielle kept slowly walking, soaking up the enchanted natural beauty before it melted away in the daylight.

She halted at the vision of a sprawling oak tree, perhaps the largest she had ever seen. It was not tall but it was wide, and at the base of it, as if being revealed by a curtain of mist, sat a man. Brielle clutched her shawl tighter around her chest. The man was sitting cross-legged, his eyes closed, his body unmoving. After a moment, she made to approach, but a twig snapped under her foot. The man's eyes shot open, dazed until his gaze found her.

"S-sorry," she stammered, shocked that he was alive. "I did not mean to disturb you."

"Not at all."

He was young, perhaps only a year older than her, with a dark head of unruly curls and kind eyes.

She turned to leave but hesitated. "Are you all right?"

"Of course."

Of course. He was simply sitting alone, unmoving, at the base of a tree, surrounded by a playful mist.

"Were you sleeping?"

"Praying."

"Oh. Aren't you supposed to kneel to pray?"

"I don't think the Divine requires us to be on our knees in order to converse with him."

Brielle arched an eyebrow, surprised. She would if she were God.

"You are Brielle. I'm Father Bastien."

"Citric's priest."

"Yes. You will be relieved to hear I am marrying your friends today."

"Today?"

"I would have married them sooner but Citric insisted that we wait for the new moon."

Had Sienna told her that the wedding would be today? Surely Brielle would have remembered if she had. But perhaps it was yet another thing they hadn't really spoken about. Sienna had told her about Father Bastien and that he was willing to perform the ceremony, but Brielle had not asked her any more about it. Guilt seeped into her veins, cold and foreign.

"Will God forgive them?" Her voice was small, timid.

Father Bastien frowned. "For creating a child outside of marriage? The child was created in love. What is there to forgive?"

Brielle pursed her lips. She was starting to question whether he was, in fact, a priest. All the priests she had ever met constantly spoke of the inherent sinful nature of people, the need to repent, and the terrible consequences they would suffer of living life outside of God's laws.

"Do you often pray under a tree?" She waved her hand, indicating the sprawling oak behind him.

"I pray wherever I like and I like it here. It's quiet, peaceful, private."

"I-I'm so sorry," she stammered, and turned to go.

"I didn't mean it like that." He laughed. "I mean, that's why you're here, isn't it?"

She considered the beautiful scenery surrounding her, the quietness of the early hour. It was indeed peaceful. "I just needed to walk."

"Something is troubling you." It was a statement, not a question.

"No, I'm fine."

She didn't know why she was lying. Habit, she supposed. The only people in her life she could ever really talk honestly with were Sienna and Henri. Yet she had not told either of them of her mother's death. Sienna would be horrified. She would feel guilty that they had not tried harder to convince her mother to come with them that night.

Henri would listen, but she didn't know whether he would understand. She knew nothing about his relationship with his own mother, whether they were close or whether she was even still alive. He had never spoken of her. He had loathed his father, though, and his father had been taken from him. She wondered what he had felt when his father died. If it had felt like this. She couldn't even put into words what she was feeling. Couldn't explain it if she wanted to.

"Do you want to tell me about it? Sometimes talking to a stranger can help."

Brielle opened her mouth to refuse, but hesitated. She looked around again, uncertain.

"Come, sit."

He indicated for her to sit beneath the tree, almost beside him but divided by a rather large raised root. She walked over, collected her skirts and sat down on the damp earth. He nodded, satisfied, then turned away slightly to offer her a semblance of privacy. Brielle pressed her lips together nervously and tried to order her thoughts. They seemed to jump at her, scrambling for her attention, competing for her voice.

"Just speak whatever is in your heart," Father Bastien suggested gently.

She inhaled a scant breath. "My mother is dead."

It was such a simple thing to say, but it was the first time she had said it out loud.

"I was told she threw herself from the high tower. That's a sin, is it not? To take your own life?"

"That's not a sin, that's a tragedy."

They sat together in a strange, comfortable silence until her thoughts quietened.

"I did not know her very well, but I despised her," she admitted. "She was ... plain. And sad. And broken. My father never loved her. To be honest, he could not stand to be near her. No one could. She was not fit to be queen. She was everything I did not want to be."

Brielle glanced around the woodland as it stirred with life beneath the sun's rise.

"I used to think if I was beautiful and strong and perfect, everyone would love me. But it turns out I was wrong, everyone hated me anyway."

It surprised her to find tears welling behind her eyes. She refused to let them fall, though. Brielle was not a fool. She knew that her ladies had never truly been her friends. She could not trust them with her secrets, but she thought that they at least admired her. Wanted to be her. But all this time they had hated her, not for her position or her beauty or her wealth, but for her arrogance, her ignorance.

"Unrequited love is the worst kind of pain," Father Bastien mused. "It's a form of torture. A slow, painful death."

Brielle wasn't sure what he was talking about, but she did not question him. She was content to simply sit here and become lost in the silence of her own thoughts.

Eventually he said, "I'm sure your mother loved you very much. And not because you were a beautiful child but because you were her daughter."

Brielle lowered her gaze to the crushed leaves at her feet. "If she did, I never felt it."

She could not call forth a single memory of tenderness from her mother. The woman had never told her she loved her or been affectionate or complimentary. She had always been consumed by her own melancholy, unable to see anything or anyone outside of it.

"Society tries to tell us who is worthy and who is not. Of love, of power, of life. They try to tell us what we should value and what we should not. Beauty, wealth, status, gender. All to control us, to ensure we live our lives by their rules. It sounds to me like your mother did not live her life by societie's rules."

Brielle looked over at him with furrowed brows.

In response to her confused look, he explained, "Society is ruled by men. To retain their power, they force women to take up the smallest space in the room, if they are permitted to be in the room at all. As long as you stand there quietly, look pretty and smile, they will permit you to breathe. They will tolerate you while you make yourself smaller and smaller until you slowly shrink away to nothing but a shadow of who you could have been. Some women accept this and bend accordingly, but others do not. Either way, there is a cost. On some days it is enough to break even the strongest of us."

"Us? You are not a woman. How do you know such things?"

"Men are not ignorant of what we do. We are ignorant of the cost to ourselves." His lips twitched in wry irony. "I am a man. In a lot of ways that protects me, in other ways it does not."

Brielle considered his words for a moment before he added, "I do not think your father didn't love your mother because she was plain or unlovable. I do not think your mother was weak. We do not choose the bodies we are put into or the minds we are given or who we fall in love with in this short life. Unfortunately, society—men—like to put rules around such things."

"Is that why you are here?" Brielle asked hesitantly.

He returned a sad smile. "I always knew I was different, but I didn't know why, until I fell in love with a man. If I had stayed at the monastery, they would have killed me for it. These people I had known my whole life, my brothers who had raised me from boyhood, they would have been the first to throw stones. But love, in whatever form, is never wrong. It is what connects us all. Our need to love and be loved."

Brielle had heard whispers about such things: men lying with other men, women sharing romantic feelings for each other, but they had always been labeled unnatural.

"It is more common than you think." Father Bastien smiled, reading her thoughts.

Brielle felt the breeze play with her hair as she reflected on his words. All her life her father had ignored her mother, pretended she did not exist, save for official occasions where he was forced to acknowledge her absence. But he also ignored every other lady at court. She had never seen him flirt or dance with anyone. She had never heard rumors about him having affairs or destroying the reputations of young ladies. Perhaps he was simply discreet, but Brielle knew how hard it was to keep a secret at court. The very walls had ears.

Once upon a time, her mother had loved her father deeply and desperately, and it broke her heart that he did not love her in return. But perhaps it was not her mother's fault that he did not love her. Perhaps he could not love her. Perhaps love was not something that could be controlled.

"Loving yourself despite what others may think of you is sometimes the hardest battle of all."

Father Bastien's words drew her attention back to him. She had always thought highly of herself, had never questioned her worth, but that was because she was born to a great destiny. She was born to rule the Southern Kingdom.

"Without my title, my crown, my kingdom ... I am nothing."

Worse than nothing, Eve had said. Ordinary, she had called her.

"Nobody is nothing as long as they are something to someone. Love. Friendship. Hope. These are the things that truly have value in this life. These are the things worth fighting for."

Their eyes met, and he nodded as if she had finally been let in on a universal secret. She had friends, people who had stayed by her side, fought for her, risked their lives for her despite her losing everything she ever had to offer them. That was love. She was loved.

Eve was wrong about her. She didn't only care for herself. She would fight for them, her friends. She would give them the only thing she had left to offer.

Hope.

CHAPTER NINE

B rielle could not tear her eyes away from the sight of her beautiful friend standing opposite the man she loved, the father of her unborn child, now officially her husband. Not even the magnificence of the grand ruin they stood in could distract her from this enchanted moment.

She had expected the ceremony to be performed in the woods, a quiet private affair beneath the trees, but Citric had insisted that the ceremony be performed here, in the large hall with the intricate tiled floor. It had been transformed into a wonder of natural beauty. Without a roof overhead, the warm afternoon light poured in from all directions. Garlands of flowers hung from the archways, scenting the room with sweet perfume. Everyone from Alkhiem had come to bear witness to this act of love, dressed in their finest clothes, the girls with flowers in their hair. Everyone held a single wax candle set into a smooth, round wooden holder.

Brielle had insisted that Sienna prepare herself in her room so that she could help her friend get ready. She was surprised when one of the weaving women interrupted them to present Sienna with a dress; the dress that Brielle had coveted weeks ago. It was a gift from Citric, the woman had said, a blessing for her special day. Sienna's face had lit up with pure joy at the sight of it. Her hands had roamed the rich material as Brielle helped her step into it. She looked absolutely stunning. The women even helped Brielle find small purple flowers to match Sienna's lilac silk sash. She wove them into Sienna's golden braid as she fashioned it into a crown atop her head.

Jameson's face when he beheld his beautiful bride walking toward him was something Brielle would never forget. He looked completely overwhelmed by the sight of her. His eyes never left her face with every step she took, and they had misted when she smiled at him. He had not been able to stop himself from stepping forward to meet her halfway, much to the amusement of the crowd. It was as if he could not bear to be apart from her for another second.

Father Bastien's ceremony was not the dry sermon of a priest but rather the honest words of a man, spoken from the heart. This was a celebration of love, not doctrine. There would be no vows more sacred than those exchanged between two hearts. Brielle's cheeks ached from smiling so much, but she couldn't help the renewed tug on her lips as she watched Jameson slip a ring on her friend's finger. The crowd erupted in applause at their kiss, which was sweet and passionate. Brielle glanced over at Henri, who returned a secret smile.

The festivities that followed the ceremony overflowed with mirth, feasting, and dancing. The music was lively with the beat of frame drums and tambourines, punctured with the fast-paced strings of the fiddle. Brielle had never heard such music before. It was wild and infectious. She felt like it was infiltrating her body, tempting her soul to dance.

The dancing was not the usual partner dances of court, rather everyone was dancing freely with everyone. Forming great circles held by hands that would break apart and come together again, skipping partners across the dirt floor, forming long lines and archways with their arms, through which people would gallop down until they galloped back up again. The dancing was pure joy.

At court, dancing was a finely tuned ritual, a spectacle whose purpose was usually political. Lords would invite ladies to dance as a form of courtship, and ladies would use the opportunity to show off years of practiced skill; their elegance of movement, the grace of their lithe bodies. All in the hopes of securing a husband.

Brielle had danced with many princes seeking to court her. She had also danced with countless foreign dignitaries and wealthy noblemen whose support her father depended on. It was expected of her to charm them, to dance prettily and smile at them. She had never questioned her duty to perform, in fact she relished her position of power, but she had never before danced for the simple pure joy of it.

She wanted to join in, but propriety kept her on the sidelines. Even though none of the other women were waiting for a man to invite them to dance. They were all joining the fray, dancing with each other as much as with the men. Still, she felt like she would be intruding if she joined them. She clapped her hands along to the beat, content to watch everyone laughing and enjoying themselves.

It was a beautiful night for a celebration. The new moon looked spectacular hanging in the sky and the stars seemed to be especially bright. Even the woodland appeared to be aware of the festivities, because hundreds of tiny fireflies flittered in the darkness amongst the trees, glowing and dancing. She had never seen them appear on any other night. It was as if the wood wanted to revel with them.

Brielle did not know what to make of this strange wood. All the tales she had ever heard about the Red Wood were dark and frightening; that it was cursed, filled with vengeful ghosts and angry spirits and blood magic. Having traveled the length of it across both kingdoms and bathed in its rivers and slept beneath its canopy of trees, she could not say that she had encountered any spirits or curses. But she had felt—something. It was almost like the woods possessed a sentience, within itself and with those who entered it. She felt like it was aware of her, somehow.

Brielle's attention caught on Sienna as she approached, a cup of spiced wine in her hand.

"Mrs. Jameson." Brielle bowed her head slightly and Sienna laughed. "Why are you not dancing with your handsome husband?"

"I needed some refreshment. The dancing is quite spirited."

"It is," she agreed, and took a moment to survey her beautiful friend. "You look stunning. That dress was made for you."

"It was made for some nobleman's wife," she pointed out.

"Or his mistress."

They burst out into laughter.

"I still cannot believe Citric gave it to you."

"And the ring." Sienna spread her fingers out to reveal a stunning gold ring with a diamond set in the center.

"What?" Brielle leaned in closer to inspect it.

"He gave Jameson a few pieces from his collection and told him that the blacksmith would melt them down and make anything he wanted. Jameson asked for this."

Brielle blinked, stunned. The ring was indeed a work of art.

"He has been more than generous to us," Sienna said.

"I am glad for it. You deserve nothing less."

Brielle reached out to touch Sienna's slightly protruding belly, even though she knew she would not feel anything through the heavy corset and lace.

"And how is the little one?"

Sienna's features softened, as if she too knew this was the first time Brielle had asked about the babe. She glanced down at her bump with pride and unconditional love.

"She is well. A little excited by all the rich food but well."

"She?"

Sienna shrugged. "There is no way to know, of course, but I have a feeling."

"Well then, she is the luckiest babe in the world to have you as her mother."

Sienna smiled softly. "Thank you."

Brielle took her hand in hers and gave it a slight squeeze. "I am sorry that was not the first thing I said to you when I learned of her."

Sienna shook her head. "It's okay."

"It's not. I have been a terrible friend. I promise to do better."

"Brielle, you have never been just my friend. You are also my queen. It changes things."

"I have been a terrible queen as well and I swear from this day on I am going to do better."

Sienna raised her chin slightly in acceptance of the proclamation.

"May I interrupt?" Father Bastien asked as he approached.

"Father, the service was beautiful," Sienna gushed.

"You have a way with words," Brielle agreed.

"Love is universal. It is easy to put into words, but I never tire of witnessing it."

"Most wedding services I have witnessed have been dreadfully dull," Brielle said.

Father Bastien smiled knowingly. "I must admit, since leaving the church I have enjoyed the freedom to explore doing things a little unconventionally. Though I suppose some would consider the rituals here to be very unconventional."

"Yes, I'm relieved I did not have to wound myself on my wedding day."

Brielle frowned. "Wound yourself?"

"When a couple wishes to be married here, they must wait for a new moon," Sienna explained.

"The people believe the power of the new moon strengthens the marriage bonds," Father Bastien added.

"The four elements must be present in the ceremony: earth, air, fire, and water."

The women all wore flowers weaved through their hair and everyone held a single candle, Brielle recalled. Father Bastien had dipped his fingers into a bowl of water before placing the tip of his thumb to their foreheads as they stood at the altar. Brielle had assumed it was a blessing using holy water, but now it seemed like it was part of some pagan ritual.

"Couples here don't exchange rings. They give blood oaths to each other. They cut open their left palms and place them on top of each other, letting the blood flow into one."

Brielle wasn't sure what to say to that. It sounded awful.

"Thankfully, Father Bastien was willing to skip that part." Sienna laughed.

"The people here have their beliefs and their way of doing things, but they always accept others who believe differently. I hope you will share a long and happy life together." Father Bastien bowed his head in blessing.

"Thank you, Father."

Brielle watched as Father Bastien walked on to join a nearby conversation. Willow's hand; she recalled she had a nasty red scar across her left palm. Willow was married, she realized. Or blood bound. Whatever they called it here. She still couldn't quite believe people willingly marked themselves, especially women.

At court, the smallest imperfection could render a woman undesirable. A scar would make her unmarriageable and therefore worthless.

Brielle turned her attention back to Sienna, whose gaze was lingering across the way. She followed her gaze to see Eve reaching out to Citric, trying to coax him to dance with her. Amusement tugged at his lips as the others around him goaded him to take her hand. He reluctantly did so, and she clutched his hand within both of hers as she led him to join the dance.

"I wonder what they are to each other," Sienna murmured as she raised the wine to her lips.

Brielle knew what she meant. Eve was clearly besotted with him. Sometimes she acted indifferent, as if he were nothing more than a passing acquaintance, but other times she looked at him for just a moment too long, her eyes holding a girlish longing. She was sixteen, after all. It was normal to entertain romantic thoughts. Most girls were married at her age.

At nineteen, Brielle was considered by some to be past marriageable age. Certainly her father's councilmen had become frustrated with her reluctance to choose a husband. It was strange to think of it. If she had been anyone else's daughter, she would be married by now, her husband chosen for her, perhaps a baby already in the cradle. She still felt so naïve to it all. Inexperienced.

She had always enjoyed the pretty compliments lords paid her and appreciated a handsome face as much as any other lady, but she had only ever felt fleeting moments of desire once or twice in her life. What she had felt with Citric in the river that day surprised her. It was strong and instinctive, as if her body knew things she did not.

With Henri it had felt more like a soul connection, a friendship which had begun with the brightest of sparks but settled into a low burning flame over many months of correspondence. Through their letters, she felt like he really saw her. They had, of course, indulged in flirtations with each other, but they were meaningless. Nothing could ever happen between them. The Old Treaty forbade it. Which made it safe for her to have some fun, but also to let herself be truly seen by him.

The way Eve looked at Citric, though, was something else entirely. It was as if they already shared a connection and she wanted it to change, to go deeper. If Citric knew how Eve felt, he did not show it. He clearly did not feel the same.

She was almost certain he didn't.

But then he betrayed no indication of what had occurred between them either. No one would ever know that he had looked at her with barely restrained desire, that they had almost kissed. He had not shown more than polite interest in her since that day in the river. He had not come to her room or tried to catch moments alone with her. In fact, he had barely spoken a single word to her. Perhaps she had misread the entire interaction, and it had been nothing more than a moment of fleeting desire. Brielle's heart sank. The thought hurt more than she would have liked to admit.

Brielle felt the heat of a body at her back as Henri came to stand behind her. It reminded her of the first night they met, when she had felt his breath kiss the slope of her neck as he tried to coax her attention away from Lady Quinne. He had tried to seduce her that night, pursued her as if he were a hunter and she the prey, but now he simply said, "Do we know their history yet?"

Brielle sighed. "Not yet. Sienna, you could ask her about it. You two seem close." She tried to keep any traces of bitterness from her voice.

Sienna's expression turned uneasy. "I know, but I don't want to use our friendship to pry."

"Well, I cannot ask her. She hates me."

"You could ask Citric," Sienna suggested.

"Why would he tell me anything?"

Sienna gave her a pointed look. Brielle's heart quickened at the implication.

"A conversation for another time, perhaps." Henri held his hand out to Brielle and his eyes sparkled mischievously.

Brielle smiled as she took his hand. She didn't know any of these dances and she was likely going to make a fool of herself, but it did not matter because he would be right there beside her, making a fool of himself as well.

They held hands even as they joined the circle and tried to mimic the steps and hops of the others. She laughed as the direction changed suddenly and

Henri almost fell over. The circle moved inward as people clapped their hands and then moved back out before breaking apart to form smaller groups of four. Everyone raised their hands to the center of their group and danced clockwise, the women now and then indulging in a spin. The smaller groups came together to reform the larger circle and the pace of the music quickened.

Having now learned the steps, Henri did not falter, even as the music rose faster and faster and others stumbled. He held her hand tight, his smile triumphant as they kept pace with the beat until its dramatic conclusion. Everyone clapped as they laughed, bent over with exhaustion and keen for refreshment.

A single lute started playing a delicate melody, and everyone cheered anew, searching for the newlywed couple. They were ushered into the center of the dancefloor and Jameson offered Sienna a courtly bow before he swept her into his arms. It was a beautiful song, sweet and joyful. Jameson and Sienna clearly did not know the steps, but it did not matter. They stepped and swayed as if they were the only two people in the world. When he leaned in for a kiss, the crowd cheered again.

Other couples began to dance around them. Henri tugged at her hand, and Brielle obliged, following him to the dancefloor. He slid his hand around her waist and she slid hers around his as he moved them in a slow circle, both of them facing opposite directions. She reached her hand up and he met it with his own. They were sharing the lead, she realized, making up the steps in the moment, each anticipating what the other would do and meeting them halfway. It was as if their bodies moved as one, as if they each knew this dance instinctively and it was only ever meant for them.

Henri turned, and their bodies came together in a firm embrace. Brielle's breath hitched in her throat. She could feel the warmth of his palm against the small of her back, the broad expanse of his chest pressing against her breasts. Something flickered across his face and she wondered if he had felt it too. Whatever had just charged between them. They were so close she could see the faint stubble lining his jaw. His hazel eyes were intense as they focused on her. Her body moved as if by his command. Her heart thundered against her rib cage as delicious warmth spread through her core.

The wanting was clear in his eyes, but there was also something else, something more. Suddenly, she wished they were alone. She wished she were brave. She wished he would never stop looking at her like that. But as the dance ended and the couples around them applauded, Henri let her go.

Henri tried to compose himself when he saw Brielle standing on the bottom step of a stone staircase that no longer led anywhere. His thoughts were still spinning from the dance they had shared last night. The feel of her soft body flush against his, the way her rosebud lips had parted when he pressed closer. The scent of her had invaded his dreams last night, forcing him to take matters into his own hands. Even now he was afraid to get too close, lest his desire manifest.

He had not been with a woman for over a year now. Despite owning the Sodisce he had not partaken in the pleasures of the women in his employ, but whatever had sparked between them last night was more than just the physical longing between two bodies. He had felt undeniably drawn to her. To be honest, he had been feeling it for a while now, this growing need to be beside her. And there she stood, resplendent despite her lack of fine clothes and jewels. Defiant against the world that would see her torn down, displaced from her throne. She was innocent and untouched and Gods be damned he wanted her. Not as a conquest or a distraction or a release, but as *his*. And perhaps he would have told her that if they were alone, but they were not, so he tried to compose himself.

Eve was standing off to the side, in front of the crumbling wall, her arms crossed as if she had been impatiently waiting for hours. Citric was leaning against the staircase, as if he did not care to be a part of this conversation and was only here because it was happening in his woodland.

Yesterday, Brielle had asked them to meet her in the ruins at noon. He presumed to discuss the proposal of Eve funding her campaign.

"What are you doing here?" Brielle asked.

Henri frowned at Brielle's perplexed expression, but before he could answer, a voice came from behind him.

"What do you mean? We are a part of this as well," Sienna insisted, holding hands with Jameson as they approached.

"It's the day after your wedding. You should be … well, not here."

"Yesterday was for celebrating our wedding, today is for making plans to reclaim your kingdom."

Brielle straightened slightly, seemingly emboldened by the confidence in her friend's voice. She returned a small smile of gratitude.

"If there is anything left to reclaim," Eve drawled, drawing everyone's attention to her. "None of you have any idea what has been happening."

"Then tell us," Henri said flatly.

Her features hardened. "After winning the battle, King Heroux took control of the combined Northern and Southern armies. Those who resisted were killed where they stood. He divided the army, taking half to the Northern Kingdom where he has remained ever since. The other half came to the Southern Kingdom under the command of his right hand, a man the people have taken to calling the Butcher."

Henri flicked his gaze to Brielle, but she was focused on Eve, her expression troubled.

"He rules the South for King Heroux, and he rules it without mercy. King Heroux immediately implemented high taxes to pay for his previous war campaigns, and to fund future ones, no doubt. The people cannot afford it. They were already facing lean harvests, now they are starving to death in the streets. Those who cannot pay their taxes are executed. Men. Women. And children."

Sienna's hand went to her belly.

"Homes have been set alight, entire families burned to death. At first there were some who resisted, but enough examples have been made now that no one dares resist anymore. Nightly curfews are in place, people are afraid to walk the streets. Not even courtiers are safe. Many tried to bribe the King's Guard to make exceptions for them, but the King's Guard are unpredictable. They have looted grand estates, defiled noblemen's wives and daughters. Usually tyranny only breaks the poor, but the wealthy are also living on a knife's edge at the mercy of the King's Guard. There is no one to stop them."

Henri had heard the rumors about the taxes and the rampant executions. Exorbitant taxes had been implemented in the Northern Kingdom as well, but the enforcement had not been as severe as the Southern Kingdom. Perhaps because the Butcher was not there to do so. On his orders, Fleur had bribed the King's Guard to look the other way and because the Sodisce was one of their favorite establishments, they had been more than happy to.

Until they had come for him.

"My ladies?" Brielle asked.

"Our positions afford us little protection. Those that were able to have returned to their country estates, but those that cannot ..." Eve faltered for words before steeling herself again. "We try to avoid the attention of the King's Guard as much as we can."

"And you?"

Eve cocked her head at Brielle with derision. "I remain at court. I can take care of myself."

Henri didn't doubt it. She looked as small as a fawn, but she moved with the strength and confidence of a stag. She had a swagger he had only ever seen men walk with, and only when they knew they could handle themselves against any enemy.

"So, what is this grand plan of yours to reclaim your kingdom?" Eve asked mockingly.

Brielle squared her shoulders as if she were trying to push the horrors from her mind. "I need an army."

"And where do you suppose you will find one?"

"I'll buy one. Mercenaries."

"Murderers with no morality or loyalty, save for themselves. Brilliant idea."

"They'll be loyal to me."

"They'll murder you in your sleep. I would."

"Eve." Citric's voice was smooth, but the warning was clear.

"The way I see it, there is one enemy but two battlegrounds: North and South," Jameson began.

"Or perhaps there is no battleground," Sienna interjected. "King Heroux won because he murdered both Kings in one blow. A kingdom without a king is easy to take. So we don't fight a battle, we just kill King Heroux."

Jameson stared at his wife as if he could not believe she had uttered such words. His expression was still somewhat stunned as he turned to Henri and asked, "How fortified is the northern castle?"

"Heavily. My father saw enemies around every corner, even inside the castle walls. You'll never get to him. If you want to kill King Heroux, you'll have to lure him out into the open."

"You mean we," Brielle said. Their eyes locked onto each other. "*We* will have to lure him out so *you* can reclaim *your* kingdom."

He knew what she was asking without saying the words. She wanted to know whether he had changed his mind, whether he wanted it. Henri shifted uncomfortably on his feet, unsure what to say, how to make her understand. His silence must have said it all because Eve furrowed her brows.

"You don't want to be king?" For once, there was no bravado or skepticism in her tone.

As he held Brielle's stare, his expression tightened. "I will fight with you. To free our people and to see you returned to your throne, but that is all."

Brielle's cheeks flushed with indignant anger. "You heard what Sienna said, a kingdom without a ruler is easy to take."

"And you want to be queen of both kingdoms, I presume," Eve said. At Brielle's wide-eyed objection she said, "Oh please, don't pretend like you haven't thought about it."

"And what is your motivation in all of this?" Brielle returned fire. "For all your talk of caring for the people, I think you might desire the throne for yourself. You claim that you are better than me, but perhaps you are just jealous."

"Jealous of what? Being despised? Looking like a fool? Almost anyone would be a better ruler than you. Even Citric."

Everyone's gaze turned to Citric, who was silently leaning against the stairway, his arms folded in front of his chest. He shrugged, the corners of his mouth tugging up into a sly grin. "Everyone loves an outlaw."

Sienna stepped forward, placing herself between Brielle and Eve. "Brielle knows that she's made mistakes. Who here is not guilty of that? The main thing is she is willing to do better. She is willing to fight for her people, and even for people who are not hers." Sienna threw a sharp look at Henri.

"As I was saying, there are two battlefields." Jameson drew everyone's attention back to the task at hand.

Henri nodded, grateful for the diffusion. "We take the Southern Kingdom first and then use their army to lure King Heroux out onto the battlefield to claim the Northern Kingdom."

"And how do you propose we take the Southern Kingdom?" Eve asked impatiently.

"Well, we already have a spy on the inside." He flashed a wry smile.

She returned a flat look.

"Perhaps we do not need an army," Brielle mused, as though an idea was forming in her mind. "My father was not paranoid. The castle is heavily guarded, but not impenetrable. Perhaps all we need is a small group of well-trained men."

Citric went deathly still. A heavy silence fell amongst them as they considered the implication of her words.

"We have already paid you a fortune in compensation," Henri said to Citric as he exchanged a conspiratorial look with Brielle.

"Compensation for harboring traitors to the Crown, not for fighting in your wars," Citric returned.

"Then what can I offer you?" Brielle asked. "Immunity from the Crown for you and your people?"

"We are already immune under Woodland Law."

"What?"

"You don't even know your own laws." Eve rolled her eyes.

Henri shot Eve a hard look before he explained, "When the Old Treaty was written, so too was Woodland Law. The law makes it illegal for anyone to enter these woods. But for those who do, they are not subject to Crown law."

Brielle frowned, clearly intrigued, but she kept her focus on the task at hand.

"You said once that you and your people are bonded by a dream; to build a home, to live your lives free of fear and persecution. That is what I want for my people as well."

"Then that is your responsibility. I have a responsibility to my people to keep them safe, to not let them die fighting someone else's war."

"This will likely become your war. I doubt King Heroux will abide by the Old Treaty or Woodland Law. He will come for your people next."

"Perhaps."

"You won't stand a chance against him alone," Henri warned.

"Many have tried to destroy my people, yet here we still stand."

"My people, your people; why does it matter whose people belong to who?" Jameson threw his arms out in exasperation. "We are all the same. We all deserve to live our lives and raise our children in a world without fear."

Sienna moved to his side, taking his hand firmly in hers.

"Rowan would do it." Eve's voice was small and sad as it cut through the tension.

Citric's eyes snapped to her in warning.

"He would fight with them, you know he would. If you won't do it for me, then do it for Rowan."

In one brutal motion, Citric pushed off the stairs and walked away. Eve inhaled a shattered breath, as if something inside her was broken.

"I will speak to him," she said, before turning to follow him.

Henri stepped closer to Brielle as they all exchanged looks.

"Do you think she will be able to convince him?" Sienna asked no one in particular.

"If anyone could, it would be her," Henri replied. Which wasn't exactly an answer, but he did not want to smother their only hope.

Brielle turned to him, her mind clearly churning something over. "Do you still have access to your network of spies?"

The question surprised him. He hadn't contacted anyone, except for Ele, since the day his father was murdered. They had all likely gone to ground or started working for someone else.

"I could contact them if I needed to." He tilted his head in thought. "I would need to pay them well, though. Not only for information, but for their loyalty. Our whereabouts are probably the most valuable piece of information on the market right now."

"What are you thinking?" Sienna asked her friend.

"I am thinking there is more than one way to wage a war. I may not know how to use weapons or fight or command an army, but that does not mean I do not know how to destroy someone."

Henri furrowed his brows, and Jameson frowned, but Sienna's mouth curved into a knowing smile.

⸙

Citric stalked into the camp, his strides long and livid. Some people cast curious glances his way, noting the dark change in his demeanor, but they knew better than to approach him. He stopped and rubbed a hand over his features as if he could wipe the emotions from his face. It didn't help. He was beyond furious. At Eve for so blatantly crossing a line and at himself for so quickly rising to her provocation. He had walked away when he should have stayed. It had been a pivotal moment and one comment had thrown him off his game.

At the sound of light steps approaching him from behind, he turned around, his expression like thunder. "That was unnecessary."

"It had the desired effect," Eve returned unapologetically.

Citric's features tightened in barely contained anger. He was not used to being manipulated, especially by those he trusted. He was always the one in control. Calculating every possible angle. Weaving narratives to suit his purposes, to protect his people.

"I told them I would talk you round," she said.

He forced his lips into a humorless smirk. "You're not that good at negotiating."

She crossed her arms defensively. "I have lived the last year of my life at the Southern court. I would say the pupil has outgrown the master."

"The pupil still has a lot to learn."

"Really? Let's see about that. Fight me for it. Fight me for your men."

Citric's eyebrows twitched in disapproval of the idea.

"What? It's the only way to settle this convincingly. You just said so yourself."

"I didn't— "

"Fight me for them!" she raised her voice loud enough for the entire camp to hear.

His eyes flashed in stern reproach. He knew exactly what she was trying to do; gain an audience, put on a show. Unfortunately, it was working. Everyone had stalled in their duties and were watching them with intrigue. She intended to force him into a corner publicly so that he could not back down without losing face.

"No." The word was firm and heavy with authority.

Eve had always looked up to him like a brother, with respect and admiration. He hoped it would be enough to dissuade her. It was not that he thought she would be helpless against him. Eve was well-trained and could hold her own against most opponents. But issuing a challenge like this and putting on a show for everyone was different to sparring in the training ground.

"Oh, don't you dare be a coward now," she laughed scornfully as she lowered her voice. "This was your doing. You brought me here and this is the outcome. It is our best chance. I am willing to do whatever it takes. You need to be willing to do the same."

"Not like this," he bit out each word through clenched teeth.

"You are a coward!" she yelled, taking a step back and throwing her arms wide.

Fuck.

Citric clenched his jaw. He closed the distance between them swiftly until his face was an inch away from hers. "I'm not going to hold back."

To his annoyance she did not flinch or look the least bit concerned as she replied, "Good. Neither am I."

CHAPTER TEN

B rielle was still refining the plan in her head when they entered the camp to find it abandoned. She halted as Henri moved swiftly to her side, his sword already drawn. There were no signs of a fight. Food was left on the tables, clothes hung from the lines strung up between trees. Nothing seemed to be disturbed. Henri scanned the area, alert for the smallest of movements.

"The training ground," Sienna whispered.

Brielle strained her ears against the silence to make out the muffled sounds of voices coming from the direction of the clearing. Henri nodded and signaled for them to be silent before leading the way through the city of tents. Even before they stepped out into the open ground, they saw them. The entire camp was gathered there, surrounding the training ground.

Citric and Eve stood in the middle of the fray, facing each other. Brielle spotted Father Bastien in the crowd, nervously biting his thumbnail. She quickly forged her way through the people to sidle up beside him.

"Father, what is happening?"

Father Bastien did not even look at her, he just shook his head as if he didn't know or couldn't quite believe it. "They were arguing, loud enough for the entire camp to hear. He was refusing her, she accused him of being a coward, then she challenged him."

"Challenged him?" Brielle blinked. "To a fight? She cannot be serious."

Father Bastien's hand shot out in gesture to the fight, emphasizing that she was indeed serious.

Eve was insane.

Citric was three times her size. He could break her in one blow.

"What's the challenge?" Henri asked, and Brielle startled. She hadn't realized he'd followed her and was now standing behind her, his gaze fixed ahead on the two people in the arena.

"I don't know. I don't know what they were arguing about," Father Bastien replied.

"His men," Henri whispered, his breath warm against her ear as he leaned in closer. "If she wins, his men will fight for us. It has to be."

Brielle turned her head to whisper back, and her lips almost brushed his. They stilled for a second before she said, "She's not going to win."

Their eyes held for a moment longer before she tore her gaze away to focus on the arena. Brielle watched as Eve took up what she presumed to be a fighting stance, planting her feet firmly into the ground as both of her hands gripped the hilt of a longsword. The sword was almost as tall as she was. Citric just stood there, his body and limbs relaxed, but his expression was furious.

Without warning, Eve swung the sword and Citric stepped back, letting it narrowly miss his throat. The crowd silenced. He dodged another swing with brutal efficiency before steel struck steel as Citric lifted his sword to meet her blow. She absorbed the impact without flinching and whirled to strike again and again, moving with impressive speed and agility, forcing him to relentlessly defend himself.

Brielle could not believe her eyes; Eve was matching him.

But then she was on the ground, Citric's hit faster than Brielle's eyes could follow. She was not sure if he had hit Eve with his fist or his sword, but her lip was split and blood had splattered across the dirt.

The look Eve shot him over her shoulder as he allowed her a moment to get up was lethal. Gone was the girlish longing. He was her enemy, and she was determined to cut him down. Brielle's heart thundered.

Eve flung a fist of dirt in his eyes before lunging at him as he staggered backward. Even as she swung the sword in an overhead blow, which he blocked, she reached for a dagger at her belt and sliced his torso. Brielle dug her nails deep into the palms of her hands as she beheld the blood smeared on Eve's blade.

Citric's lips pinched into a hard line, his eyes glazed with fury. Eve returned a feral grin.

Citric cocked his head and began to pace the outer line of the arena, like a predator taunting her. To Brielle's horror, Eve refused to move, letting him circle her, her eyes shrewd as she listened for his footsteps behind her. It was all Brielle could do not to scream in warning as he attacked her back, but Eve lifted her sword to block the blow at the same time as her elbow lifted to smash into his face. She whirled around, sending a knee into his gut before throwing all her weight into the blow that saw his sword fall from his hand. He tackled her and her head hit the ground with a sickening crack.

Brielle pinched her eyes closed, wincing against the sound. When she opened them, Citric was straddling Eve, pinning her wrists to the dirt in a vise grip, turning her fingers bloodless. But in one swift motion Eve arched her hips, sending him careening forward, his hands forced to brace to ensure his face would not hit the dirt. Eve grabbed at his arm as her leg encircled his leg and the manoeuver toppled him over onto his back. She flung herself on top of him and he made to shove her off, but then he stilled at the dagger now poised to penetrate his heart.

Eve had whipped it out faster than a breath, from where Brielle had no idea. The crowd was still, silent, shocked. Brielle's own eyes were wide with disbelief as Eve stared down at Citric, her expression murderous.

The air was taut, charged with danger and laced with fear that she might actually do it. After a moment, though, she stood, allowing him to pull himself out from underneath her. Without a glance at the crowd, without even a word, Citric stalked away from the training ground. Eve stared after him, her expression slowly softening, and Brielle could not help but wonder what her victory had cost her.

The atmosphere in the camp was tense. After the fight, everyone had slowly dispersed, returning to their respective duties in silent shock and palpable unease.

Henri exchanged a look with Brielle, but there was no time for words because when Eve walked off the training ground in the direction of the woods, Henri immediately followed her. He hung back a short distance out of respect, giving her some space to breathe and decompress from the adrenaline, but he knew that she knew he was there. He did not try to hide himself or silence his footfalls. He simply watched and followed as she wandered into the woods behind the ruin, seemingly knowing exactly where she was going.

Suddenly, she stopped and crouched to the ground. When he finally approached, she was pulling up a small plant.

"Sneaking up on me is unwise."

"So I see. You were impressive out there. Who taught you how to fight?"

Eve didn't reply. She simply tore some of the leaves off the plant and began chewing them. Henri considered his options. He wanted to be direct, to demand answers to specific questions, but he knew that if he did that, she would give him nothing. So he tried a different approach.

"Citric," he guessed.

She did not correct him.

"When you lived here."

"I never lived here."

Henri cocked a skeptical eyebrow. "Everyone in the camp knows you and you clearly know the way of life here."

"I visit from time to time," she said dismissively.

"Why?"

Eve stood up, her eyes searching the ground, before she walked over to inspect another patch of plants.

"Citric," he guessed again.

She did not correct him.

"You challenged him for his men."

"It was the only way," she said defensively, but her tone also held regret.

"Rowan was not enough?"

She threw a sharp look over her shoulder in warning. "You don't know what you're talking about, so don't speak his name."

"I know you both cared about him and you both lost him."

Shadows danced across her face. Memories. Sad ones.

"How did he die?" he asked gently.

Eve turned back to inspecting the plants. Henri tried to swallow his frustration, but to his surprise she replied, "In battle."

Enough time passed that Henri thought she would not say more, but eventually she added, "That's how they met. Rowan was a lieutenant in the Southern army, being a nobleman's son. Citric was a bowman in the Northern army, a commoner but popular among the soldiers, famed for his skill. They became friends when both armies joined forces against the threat of Gudrun."

Henri remembered that battle. It was the first battle he had been allowed to wet his sword in. With the combined armies of the Northern and Southern Kingdoms, they grossly outnumbered Gudrun's men, so his father had deemed it safe enough for him to join the lines. It had been a slaughter. The battle was over within the hour.

"You were there." She looked at him pointedly, her tone accusing, the plants held limp in her hands.

"I was."

"But all you remember is victory."

"Victory or no, war comes at the cost of lives," Henri said carefully.

"And certain men's lives are more expendable than others."

"Never."

Eve glanced away, her features tight with anger. Henri waited.

"Some say he was drunk or impatient, but I think he was just arrogant. So confident was he of his victory that he thought a third of his army could deliver it to him. Such was the might of the Northern King."

Henri frowned, confused, but her words stirred memories in his mind. Watching his father standing in a war tent, raging against his commander. The commander reluctantly yielding to his demands, ordering a single company of men to move out to engage the enemy while the rest of the army remained in the camp, himself and Nathaniel included. He had watched that single company march out, but he could not remember the soldiers' faces. Or what happened next.

"It was a doomed plan. As a lieutenant, Rowan could have stayed at the rear of the company, out of immediate danger, but instead he chose to lead his men into battle. He knew they would all die that day. He wanted to share in their fate. He was twenty years old."

Henri's heart ached at the raw pain etched on her young face.

"Citric saw him fall and risked his own life to retrieve his body. He took three arrows in the back, but still managed to carry Rowan off that bloody field. Then he deserted."

Henry's brows arched in surprise. Desertion from the army was a death sentence. Citric would have been hunted, there would have been no safe place for him anywhere. Except the Red Wood.

"He tried to bring Rowan's body home to me, but the journey was too long and his wounds were too great. He buried Rowan in an unmarked grave at the base of a black thorn tree."

Eve's eyes glistened, but she steeled herself against the shaking in her voice. "Rowan was the only family I had left. My mother died when I was young, my father died a year before Rowan. Without Rowan, I stood to lose everything; my home, my title. It would have all gone to some distant male relative I had never even heard of, and my fate would have been at his mercy. But Citric made Rowan a promise; that if he died, Citric would protect me. So Citric became a long-lost relative and laid claim to my family's estate. No one questioned it, especially when he sent substantial funds to run the estate and keep me in high society. He even wrote a letter of introduction for me to the court."

New money, he recalled Brielle telling him. Stolen money, it seemed.

"Rowan believed in duty and loyalty, but he also believed in justice and equality. That no man's life is more important than another. If he were alive today, he would fight with us."

Henri considered for a moment. "That was not enough for Citric?"

"Citric," Eve breathed and pressed her lips together, hesitant to say more. "Citric has lost more than most people ever will. He understands that by sending his men into this battle, he is risking not only their lives but everything he has worked so hard to protect."

"Yet you would ask him to risk it?"

"Yes." Her tone was firm, resolved. "Because while I owe him everything and I care for him deeply"—she averted her gaze to her hands as if she was ashamed to admit it—"I am still Rowan's sister."

Henri nodded, suddenly in awe of the young girl who stood before him. "He would be proud of you, the woman you have become."

Eve slowly raised her eyes to him.

"Though he might be a bit concerned that you've started eating leaves."

Eve's grief cracked with a bemused smile. "It's called Olevia, it's good for pain."

Indeed, her lip was swollen, and her cheek was beginning to bruise yellow and green. The fight had been brutal. He had no doubt she had wounds on her body he could not see.

"Let me help you," Henri offered, and began scanning the ground for more of the plant.

They searched together in companionable silence, letting the emotionally charged air dissipate on the wind. Henri was surprised she had revealed so much to him. Perhaps he had caught her in a rare moment of weakness. Perhaps she would regret it later, being so honest with him. Either way, he was grateful for it. If Brielle's campaign had any chance of success, they needed to know who they could trust.

Crouched down inspecting a patch of plants, Henri's attention caught on a stone slab in the ground, almost completely hidden by vegetation. He brushed the undergrowth aside and ran his hand over the smooth stone. It looked like a foundation stone.

Henri furrowed his brows as he cast his gaze further along the ground until he spotted another stone slab peeking out from underneath the soil, perfectly in line with the first. He walked over and crouched down to inspect it. Glancing back at the ruins, he calculated the distance in his head because these stones looked like the foundation of a wall. And the distance between the stones and the ruin suggested that this had been no ordinary wall surrounding a grand house. It looked like an inner curtain wall of a castle.

When Brielle woke the next day, it was as if the world had changed. The camp was busy with men preparing to leave: packing their bedrolls, sharpening their weapons, ensuring their mounts were ready for the long journey. Citric had announced last night that a select group of thirty men would be leaving in two days to join her campaign to reclaim her kingdom. He would risk no more than that. The men left behind would guard Alkhiem and ensure that life here continued, no matter what befell the small company.

Unsettled murmurs had broken out amongst the people, and Brielle's cheeks had warmed as their collective gaze fell upon her. She could only guess what they were thinking, none of it favorable to her. In that moment, part of her wished she could hide under a rock, but the queen she needed to be stood firm, unapologetic. Henri had been at her side bearing the weight of their gazes with her, his unyielding expression lending her strength. Despite their murmurings, though, the people had not challenged Citric's command and now they were openly preparing for war.

It felt surreal.

For months now, all she could think about, every choice she had made, was in pursuit of reclaiming her kingdom. She had faced every indignity, every setback, every challenge, even from those closest to her, and she had never wavered in her conviction. But now it was actually happening.

She knew she should feel proud, vindicated that she had finally clawed her way to this defining moment. Instead, she felt so many things it was hard to keep her thoughts straight and her breakfast from coming up. She maintained her composure, though, as she walked through the camp, taking in the sight of the men who would risk their lives for her, perhaps even die for her. Harder to look at were their wives helping them pack for the journey and the children playing at their feet, unaware of what was happening around them. Brielle avoided their gazes as much as possible, her insides churning with nerves and dread and regret and resolve.

She found Henri sitting on a stump outside his tent, taking a whetstone to his sword. When he saw her, he said, "Jameson left at first light for Clontarf."

Brielle merely nodded. Jameson was carrying a letter from Henri to Ele asking him to revive Henri's network of spies. He was also carrying a substantial amount of wealth, enough to pay this network of spies and buy their loyalty. Eve had requested the funds from Citric and he had handed them over to her without a word of protest. Brielle had watched the interaction between Eve and Citric. It was cold, formal. Eve had tried to look indifferent, but her performance was not convincing.

"What is it?" Henri stopped sharpening his sword and looked up at her, concerned.

Brielle inhaled a shaky breath. "It's beginning to feel real. These men," she said, glancing around at the people who had offered them sanctuary, and who were now preparing for war. "They may never come home."

Henri held her gaze but offered no words of comfort. She wanted to ask him for reassurance that she was doing the right thing, that she was justified in asking this of them, but she was too afraid of what his answer might be. Brielle cleared her throat, trying to push the avalanche of thoughts from her mind.

"I need you to do something for me."

She had been thinking about this all night. In fact, ever since she had witnessed Eve defeat Citric in the training ground. She had never seen a woman fight before. She would have never believed it possible without seeing it with her own eyes. As much as Brielle disliked Eve, and the feeling was clearly mutual, she had to admit that she admired her. Eve had survived the invasion of the King's Guard at court, she had traveled alone for weeks in the Red Wood to reach them, and she was risking her life coming to Brielle's aid and fighting in her campaign.

At such a young age, Eve was more resourceful than Brielle was or could ever hope to be, with more courage than anyone Brielle had ever met. She could protect herself, and she was willing to fight for what she believed in, even at great personal cost to herself. It killed her to admit it, but Brielle wanted to be like her.

That was the kind of queen her people deserved. Citric was right. She could not expect others to fight for her if she did not fight for herself.

"I need you to teach me how to fight."

Henri frowned. "Why? You're not going to be anywhere near the fighting."

"I might be. We do not know what is going to happen."

"That's not going to happen," he insisted, as if he would die ensuring that it didn't.

"In any case, you are the one who told me rulers face unknown threats every day. I need to be able to fight. Or at least defend myself."

"One day is not enough time to teach you."

"Anything is better than nothing. Teach me enough to at least give me a chance."

Henri continued to stare up at her, unconvinced.

"Please."

The word seemed to loosen his resolve slightly, perhaps because she rarely used it. Henri glanced around them and laid his sword to rest against the tent pole behind him.

"Not here. Or the training ground."

He inclined his head to the woodland, and she followed his lead as they made their way through the camp. As they passed Eve talking to a group of women, Brielle noticed her pause in conversation, her eyes following them curiously. She wondered how Eve was feeling this morning. She knew these people better than Brielle did, she was close to them, and she was equally to blame for bringing this war to their door. Was she feeling the queasy combination of guilt, fear, and nervous dread? Perhaps what Eve was feeling was worse.

Brielle continued to follow Henri as he led them deep into the woods. Finally, he stopped and turned to her.

"We start with the basics: fighting stance. Always make sure you are in a good position to think, move, and fight. Fill your space at all times. Do not cower or shrink yourself when you are threatened. It reduces your power and makes you look weak. Do not let anyone force you to take up less space."

Women are forced to take up the smallest space.

Father Bastien's words echoed in her mind. Brielle nodded firmly.

"There are two things you need to remember: protect your head and stay on your feet. If you stay on your feet, you have the option to move or run. If you hit the ground, your options are reduced."

Brielle recalled Henri trying to tackle Citric, and Citric knocking Eve to the ground so hard her head had made a sickening cracking sound. In both fights, they had tried to turn the tide by knocking their enemy off their feet.

"Place one foot in the front, one foot in the back, hip width apart."

Brielle followed his instruction and tried to look down at her feet as she positioned them, but they were hidden underneath her dress. Perhaps this was why Eve wore men's pants. She had never thought about it before, but dresses were quite restrictive of movement.

"This stance allows you to remain balanced but also to pivot." He demonstrated, swiveling to either side. "Make sure your knees are bent slightly. That way you can exert force and absorb force."

She felt ridiculous. The stance was awkward and unnatural.

"Now you need to learn how to breathe."

"What?"

"You need to make sure you keep your breathing even. When we feel angry or scared, our breathing changes. We take short sharp breaths, this reduces our power. No matter what happens, no matter what you feel, you need to keep your breathing even."

Henri demonstrated, taking in full, measured calm breaths. Brielle followed suit.

"Good. Footwork."

Henri showed her a sequence of maneuvers with his feet, gradually adding options for how to move her arms and then her whole body. It was a lot to remember and every movement felt strange, foreign. She didn't seem to move right, no matter how simple it looked. He was constantly correcting her, telling her to drop her chin, keep her elbows down, her weight balanced. She felt as if they had hardly done anything meaningful in the past hour, yet she was exhausted and sweating profusely.

They were taking a much needed break when she asked, "How did Eve win against Citric? She's so small compared to him."

"She was fast. And smart. She used gravity against him. She also remembered a simple rule; once you have an arm and a leg, your opponent is immobilized."

At her questioning look, he demonstrated by making a move to grab her arm and restrain her leg with his own. She tried to pull herself free, but they were firmly interlocked. Brielle stopped struggling and their eyes caught, their faces so close she could feel his breath on her cheek. Henri loosened his grip slightly but didn't let her go, didn't seem to want to. His gaze slid to her lips, so close to his own, slightly parted and breathless. Brielle felt the air charge between them like it had the other night when they danced together. That night, she had wished they were alone. She wished she were braver. But today she felt differently.

"You knew, didn't you."

"What?"

"About the taxes, the executions. What was happening to the people."

Henri didn't reply, but she could see the answer in his eyes.

"You did nothing."

He released her, putting some distance between them. "There was nothing to be done."

She shook her head in disbelief and disappointment. "You are the Prince of the North."

"Not anymore."

"You could have done something."

"We've been over this." He scowled. "I made a choice. You don't have to agree with it."

"I don't!"

"That's fine."

"Just tell me why," she demanded, unable to keep the hurt from her voice. "Why do you not want to be king?"

Henri shifted on his feet and opened his mouth, as if he were trying to find the words.

"I'm curious as well."

They turned to see Eve standing in the distance, her keen eyes drinking in every detail.

Brielle straightened, schooling her features into cool neutrality. "Henri was just teaching me how to defend myself."

"Really? From where I'm standing, you were the one attacking him."

Brielle shot her a scathing look.

Eve strolled over to them, swung a crossbow around from her back, and held it out to Brielle. "This is for you."

She blanched. "Me?"

"You won't be able to defend yourself against an attack. You're too weak, and there's no time to teach you. Better to kill them before they can get to you."

Eve held the weapon out to her, pointedly. Brielle reluctantly took it, feeling the weight of it in her hands.

"It's heavy."

"It's light compared to most weapons. Keep it strapped to you at all times, you'll soon get used to its weight."

"It's a good idea," Henri admitted to Eve before turning to Brielle. "You'll need to practice hitting a target."

"These are also for you." Eve held out three slim short daggers. "Boot, bodice, and belt."

Brielle hesitated. The blades looked frighteningly sharp. "I'll stab myself."

"What a pity."

Brielle gave her a flat look as she snatched them from her. Eve smirked before turning to make her way back through the woods to the camp.

"Eve," Brielle called out to her, forcing herself to swallow her pride. "Thank you."

Henri and Brielle returned to camp hours later when her arms were so heavy from practicing with the crossbow that they felt like dead weights dangling from her shoulders. Her aim had improved slightly, but only over short distances. She would need to practice more. Right now, though, she didn't know how she was going to lift her dinner to her mouth.

Spotting Jameson in the stables, they wandered over to find him brushing down his mare. Sienna stood by the stall in silent company. No doubt she had spent the day packing and preparing to leave. A heaviness pressed on Brielle's chest at the thought of it. She was putting everyone she cared for in grave danger, just as Citric had foretold.

Sienna smiled at them as they approached, but her expression quickly changed.

"Are you all right? You look ... unwell."

Brielle could only imagine how disheveled she looked; exhausted and sweaty. "I'm fine."

"Ele?" Henri directed the question to Jameson.

"He's fine. More than fine, actually. Things have changed a lot since you left. Ele now runs the Sodisce."

Brielle's brows shot up in surprise. The boy was barely ten years old!

"He has built quite the reputation for himself. People refer to him as the *Petit Maitre*."

"The Little Master," Brielle murmured in wonder.

"It was difficult to get a meeting with him."

A proud smile spread across Henri's lips. "He was always a quick study."

"He gave me a message for you. He said to tell you that he still serves you and always will."

Henri nodded, his features betraying a sudden wave of emotion. Clearly, he still cared for them all a great deal. Brielle wondered if he wished he were with them right now rather than here with her. She was grateful she didn't know the answer. The truth might break her heart.

"Do you need help with anything before we leave tomorrow?" Sienna offered.

"No, thank you. But I have one request of you." Brielle inhaled a steadying breath. "I need you to stay here."

Sienna cocked her head to the side as if she didn't understand. "What?"

"You are three months pregnant. The journey is too long, and the campaign is too dangerous. I cannot ask you to risk your life for me. I will not ask you to risk hers."

Sienna held her gaze for a moment, her expression torn. Brielle knew she wanted to be by her side, would never have considered not going with her, but her hands fell to her slightly swollen belly and Brielle could see her resolve waning.

"My duty is to my people; your duty is to her."

Sienna's face crumpled as she pulled Brielle into a fierce embrace, tears spilling down her cheeks. Brielle held her as if she would never let her go. She pinched her eyes closed, committing this embrace to memory, sewing it into the fabric of her heart so she could carry it with her always. When she opened her eyes, Jameson dipped his chin in silent thanks. She blinked back in acknowledgment. When they finally parted, Brielle forced a reassuring smile.

"You will be safe here. These people love you. They accepted you the moment you walked into this camp."

Sienna laughed even as she sniffled and wiped her damp cheeks with the heel of her hand. Having collected herself, Sienna turned to Jameson, her expression suddenly serious.

"I charge you with the safety of your queen." She looked to Henri. "Both of you."

Henri bowed, accepting the oath.

"We will keep her safe," Jameson swore and placed a kiss on her brow.

CHAPTER ELEVEN

Before the first rays of dawn appeared, the company had mounted their horses while the rest of Alkhiem gathered to witness their departure. There were no tears, no wailing or farewells to be said. Those had been done last night in the privacy of tents, in the pleasure between sheets, in savoring the ordinary moments of life that normally went unnoticed. Now there was only duty, what must be done. Henri had experienced this moment many times in his life. He had fought with enough armies in enough battles that the thoughts and feelings laying heavy in the air were no strangers to him. He recognized and welcomed them as familiar old comrades.

Citric led the company as they moved out, with Eve trailing slightly behind him, as if she would ride by his side but was afraid he would not want her there. Brielle took position in the middle of the group, riding between Henri and Jameson. By rights, she should be leading the company. This was her campaign, after all. But she made no effort to move to the front. She seemed content to acknowledge that these were Citric's men, not hers, and they were only here because he ordered them to be.

Sitting straight-backed in the saddle, her crossbow slung across her back, Brielle almost looked like a warrior queen. Her face was a mask of calm, seemingly unperturbed by what lay ahead. But Henri knew her better than to believe the mask. He could see the fast undercurrent of emotion beneath the cool, calm exterior. She was terrified. And with good reason. They were likely traveling to their deaths.

The company rode in silence as the woodland woke to the dawn. It would take weeks to cross the Southern border, even longer to reach the castle gates.

They would travel from sun's rise to sun's set. The journey would be long and wretched; they always were.

Henri had met most of the men Citric selected to form the company, had drunk with some of them in those first days of entering the camp and had sparred with others since joining them to train, but he did not really know them. They would get to know each other, though, as soldiers were often forced to, thrown together by a common cause or, at the very least, a common order. Talk would be tentative at first, but over time they would learn the names of each other's wives and children, the towns in which they were born. They would share stories, usually of past battles, of conquests both on and off the killing field. They would get to know each other's strengths and weaknesses, motivations and fears. Enduring the wretched journey together would bond them so that by the time they faced the enemy, they would face him as one.

At least, that was how it usually went.

Days passed, and the men remained distant. They were pleasant but not friendly, and largely kept to each other, only speaking to Henri, Jameson, and Brielle when they had to. It was beginning to make Henri feel uncomfortable. He understood they did not believe in this campaign. They did not care for either kingdom, and Brielle was not their queen. They resented being torn away from their families, their home, but they did not direct that resentment at Citric despite the fact that it was his pride which had damned them to this cause. Nor did they recoil from Eve, who was equally to blame. They followed his every word without complaint and treated her like one of their own.

It was clear that lines had been drawn before the company had even left Alkhiem. The men would journey with them, they would fight with them, they would even die with them, but they would never accept them. Henri told himself that it did not matter, that it should not bother him, but for some reason it did.

Brielle lowered her weary body to sit on her bedroll, wincing from the pain of solid ground against her stiff backside. Once she reclaimed her kingdom, she was never riding a horse again. Fine cushioned carriages were the only way to travel. She would also never sleep outdoors again, though the thought of sleeping in an actual bed, in a room with four walls, seemed foreign to her now. She was so used to being out in the elements, feeling the cold and the wind against her skin, hearing the rustle and the calls of the animals at night. It would take some time for her to adjust to court life again.

Brielle lifted her face to the night sky as she clasped her hands around her drawn-up knees; she would miss this view. Above her, a million stars sparkled like diamonds, stretching across black silk for what seemed like forever. Brielle bathed in the wondrous sight even as she tried to rub some heat into her bare arms. The campfire provided some semblance of warmth, but even so, the night was frigid.

No one had packed tents. They were too cumbersome to carry and wholly unnecessary. Everyone simply laid their bedrolls out around the fire. There was no privacy in war, apparently, no small creature comforts. Brielle had not complained, though. Her world had changed so much these past few months, very few things bothered her anymore. She had learned how to adapt, how to survive. The things she could accept and the things she refused to accept. And they were not the same as what she had believed before. What society had taught her was acceptable.

Henri sat down on the bedroll beside her, stretching his legs out in front of him and loosening his cuffs. Jameson was already asleep on her other side. She had hardly spoken to Henri in the past few days, despite the fact that he rarely left her side. Their argument had put a distance between them that neither of them seemed to want to bridge.

She could not understand him, how he could have remained in hiding, enjoying the pleasures of the Sodisce while his kingdom was ravaged, his people executed in the streets. How could he have been so unaffected by it? How could she trust him to care about it now? She knew the question was unfair. He was here. He had pledged his loyalty to her, but for some reason, it still did not feel like enough. She wanted him to *want* to be here. She wanted him to lead this campaign beside her, as a king.

Brielle wondered what he would do when this was all over, if they were fortunate enough to reclaim her kingdom. Would he really return to the Sodisce and live his life as if he were a born commoner? Would she be forced to let him go? The pain that struck her heart was sharp. She did not want to think about it. She did not want to think about who would rule the Northern Kingdom in his place. Because even if they were successful in reclaiming her kingdom, the danger would not stop there.

If Henri was king, she would not need to fear for her borders, her right to rule would not be challenged. No other king would afford her such peace or respect. She would always be seen as weak, unfit to rule because of her sex. She would need to marry quickly. To at least give the illusion of a man ruling by her side, even when she had no intention of allowing her husband to take her throne. She would need to choose wisely. A man without ambition was hard to find. She would need allies. To form a council who would accept her, protect her, and respect her.

A council of men.

Brielle groaned inwardly; the task was impossible.

"Eve told me something today," Henri said quietly, his words startling her from her despondence. "About your mother."

Brielle's spine stiffened. "I did not realize you two spoke to each other."

A lie. She had noticed the way his eyes sometimes followed Eve, as if he was casually monitoring her wellbeing. Noticed the brief words they exchanged, which were wholly unnecessary and evidenced some sense of personal interest. Something had changed between them after Eve's fight with Citric. It was as if they had reached an understanding of sorts. They were not friends, but something in between.

"Why didn't you tell me?" Henri asked.

"I suppose we no longer tell each other everything."

It was the truth, but she hoped the words stung.

He hesitated. "I'm sorry."

For everything, his tone said. Not just her mother.

Brielle sighed. "We were not close, my mother and I. In truth, I despised her."

Henri nodded, not a trace of judgment on his face. "I despised my father as well."

Brielle had yet to reconcile her feelings about her mother; anger and resentment, shame and regret. She wondered if she ever would.

"When your father died, how did it make you feel?"

Henri thought carefully for a moment. "When I realized my father was being murdered, I ran to him. I would have given my life to save his. But afterward I felt ... relieved. I was not sad or angry. I didn't shed a single tear. When my mother died, I cried for days."

Brielle glanced over at him to find his expression solemn and earnest.

"You have never spoken of her before."

"It's difficult for me to speak of her," he admitted. "She was executed for treason. My father accused her of being unfaithful. She maintained her innocence until her last breath. I was only a boy, but I was made to watch the axe fall."

Brielle's eyes widened in horror.

"The ladies of the court did not even wait for her body to turn cold before they swarmed around my father like bees to a hive. All of them were eager to be the next queen, even if it meant their head could one day end up on the same chopping block. That was the day I realized the power of the Crown. Its corruption. It made my father distrustful and callous. Hungry for power and the need to control everything. It stripped him of his humanity, his compassion, his ability to be a husband and a father. It made him a murderer."

Brielle furrowed her brows. "That does not mean it would do the same to you. You are nothing like your father."

"No, I am not, but I have failed to protect everything and everyone I have ever cared about. That is enough of a legacy that I would not entrust a kingdom to me."

"That is not true," she protested. "You protected me. Your warning saved my life."

"You saved your own life. Your courage, your stubbornness, are the only reasons you are here tonight."

His eyes searched hers, conveying the conviction in his words. She did not pull back as he reached out to brush a strand of hair from her face, the movement gentle and intimate.

"You are a true queen."

"And you could be a great king."

Henri scowled and sat back, frustrated. "Do not tell me what I could be."

"You may not believe it because your father never said it to you, but—"

"Enough!"

Brielle pinched her lips together and averted her gaze to her hands.

He exhaled, pinching his eyes closed in regret. "I'm sorry."

She shook her head, dismissing his apology as though his words hadn't hurt. They had, and he saw it.

"You don't need me, Brielle. You think you do but you don't."

"I do," she insisted. "I will always need you."

Their eyes held each other's, neither one of them willing to let go. She did not know how to convince him, what words to say. If only he could see himself the way she saw him. If only he could want the things that she wanted, then maybe they would have a chance.

Brielle cupped the water in her hands and splashed her face, washing the dust and sweat from her skin. The river was not wide, but it was enough to water the horses and fill up the waterskins. It also allowed the company an excuse to rest for a few minutes after traveling since sun's rise.

Brielle plugged her replenished waterskin and carefully made her way over the slippery rocks to a nearby tree. She kept a watchful eye on her white mare as it lapped at the water with its comrades. The men were scattered along the riverbank, either sitting on the soft ground or walking along the edge of the water in an effort to stretch their legs. Brielle was content to simply stand under the tree and take in the beautiful view.

Everything was so green here. From the woodland floor to the rocks and the trees, everything was covered in moss. Several trees leaned out over the narrow river, their branches reaching for each other. Brown leaves slowly drifted along the surface of the water. The water was still in this part of the river, but farther downstream she could hear the faint trickle of water cascading over rocks. Still, it was so quiet she would not have known that a river was here without Citric guiding them to it.

His knowledge of the Red Wood was remarkable. Eve and the others knew the wood well enough, but Citric seemed to know every mound of dirt, every river, every plant. He knew which fruits and flowers were edible and which were poisonous. He knew which vegetation had medicinal properties. It was as if he had grown up among these trees, when she knew he had not.

Henri had told her what he knew of Citric; that he had been a soldier in the northern army, a famed bowman, until he deserted and was forced to live in exile in the Red Wood. She had witnessed his skill with the bow several times. When the opportunity for fresh meat presented itself, he did not miss. The other men hunted along the way as well, when they saw a bird flying overhead or spotted the signs of a beast nearby. They even fished when Citric alerted them to a nearby river. This river, however, seemed too small for any worthwhile game to live in.

Brielle's attention drifted to Citric, who was standing beside his horse at the riverbank, affectionately stroking its side and murmuring to it as if it could understand every word he said. She still couldn't quite reconcile Citric in her head. He could be so gentle at times, thoughtful enough to consider a young woman on her wedding day. And yet at other times, he could be brutally violent, willing to fight a sixteen-year-old girl half his size just to defend his wounded pride.

As if sensing her eyes on him, Citric looked over at her. It was too late to pretend that she hadn't been staring at him, so she met his gaze unapologetically. He turned back to his horse, and she glanced away, mentally kicking herself for getting caught. It didn't matter if she couldn't understand him, she told herself. After they reclaimed the Northern and Southern Kingdoms, Citric would return to the Red Wood and she would never see him again. He would be glad never to see her again, of that she was certain. He would probably never even think of her.

"Will you miss my woodland when you return to your kingdom?"

Brielle turned to find Citric walking over the rocks toward her. The sunlight cast his long red hair into copper hues. Several days' worth of growth lined his chin, his jaw, and above his mouth. Though it was a shade darker than his hair color, almost brown.

She was staring again.

"I will," she admitted quickly. "It is so beautiful."

It was ironic to think that months ago, when she first entered the Red Wood, she had hated it. She loathed sleeping on the ground and bathing in rivers. Too focused on what had been taken from her, she had failed to notice the beauty surrounding her.

"The land is so rich and fertile here, full of life. From what little I have heard of my kingdom, my lands are not the same. My people are struggling to produce a good harvest, to feed their families."

Citric clasped his hands behind his back, his expression slightly puzzled. "It has been that way for years."

Brielle gave a curt nod and averted her gaze. "I didn't realize."

"Would you have cared if someone told you?"

Brielle didn't reply because they both knew she wouldn't have. She had been so naïve. So wrapped up in her own personal ambition and what she thought was important for a ruler to be that she had failed to see her people. What seemed like a mundane issue or trivial dispute to her could be someone's livelihood, the difference between a full stomach or starvation.

"I care now," she said firmly.

A smile tugged at Citric's lips and he cocked his head to the side as if he did not quite believe her.

"I will find a way to make the land more productive," she insisted.

They stood in uncomfortable silence for a moment before he said, "Your people farm the land. My people care for the land. The land knows the difference."

⌘

Weeks later, Brielle looked out into the distance to behold her city, her home. It was mere miles away and in the dawning light looked no different from when she had left. Except everything was different. She had left that night in a boat rowing silently down the river, barely escaping with her life. Now she was standing on the edge of the Red Wood, looking out at her birthright, willing to risk her life and the lives of people she cared about to take it back.

They had arrived last night and made camp as they always did, but this would be their final outpost. Exhausted, the men had retired early, but Brielle was unable to sleep. She could feel it, her destiny calling to her, so close she had to see it for herself. She had had a lot of time to think on this journey, to reflect on her life and her choices up to this point. She had time to think about the future she wanted. Now was the time to become the queen she wanted to be. There was no room for doubt. She would be Queen of the Southern Kingdom or she would die fighting for it.

At dawn, the camp began to stir from sleep and everyone gathered around the smoldering embers of the campfire to eat porridge. Brielle had made it, being the first one to wake. She had made a point of learning everything she could on this journey; how to pack her own bedroll, how to brush down her mare, how to gather and prepare simple meals. She had stopped short of gutting fish and skinning animals. She just couldn't bring herself to do it.

Tearing her eyes away from her kingdom, Brielle joined the men to eat breakfast. As always, the men sat apart from Henri and Jameson, preferring to keep company with each other. Initially, she had found such behavior to be rude and disconcerting, but now she accepted it. After all, she did not need them to like her. She needed them to fight for her.

Henri and Jameson murmured greetings to her as she sat down beside them. They had rarely left her side the entire journey. So much so that there were times when she had to explicitly tell them she was wandering off to relieve herself and did not require an escort or an audience. She understood they had been charged with her protection, but over time it began to feel like more than that. It was almost as if they did not completely trust the men they traveled with. Or perhaps this was just the way things would always be as queen. Henri had warned her as much; that she would face unknown threats to her life every day.

"So." Citric leveled his gaze at her across the smoking remains of the campfire. "We are here. What is your plan?"

Everyone's attention turned to her, but no one's gaze was more assessing than Eve's. Like the men, Eve had kept her distance the past few weeks, only exchanging basic words with Henri now and then. Whatever comradery or concern had spurred her to give Brielle the weapons that day had not shown itself again. She was not hostile toward her, just indifferent, which Brielle supposed was an improvement.

"First, we need to get into the city undetected," she said, resting her porridge on her lap. "We need to do it gradually, a few of us going in every day, no more than three or four. We are less likely to be noticed that way. Everyone will stay in different boarding houses, taverns or inns, and there will be a few central points in the city for communication at certain times of the day. That way if one of us is compromised, the others will not be."

"I have drawn a map of the city," Jameson added. "We've already chosen the communication points."

"And once we are all inside, how are we going to get into the castle?" Citric's tone remained steady, but she could hear the note of skepticism underneath.

"Eve will let us in," Brielle said simply, turning to Eve. "You return to court today."

Eve flicked her eyes to Citric as if waiting for his approval.

"Even with entry into the castle, thirty men against the King's Guard are foolish odds," Citric pointed out.

"We do not need to fight the King's Guard, we only need to kill the Butcher. Once he is dead, the King's Guard will be forced to choose a side: remain loyal to King Heroux or join us. Given the way King Heroux has been ruling, I think they will join their queen."

"Perhaps, but between us and the Butcher is a garrison of King's Guards."

"Then it is fortunate that in five days' time a large portion of the King's Guard will leave the city."

She held Citric's stare even as the men exchanged questioning looks. Eve frowned as she sat forward, resting her elbows on her knees. "Why?"

"Because there will be a sighting in Doranth by several trusted informants. Haven't you heard the rumors? The Queen of the South and the King of the North have joined forces and are gathering a large army to challenge King Heroux. There have also been rumors that King Heroux is unhappy with the Butcher's performance lately. His failure to gather enough taxes and keep the common folk in line could be forgiven, but if he fails to retrieve enemies of the Crown ... I hate to think what King Heroux might do."

Brielle's lips curled into a devious smile.

"You've been spreading rumors?" Eve asked.

Brielle returned an innocent look. She knew better than anyone how quickly gossip could destroy someone. Reputation was everything.

"Doranth is three days' travel," Eve said slowly, as if thinking out loud.

"Plenty of time to take the castle," Brielle said.

Citric considered the plan for a moment. "And what is to stop the Butcher from joining the King's Guard to personally retrieve you?"

"There will be too much rebellion in the city for him to risk leaving." In answer to his questioning look, she explained, "Over the next few days, whoever is in the city will need to stage some acts of rebellion; nothing too dramatic but enough to get the attention of the King's Guard, and the Butcher."

The men murmured amongst each other, weighed the plan between them, before looking to Citric for the final word. His expression was serious, but unreadable. If he rejected the plan, Brielle did not have another. She tried to remember to breathe as she waited for his response.

Finally, he turned to Eve and said, "This plan depends on you. You are our eyes and ears in the castle. You will also need to be the Butcher's shadow, to know where he is at all times and ensure that when we enter the castle, he is where we can reach him."

It was more words than he had spoken to her in weeks. Eve simply nodded, determined to do what was necessary. Citric's gaze lingered on her a moment longer and when it slid to the ground at his feet, he looked defeated somehow.

"Then let's discuss the details."

Brielle fitted the arrow into the deck of the crossbow and lifted the weapon to her eye-level. She was used to the weight of it now, having carried it across her back for the past few weeks, but she had not had an opportunity to practice using it since the day they had left Alkhiem.

After traveling in constant company for the past few weeks, she was desperate for some time alone, and practicing was the perfect excuse for it. She had informed Henri and Jameson of her intentions and ordered them not to follow her. Henri had been less than impressed. If she was honest, Brielle needed more than just a break from the constant company. She needed some space to breathe, to steady herself. The departure of several of the men this morning, along with Eve's return to court, meant that the wheels of her plan were firmly in motion.

It had begun.

Everything felt more real. More dangerous now. Brielle tried to inhale a settling breath and ignore the nervous energy coursing through her veins. She had marked some targets on trees at different distances in different directions. She was fairly accurate across short distances, but needed to improve on longer ones. Once she was satisfied with her accuracy, she would practice getting quicker at loading the crossbow so she could hit multiple targets swiftly. Part of her felt stupid for doing it. Perhaps she might never need to shoot a single arrow. Perhaps she would and all the practice in the world would not help her aim true in a moment of threat. Brielle clenched her jaw tight in determination and let the bolt fly.

It missed.

She sighed as she lowered the crossbow, giving her stiff arms a welcome reprieve.

"Your aim is too high."

Brielle whirled round to find Citric leaning against a tree behind her. She had not heard a single sound to betray his approach. She wondered exactly how long he had been standing there watching her.

"I can see that," she huffed, annoyed at the intrusion.

"Then lower your arm."

She returned a withering glare. "Is there something you want?"

"To see you hit the target."

Brielle turned her back on him and begrudgingly fitted another arrow. Trying to ignore his watchful presence, she lifted the weapon, taking extra care with her posture before releasing the bolt.

It missed.

Brielle gripped the weapon hard in frustration. She could feel Citric's critical gaze burning into her back.

"This would be easier without an audience," she seethed.

"But you will likely have one if you are attacked."

She refused to turn around even as she heard him approaching.

He came to stand beside her and folded his arms across his chest. "Try again."

"I would prefer not to."

He shrugged. "Then you will die."

Brielle gritted her teeth. How she hated him.

She loaded another bolt and lifted the weapon to her eye-level. Citric glanced at her sidelong, assessing every detail of her stance, before adjusting her posture and aim slightly with the nudge of a finger. She released the bolt.

It hit the mark.

Brielle scowled. She almost wished she had missed.

"Who taught you how to shoot a bow?" she asked.

"I did."

She resisted the sudden urge to smack him with it.

"It's a good choice." He inclined his head to the weapon still clenched in her white-knuckled hands. "Range weaponry is good for people who don't have fighting experience. Or muscle. It's lightweight and doesn't require draw strength."

"So glad you approve," she drawled.

"What made you change your mind?"

Brielle knew what he was referring to; that day in the training ground when Citric had offered to teach her how to fight and she had turned him down flat. The very thought of holding a weapon had been abominable to her.

"I want to be able to fight for my kingdom. And defend myself."

The corner of his mouth tugged up in wry amusement.

"What?" she snapped.

He shook his head. "You are beginning to surprise me."

Brielle pressed her lips together. She had to admit she was beginning to surprise herself. His amusement quickly faded, replaced by a serious expression.

"Your plan has merit but many things could go wrong."

"I know."

The many things that could go wrong had plagued her mind these past few weeks, robbing her of much needed sleep. She had tried not to let herself think too much about how she would feel if one of them—all of them—were compromised.

Captured.

Tortured.

Killed.

For her.

They had made it clear that they did not care for her, would not be here if it weren't for Citric, but still. They were men with wives and children and families. The loss of even one of them would be a gaping wound for Alkhiem, a community she had come to respect.

Brielle swallowed nervously and rolled her shoulders as if trying to shrug off the thoughts.

He watched her, his eyes softening a little. "A ruler must make difficult choices, even if those choices mean hurting the people they care about the most."

Brielle met his gaze. She knew that. She had come to learn just how much she was willing to risk for what she wanted, what was rightfully hers. There was no judgment in his expression, only bleak understanding, perhaps even a little pity. She loaded a bolt and adjusted her stance before releasing it into the air.

It hit the target with force.

CHAPTER TWELVE

"There they are!" Brielle shouted excitedly.

Henri and Jameson sprinted from the camp to join her on the edge of the clearing. Her attention was focused on the city gates in the distance, as lines of the King's Guard rode out in perfect formation.

She had been waiting for this sight for two days, her stomach roiling with fear that the Butcher would not take the bait. Or worse, that he would decide to ride out with them. They had received word from Eve that the rumors had reached his ears, but for some reason, he had hesitated. A whole day had passed, rubbing her nerves raw, but now the evidence was clear. Her plan had worked; a large company of the King's Guard was leaving the city.

Citric strolled up behind them, casting his gaze out into the distance where the King's Guard continued to pour through the gates. Brielle beamed at him, relieved and proud that her plan had worked, but he looked unimpressed. Perhaps he had been hoping that her plan would fail and his men could return home. She slid her attention back to the city gates, ignoring his mood.

"Is the Butcher among them?" Citric asked.

"It's hard to tell, given we don't know what he looks like," Henri replied.

Normally a commander would stand out, his expensive armor or the plume of his helmet signifying his importance, but so far Brielle had not seen anything that distinguished one soldier from another.

"Eve will send word," Jameson said, even though everyone knew that.

It was the only time Brielle felt any sense of relief from the nervous anxiety that coursed through her veins every hour of the day. The messages from Eve were brief, encrypted, but they gave reassurance that everything was in place. That everyone was still alive.

So far.

Brielle drew in a steadying breath. "We enter the city as soon as we know for sure that the Butcher is there."

Citric turned to walk away, seemingly resigned to the decision. He tossed over his shoulder, "Brielle and I will stay at the tavern. You two take the boarding house."

"The hell you will." Henri turned around, his face incredulous. "Brielle is coming with me."

"So if you are discovered, they can have you both? No."

Henri took a step toward him, his fists clenched at his side. "I'm not asking for your opinion."

"Citric is right." Brielle moved to position herself between them. "If one of us is recognized or compromised, the other has to lead this campaign."

"If something happens to you, this campaign is over," Henri said to her before flicking his gaze to Citric. "Citric knows that."

Citric lifted a brow, amused. "You choose now not to trust me?"

"I have never trusted you."

"Citric is right." Jameson placed a steadying hand on Henri's shoulder before lowering his voice to a whisper. "It's one night."

Their eyes fastened on each other with deadly intent before Henri stalked off. Brielle released a shaky breath. She exchanged a pointed look with Jameson, and watched as he followed his friend. They had become close lately. She had noticed it in Alkhiem, but it had become even more evident the past few weeks traveling together. They trusted one another, shared a knowing that only friends had. She was not surprised. They had much in common. Both born to the life of a courtier, both sharing the same moral code, the same fierce loyalty to the ones they cared about. Both desiring a simple life. Perhaps Henri was even a little jealous of Jameson. He had everything Henri desired; a beautiful wife, a child on the way.

"Do you think you will be recognized?" Citric's words cut through her thoughts.

"No. I hardly recognize myself these days," she murmured, her attempt at humor falling flat. "Even if someone did think my face familiar, they would not think me capable of this."

Everyone had expected her to flee the continent the moment her father was cut down. To give up her kingdom without complaint, without even making a sound, as if it were never really hers to begin with. No one would believe that their perfectly manicured princess with her garden tea parties and her silk gowns would be capable of clawing her way into a war. Of living amongst common people, thieves and outlaws, of devising a battle plan and risking her pretty neck.

She could hardly believe it herself.

She had not looked in a mirror for months, but she was sure she would not recognize the face staring back at her. Citric's eyes lingered on her as if he could read her thoughts, as if he could see it too; the change in her. The heat of his gaze made her cheeks warm.

"You are probably more recognizable than me," she pointed out. "Your face has been on broadsheets for years. Not many men have long copper hair and a scar on their cheek."

He cocked his head, as if accepting her challenge, before unsheathing the dagger at his side. Pulling his long hair over one shoulder, he sliced it clean with the blade.

Brielle sucked in a breath of horror as it fell to the ground. She surveyed the jagged cut in disbelief, his hair now slashed just above his jawline. It made his features sharper, his eyes more intense. Less wild, more—striking.

"Do you like it?" he asked.

She felt her insides flutter. "It's fine."

A sensuous smile spread across his lips. "I could cut yours for you if you like."

"Don't you dare."

He laughed as she marched past him. She needed to put distance between them right now. She did not trust herself around him when he looked at her like that, and she could not afford to lose focus at this critical point in the plan. By all accounts, they were probably going to be in the city by nightfall, preparing to take the castle in the early hours before the dawn. This could be her last night before she reclaimed her kingdom. She could not allow herself to be distracted by—well, him. Especially as he clearly did not mean anything by it more than the simple pleasure of seeing her disarmed. She had no time for his games and absolutely no intention of being his plaything.

Brielle did not mean to wander off to where Jameson was placating Henri, but when she spotted them ahead, she halted. At the same moment, they saw her, and she knew she could not walk away. Jameson dipped his chin to her before he walked off, giving them a moment together. Brielle wished he hadn't. Henri was clearly enraged. She wasn't sure why, but she definitely did not want to find out. Besides, he was being illogical. She had not thought about it until Citric had said it, but it made perfect sense that she and Henri should not stay together.

"The plan is a good one," Brielle insisted, preempting his argument.

"I take no issue with the plan."

"You take issue with Citric," she said, strolling over to him. "Why do you not trust him?"

"Why do you?"

The words sounded like an accusation.

Brielle had assumed he was mad at Citric, but now she was beginning to think he was mad at her as well.

"Citric wants what we want; this campaign to be over with so his men can return home safely."

"I know what he wants." He scowled.

She tightened her lips in frustration. "I do not want to fight with you, I do not want to part ways like this."

"Then don't. Come with me." His voice was insistent, hopeful.

"And risk everything just so you can feel better? No."

His features hardened as he looked away.

"Henri, what is this really about?"

A muscle feathered in his jaw as he shifted on his feet. "I can't lose you too."

The words were almost a whisper, as if he were ashamed to say them. He was afraid, she realized. He had told her weeks ago that he had failed to protect everyone he had ever cared about. And now she was asking him to leave her side, to entrust her safety to someone else. Her anger dissipated as she closed the distance between them. She reached for his fingers, holding them lightly, unsure whether he would welcome her touch.

"I cannot say what will happen tomorrow, for either of us."

Henri stared down between them at their entwined fingers as if he were savoring the sight of it, the feel of her fingers against his.

"It is not just tomorrow I fear."

Brielle's eyes searched his, questioning.

"Brielle! Eve has sent word!" Jameson called out to them breathlessly, holding a letter up in his hand. "The Butcher remains at the castle. We must go, now."

They had made it through the city gates without so much as a question from the guards. Henri supposed they looked like every other exhausted traveler and sword for hire. Even so, he pulled his hood closer to his face. He could not afford to be recognized. Jameson, on the other hand, had chosen to wear the fine clothes of a courtier. After all, no one knew about his role in helping Brielle escape sanctuary or living with a band of outlaws these past months, plotting a campaign to overthrow the King. No one would question where he had disappeared to, and if they did, he could easily give an array of plausible explanations. He was a Lord's son, they would believe him.

They moved through the streets, casually heading in the same direction but keeping a distance from each other. While Jameson's absence could easily be explained, his association with a cloaked stranger might stir suspicions. They were to make their way to the boarding house where Jameson would pay for a room and Henri would join him later, sneaking through a back door or an open window. Whichever route would keep him unseen. There they would wait and count the hours until it was time to move on the castle.

Henri already knew this would be one of the longest nights of his life. No one had ever told him when he was training to be a soldier that a large part of any battle was waiting. The mental battle was sometimes harder than the physical one. Staying calm but alert, not allowing the mind to travel down paths of death and defeat, staying focused on the duty ahead, clinging to the conviction that one would make it out alive. If the battle was lost in the mind, the body would surely follow.

Screams split the air and Henri halted, his senses immediately alert. Up ahead, people were running toward him, fleeing a commotion he couldn't see. He glanced across the street to Jameson, who looked back at him. Within the fleeting exchange, they acknowledged that they should not go anywhere near the chaos, but also decided that that was exactly where they would go.

Henri moved fast, dodging several people while also keeping his hood covering his face. He could hear the sounds of fighting, the wringing of metal, doors splintering, women wailing and children crying. What he saw next stopped him in his tracks.

The King's Guard were searching homes and pulling people out by the scruff of their necks, throwing them to the ground, where they beat them mercilessly with their boots and batons. Other soldiers hauled the people to their feet only to force them to their knees, forming a line in the middle of the street. Henri searched over his shoulder for Jameson, their eyes locking onto each other in alarm. This was bad. Very bad.

A man stood with his back to them, watching the scene unfold with cool authority. His clothes were well made and entirely black, his light hair the only color on him.

The Butcher.

This was an execution, Henri realized as he surveyed the guards instructing family members to stay inside or they would burn their houses to the ground. Their loved ones were already praying as they kneeled in the dirt, waiting for certain death.

Henri glanced around. Most people had fled or were watching from the safety of their homes, but an older man stood firm, wearing an apron as if he had left his shop to come out and bear witness to the atrocity. He looked resigned to the brutality of what was occurring in front of him, as if he had seen it many times before.

Henri sidled up to him, keeping his head down as he asked, "What is happening here?"

"Some rebels have been stirring up trouble the past few days," the man replied. "The Butcher means to make an example of them."

"But these look like ordinary folk," Henri protested.

"They are. I know every one of them. They would never do such a thing. They have families to protect, but it doesn't matter. This is not about justice."

Henri could hardly believe his ears. He glanced around at Jameson, who had moved in a little closer to him, his hand ready on his sword, as if waiting for Henri to give a command. They were both well armed with swords and daggers. They could take on several of the King's Guards, perhaps buy enough time for some of the people to escape. But if they did that, they would not escape, and if they were caught, the King's Guard would certainly recognize him. It would put the entire campaign at risk. And they would kill him.

A movement caught his eye, and he watched as the Butcher slowly stalked over to the line of people kneeling in a row. A short star axe dangled from his hand. There was nothing Henri could do, not without putting everything and everyone at risk. Bile rose in his throat as the Butcher positioned himself behind the first of them, and this time, Henri could not look away. With brutal efficiency, the Butcher struck the back of their neck with his axe, moving along the line as if he were hammering in nails, their bodies falling forward at his feet. But it was not the ruthlessness that stopped Henri's heart in his chest, it was not the desperate screams of the family members made to watch their loved ones being slaughtered in the street. It was the face of the man they called the Butcher, a face he knew as well as his own.

Brielle and Citric walked through the city gates hours after Henri and Jameson had passed through them. They were the picture of a common husband with his young, modest wife. At least that was what they were trying to portray. For Brielle, it was easy to hide her face behind the hooded cloak, to lower her eyes demurely as the King's Guard tried to get a look at her to satiate their curiosity.

Citric, however, could never look common. Dressed in normal clothes, his leathers packed away in their travel bag and his sword strapped to his saddle, he still looked like a warrior as he led his wife and horse through the gates. The King's Guard surveyed him warily but let them enter with barely a question. The sun would be setting soon and no doubt they had watering holes they wanted to frequent.

Citric strolled through the streets as if he had walked them a dozen times before. He had not. This would be his first time in the city, he'd told her that afternoon as he'd studied the map Jameson had drawn. It outlined the various places the men were staying, the communication points, routes to the castle, and potential escape routes should things go wrong. Brielle had studied it so thoroughly it was permanently imprinted behind her eyelids.

Despite Citric's ordinary clothes and casual gait, Brielle noticed the second glances they were receiving, the frightened looks and the quickened steps. It was the scar. Or perhaps it was the hair. After chopping it off, he had pulled what remained into a tight braid down the middle of his scalp. It made him look particularly fierce.

"Smile," she hissed at him under her breath. "You are drawing attention to us."

He took her hand in his and she stilled at the gentle touch, but her heart almost skipped a beat when he smiled down at her. It was an easy smile laced with a secret; a lover's smile. Brielle immediately lowered her eyes, grateful that the hooded cloak was hiding her blush. His touch was like an iron brand. She was keenly aware of the heat of his hand around hers. She tried to ignore it, and cherish it, as they walked through the streets.

They paid for the keep of his horse at a nearby stable before making their way to the tavern. Noise hit her with force when they walked through the door. The place was crowded, the patrons already merry with ale. A gamey aroma made her stomach grumble, even though she knew the quality of the food would be questionable at best. Brielle waited patiently behind Citric as he paid for a room and followed obediently as he led her up the rickety wooden stairs to the second floor. He held the door open for her, and she gingerly stepped inside.

The room was small, smaller than the room in the Sodisce, only large enough for a table with two chairs and a bed.

One bed.

Brielle opened her mouth to protest, but Citric said, "I'll take the floor."

She glanced around the otherwise empty room, searching for—

"The bathrooms are communal," Citric explained, dumping their travel bag on the worn floorboards.

"What!"

"I'll get us some food and fresh water for washing. Take that chair and wedge it underneath the bolt after I leave. I will knock like this"—he demonstrated a series of knocks on the door—"when I'm back. Do not open the door for anything else."

She nodded mutely. He closed the door behind him and she immediately wedged the chair underneath the bolt, checking its hold. A decent body ram would have the door and chair splintered into a million pieces, but even so, it made her feel better to have it there.

Brielle lowered her hood and removed the cloak from her shoulders. They had made it. Everyone had made it. Now there was nothing left to do but wait until the early hours before dawn. She doubted she would sleep tonight. Her insides felt like waves in a foul storm. She didn't know if she would be able to eat anything either, but she would try. She was no use to anyone weak.

She sat down on the bed, feeling the thin mattress give way beneath her. She wrung her hands nervously as she listened to the raucous sounds from the tavern below. Tomorrow, her fate would be decided. She would either reclaim her kingdom or she would die. She knew the plan was sound, but the odds still seemed against them. Brielle pinched her eyes closed against the doubts that plagued her mind. She would not entertain them. Tomorrow she would be queen. She would wear fine gowns and sleep in her old bed and bathe in rose scented water.

Brielle opened her eyes to the small vacant room. It would not be the same, she knew. Nothing would ever be as it once was. Her father would not be there, walking the halls and keeping the councilmen in line. The absence of him would be everywhere. She would no longer be free to spend her days sitting in the sunshine with her ladies, enjoying court gossip and soaking up the attention of handsome lords. She would be a queen, presiding over the council, debating laws, listening to her people's complaints and dispensing justice. Ruling her kingdom. Sienna would likely not be by her side. She may choose to live miles away at Jameson's country estate. She would enjoy that, Brielle thought; running her own household, making a brood of children, living free of the politics of court life.

Brielle would be alone.

Until she married, of course. If not a prince, then a man from a noble bloodline, willing to act as queen's consort and nothing more, but able to assure the councilmen of his wife's capability to rule. A man she could trust if not love. Both seemed implausible. Perhaps she would win the battle tomorrow only to lose her crown on the day of her marriage. The thought was enough to make her consider avoiding marriage all together, but that prospect was even more dangerous. The councilmen would never allow it; a woman sitting on the throne, alone, ruling over them. Besides, she would need to produce heirs to ensure the line of succession. If she did not choose a husband, her kingdom would revolt against her.

The raps on the door startled her. Brielle removed the chair and yanked back the bolt. Citric opened the door, a tray of food in his hands, and instructed someone to wait in the hallway. Brielle immediately moved behind the door to avoid being seen while Citric deposited the tray onto the table. He went outside to retrieve a large bowl and a jug of water from the servant. She heard the clink of a coin as he tipped the servant before bolting the door closed behind him.

Citric set the bowl and jug of water down next to the tray of food. Brielle walked over to inspect the contents of the two bowls; stew by the looks of it.

Rabbit by the smell of it. She wrinkled her nose in disgust and reached for a hunk of bread, tearing small pieces off it and popping them into her mouth. She would work her way up to the questionable stew.

Citric poured some water into the large bowl and held a washcloth out to her.

"Ladies first."

She halted, the bread lodged in her throat.

"I promise not to look." The corner of his lips lifted into an amused smile.

Brielle narrowed her eyes at him before waving a hand to indicate that he should go first. As she resumed her spot on the bed, Citric tugged his shirt out from the waistline of his pants and pulled it over his head in one swift motion. Brielle allowed herself to look at him, to take in the sight of his muscled back and strong, defined arms. She doubted she would find a husband that looked like *that*. The man would probably be twice her age and soft around the middle. Or younger than her nineteen years so that she could at least try to mold him during the formative years of his boyhood.

Citric dipped the washcloth in the water and began wiping his face, his chest. The bread was forgotten as she watched him, butterflies stirring to life in her stomach as her senses heightened. She would likely not feel such stirrings about her husband. She would probably recoil at the thought of his touch and yet have no choice but to let him touch her. That was the problem with marriage; it offered protection from some threats in exchange for submission to others. After tonight, her life and her choices would not be her own. She would have a duty to her Crown, to her people, and she would have to make the necessary sacrifices no matter the personal cost to herself. Tonight, though, she wondered if she could make a choice for herself. She wondered if she would be brave enough.

Citric was drying his damp skin with a hand towel when Brielle rose from the bed and padded over to him.

"What is this from?" She touched her fingers to a deep white scar on his shoulder.

He stilled at her touch but turned his face toward her. He hesitated a moment before answering. "An arrow."

"You were shot?"

He didn't reply, but she noticed his muscles had tensed.

Her gaze roamed his back as her fingers found another two deep scars. "And these?"

She could hear his breathing had become slightly uneven.

"I was a popular target that day."

He had taken three arrows in the back. Despite her curiosity, she did not enquire about the circumstances. Her eyes continued to roam his magnificent body as she slowly moved around him. He stepped to the side, as if allowing her the opportunity to look all she wanted. The move sent a nervous thrill through her core.

"And this?" She ran her fingers along a thin pink scar between his ribs.

She was standing so close now she could feel the heat of him. If she raised her eyes, his face would be inches away from hers. She dared to look up at him even as her heart thundered in her chest. His eyes were fixed on hers, hungry and intense. As if he knew exactly what she was doing.

"A knife."

She nodded slightly, unsure what to do next despite coming this far. He seemed to sense it because he slid a hand up behind the nape of her neck, lacing his fingers through her hair as he pulled her to his lips. The kiss was not light, but she somehow knew he was holding back, being gentle with her. He would know that she had never been kissed before, had never done anything like this before in her life. His lips tasted hers as his tongue tentatively explored her mouth. The sensation was overwhelming, as if every thought had fled her mind but every inch of her body had caught fire and all she could feel, think, and know now was this—him.

More.

She wanted more. Brielle opened her mouth to him and he gladly met her request, the kiss deepening in hunger. His hands held her firmly, but her hands began to roam, traveling over his rib cage around his muscled back, pulling him into her, welcoming the solid warmth of him. She suddenly wanted to know how his body would feel against her bare skin. She *needed* to know. Brielle's fingers deftly loosened the laces at the front of her dress, the movement causing Citric to stop and look down between them. He watched as she released the laces of her bodice, letting it fall to the floor at her feet, leaving her standing there in only a loose white chemise.

"Brielle." Citric's voice was strained, as if he was struggling to control himself. "Are you sure you want this?"

"Yes," she breathed as her hands moved to the waistband of his pants.

His fingers clasped around them, halting her. "You weren't sure in the river that day."

"That was a lifetime ago, things have changed."

He exhaled, as if debating her words in his mind. "Nothing can come of this," he said firmly. "Tomorrow everything will change again."

"I know. But tonight I choose this. I choose to take what I want because I can. You will owe me nothing and I will owe you nothing." His eyes searched hers, seeking the truth in them. "It's one night," she promised.

His mouth claimed hers as if her words had unleashed him. His hands seized her body, exploring every curve. Brielle's fingers fumbled with his pants until his own hands took charge, releasing them to the floor even as he maneuvered them both toward the bed.

The mattress gave way as their bodies crashed on top of it. Brielle wriggled back to hitch up her chemise and Citric helped her pull it off. She froze as the chill in the air hit her bare skin, along with the knowledge that she was completely naked before him. She fought the urge to cover up her most private parts, even as his eyes devoured her. Citric brought his body over hers and her legs instinctively parted for him.

She gazed down between them, and the sight of his manhood made her gasp. He lowered his mouth to her neck and began tasting her with his lips, his tongue, his teeth. Her insides thrummed, pulsing like a drumbeat. She could feel him moving against her sex, slow and rhythmic, the sensation kindling an internal fire building inside her. She arched against him, wanting to feel more, desperate for the friction.

Sensing her need, he shifted slightly and then she felt his finger inside of her. She bucked a little, unprepared for it, but then the rhythmic motion melted her core and disabled her objections. She never knew any of this. That it would feel this way. That her body was capable of such things. Citric slid a second finger inside her and she groaned, every nerve in her body igniting with excruciating pleasure.

She couldn't think, could hardly breathe. His lips found hers and the kiss was demanding, greedy. As if he could not get enough of her. Brielle responded in like, her hunger ravenous. She reached down between them and put her hand around his manhood, surprised by her own boldness but unable to stop herself, to resist this primal need inside her.

Citric groaned at her touch, their kiss breaking apart for a second, long enough for Brielle to witness her power over him. It was intoxicating. The knowledge that he wanted her so badly. She fumbled trying to guide his manhood to her entrance, but at her silent demand Citric retrieved his fingers and began sinking himself gently inside her.

Brielle winced as he began to fill her, little by little, his movements slow and deliberate. Feeling her body gradually give way to him, she tried to relax, pulling her knees up tight against his hips, drawing him in closer and holding him firm. His movements built, driving harder and deeper, pushing her to an edge that she wanted desperately to soar over. Her fingers dug hard into his muscled back as she gave herself over to him completely and every nerve in her body exploded into release.

CHAPTER THIRTEEN

Henri violently jerked the guard's jaw up as he sliced his throat. The body slumped to his feet, and he quickly bent down to drag it over into the shadows beneath the castle wall. Jameson had taken out the other guard and now two trails of blood were smeared on the cobblestones, disappearing into the shadows. Two of Citric's men stripped the guards of their uniforms, trying to avoid the blood where they could. Within minutes they had resumed the guards' posts, their uniforms slightly ill-fitting. Henri remained in the shadows, scanning the surrounding area, listening for the smallest of sounds, waiting for the rest of Citric's men to appear.

The postern gate within the castle wall was their only chance of getting inside the castle. It was originally designed to be used in the event of a siege, its location known only to the royal family. It was a blessed relief when Brielle had informed him about it, their only other option being the gatehouse and that was clear suicide.

Henri's senses sharpened at a flicker of movement in the distance. He watched and waited, but relaxed a little when Citric's men began to emerge. Henri stepped a foot into the moonlight and nodded to them as they passed through the gate. Each of them would silently make their way to various points within the castle in order to monitor the movements of the King's Guard and send up a warning should anything go wrong.

Brielle's plan was not complicated and involved little loss of life; primarily, the Butcher's. Henri's stomach sickened at the thought. He hadn't been able to stop thinking about it since the moment he had seen his face. He had frozen in shock, so much so that Jameson had had to drag him from the scene before they drew too much attention. The Butcher had looked directly at him, as if he could sense him somehow despite the hooded cloak. Henri and Jameson had not spoken of what they'd witnessed. There were simply no words for what their eyes had seen, and for the second time in his life, Henri questioned whether he truly knew anything at all.

A mournful, animalistic cry pierced the air, sending a wave of gooseflesh along his arms. A light birdcall answered back, from one of the new King's Guards. Then Henri saw her emerge from the darkness; a leather breastplate over her simple cotton dress, a crossbow strapped to her back, and three daggers no doubt hidden beneath her clothes. Her long hair was braided and wound tight into a bun. She looked achingly beautiful bathed in the silver moonlight, like an avenging warrior queen. He was barely aware of the fact that Citric walked beside her.

Jameson's hand clamped down on his shoulder, breaking the spell. He gave him a knowing look that also served as a warning. He needed to focus. One wrong move and this entire plan would fall apart and none of them would make it out alive. Henri nodded in acknowledgment and Jameson disappeared inside the castle wall to take up his position.

"Is everyone inside?" Brielle whispered to him as she approached.

"Yes."

"Then let's go."

She pushed past them through the postern gate, keeping to the shadows of these familiar walls. Henri followed closely behind her, with Citric trailing behind them, as she led the way to a door at the bottom of a tower. After quietly easing open the door, Brielle jumped, startled.

"Eve."

Eve didn't reply as she swept her gaze over the three of them, as if assessing them for injury. Henri's features tightened in barely restrained anger at the sight of her, but she didn't seem to notice and now was not the time to confront her. She turned and began ascending the servants' staircase, holding a candle to light the way. Using the servant's staircase was Eve's idea. She had assured them it was unlikely anyone would be using it at this early hour, but she had also warned them they would only have a small window of time before the servants would wake to start their day. About an hour before sun's rise, she'd said.

They halted at the top of the narrow stairs as Eve opened the door slightly to peer out into the hallway. She closed the door softly, her face stern, but he knew her well enough by now to recognize the flicker of unease across her features.

"What's wrong?" Henri demanded.

She hesitated, as if she didn't want to say the words out loud. "He didn't go to his bed tonight."

The Butcher.

"Where is he now?" Citric asked.

"In his private study."

"He's been there all night?" Henri asked. She nodded. "What is he doing in there?"

Eve shrugged, her eyes uncertain. The movement reminded him just how young she was and how much courage she had to be here tonight and to do all that she had done. She was right to be concerned. It was not like him to not sleep. It was like he was waiting for something. The thought was unsettling.

"It doesn't matter. In his sleep or awake, it makes no difference," Citric insisted as he pushed through them to the top of the stairs.

He opened the door slightly to peer into the hallway before slipping out. Henri moved to follow him, but Brielle grasped his arm and their eyes met for the briefest of moments. He tried to convey everything he wanted to say to her in that moment; that they would both survive this, that they would see each other again. Her heart must have heard his because she released him and he entered the hallway.

Citric moved fast. He was already at the end of the passageway, a dagger ready in his hand. He moved like a predator, silent but swift and agile. His bow and quiver were slung across his back and a longsword hung from his belt. Henri knew he had other weapons hidden on his body. The man himself was a weapon. Henri caught up to him and followed his lead as they made their way through the castle halls.

The castle was familiar. It had not been so long ago that he had been here with his father to call on the alliance with the Southern Kingdom to defeat King Heroux. Yet in some ways it felt like a lifetime ago, another person's life entirely. He had had no purpose then. His only interests were finding escape where he could and avoiding his father as much as possible. He had no idea what his life would become, what choices he would be forced to make. He could not have foreseen that he would be faced with this choice tonight.

Citric halted suddenly in the shadows and Henri realized they were standing across the way from what had to be the private study. His stomach lurched and he thought he might retch right here in the hallway, but he swallowed the bile that rose in his throat and tried to compose himself. Citric moved to step out of the shadows, but Henri thrust a hand out in front of him.

"I'll do it. You stay here and guard the door."

Citric furrowed his brow in question, but he nodded. Henri looked over at the door that he would give anything not to walk through. Taking silent steps to cross the hallway, he rested one hand on his sword, the other on the door, and opened it.

Henri slid inside fast as a breath and moved into a defensive stance. Nathaniel slowly rose from his chair at the desk, his face a cool, emotionless mask. He wore the same black clothes Henri had seen him dressed in yesterday. Clearly, he had not bathed or slept since. His presentation was pristine, though; he had always been fastidious about being presentable. Henri's eyes searched his body for weapons but only noted the sheathed sword laid out on top of the desk, as if he had purposely removed his belt and put it there.

"Why have you come?"

Nathaniel's words surprised him, his tone even more so. It was indifferent, as if they were strangers, but not quite. Henri didn't know what he had expected him to say, but those words were not it.

"Isn't it obvious?" Henri stalked closer, his steps careful, his sword ready.

"You wouldn't have come on your own."

True. He wouldn't have done any of this on his own; rebelling against oppression to defend the innocent, fighting to reclaim what was stolen from him.

"Where is she?"

The words were damning. The shame of his inadequacies burned inside him.

"Nearby, waiting to reclaim what is rightfully hers."

Nathaniel averted his gaze, as if the knowledge wounded him somehow.

"Where is the commander?" he countered, eager to change the subject.

Nathaniel met his eyes again, his stony features returning.

"My father promised King Heroux three heads that day, but only delivered two. King Heroux does not tolerate incompetence. He sentenced my father to death right there on the battlefield."

Henri tensed. The commander had always been a force in his life, unavoidable and indestructible. A domineering presence eclipsed only by his father. It was inconceivable to think that he no longer walked this earth.

"My father insisted that I be the one to kill him. One might have thought he did so for some sentimental reason, but in truth, it was a punishment. He knew who was to blame for your escape. Life, it seems, has a sense of irony. So many times I dreamed of killing my father and in the end he controlled that too."

Henri remained still, even as the words stirred his insides. It was more than his friend had ever revealed to him in a lifetime. He had known he hated his father, but he had not known he wished him dead. He didn't know what would cause a son to want that. Henri had hated his own father, but he would not have wished him dead.

Henri tried to ignore his thoughts, to convince himself they did not matter.

"And you became King Heroux's lackey."

"I had no choice."

"There is always a choice."

Just like he had had a choice. To fight for his people, to reclaim his kingdom, to defend those innocents in the street yesterday. But he hadn't.

"You are right. I could have chosen death," Nathaniel said.

"Instead, you chose to become a murderer."

"No man can claim that his hands are clean."

"That does not excuse what you have done."

"I am not trying to atone."

Indeed, there was no remorse on his face, no regret in his tone. They could have been talking about any mundane topic and he would have looked and sounded the same.

Henri shook his head, suddenly disgusted with himself. "Did I ever know you at all?"

There, a flicker of emotion. "No." The word was quiet, sad.

Time and silence stretched out between them like distance. Henri knew he should kill him. He had come to kill him. There was nothing more to say, but still he could not will his limbs to move closer, to strike out. Standing in front of him was a traitor, a murderer, and his closest friend.

Henri's voice trembled as his heart cracked open. "You should have come with me that day."

He hated the emotion in his voice, the fact that they both knew his words were only delaying the inevitable.

Nathaniel nodded solemnly. "Something else I dream about."

Warning bells sounded throughout the castle a split second before the door splintered open and Citric's arrow flew. Nathaniel fell forward, his teeth gritted in pain at the arrow lodged deep inside his shoulder. His hand hovered over his sword on the table, as if he would have drawn it but had not been able to match the speed of Citric's assault. That same hand now reached up to grip the arrow. He snapped it in half, tossed the fletching across the floor, and then splayed his fingers across the table for support.

"Why is he still alive?" Citric demanded, another arrow nocked and ready.

Henri stared at the blood seeping out of his friend, the pain etched on his face. Nathaniel looked back at him sternly.

"What happened?" Henri asked, even though he knew Citric would not be able to answer him with any definitive truth.

"Someone must have been compromised."

It was a logical assumption, one they had both reached.

Brielle.

"In less than a minute, the entire garrison of the King's Guard will be upon you and your men," Nathaniel said, his voice strained. "I will give you this one chance to leave with your lives."

Citric pulled his bowstring tighter. "I would rather kill you."

"Do it," Nathaniel snarled.

Henri stopped breathing. He wished time would have stopped too, but it seemed to speed up as the thunder of boots echoed down the hallway. He pivoted to defend Citric's back as the King's Guard poured into the room.

"Stop!" Nathaniel roared, and the guards held back even as they surrounded them, their swords barely restrained.

Henri counted near a dozen and knew that more would come. They would be combing every inch of the castle, searching for traitors. His thoughts leaped over each other, wondering what had gone wrong, who had been compromised, who was already dead, if any had managed to escape.

Brielle.

He prayed to God she had escaped through the servants' passage. She wouldn't have wanted to, would have probably fought against it, but hopefully Eve had convinced her to run. He would give anything, swear any oath, break any bone in his body to know that she was still alive, that she would survive this.

"Your men are not faster than my arrow, Butcher." Citric's voice held a deadly promise.

Henri did not know what was going on behind him, what Nathaniel was thinking or doing, what his silence meant. His attention was fixed solely on the dozen guards in front of him, determining who was the biggest threat, who he would take down first, how many he could end before he would take a fatal wound. He knew he was in the last minutes of his life, but that did not matter. His life was of little consequence.

"Stand down."

Henri did not understand the words. Neither did the guards, for they made no move to follow such orders.

"I said stand down!" Nathaniel commanded.

The guards reluctantly eased their positions and lowered their weapons a fraction. Henri remained in a defensive stance, his sword at the ready.

"The King's Guard now answer to a new King," Nathaniel instructed, his breathing labored.

Henri did not have to see his friend to know that his blood loss was weakening him. It would not be long before he bled out.

"A wise decision," Citric said. "Though I would clarify one thing."

Waiting in the narrow, dim servants' staircase was nothing short of torture. Every second felt like it was being drawn out, stretching her nerves until they were tighter than a bowstring. Her eyes kept involuntarily darting to Eve's face, half illuminated by the glow of the single wax candle. She didn't know why. Perhaps she was seeking some kind of reassurance, or perhaps because Eve was the only thing to see in the passageway.

Eve did not meet her gaze, though, and her expression did not comfort her. She looked like a skittish deer being cornered by a hunter, unsure of whether to stay hidden or flee. Brielle wanted to say something to distract them both, but there was nothing to say. Instead, she forced herself to take in Eve's appearance. She was dressed in a fine gown, her hair parted down the middle and tied back against the nape of her neck in a modest design. The style was feminine, but her features were still sharp, her expression stern. Brielle had to admit she preferred her in leathers and pants. It suited her better.

Eve huffed and shifted her weight impatiently. Brielle studied her for a moment before searching for the right words to say.

"Citric will be fine."

"Of course he'll be fine," Eve snapped.

Brielle pressed her lips into a thin line. Perhaps once she was queen, she would give Eve permission to leave court and live wherever she liked. The Red Wood seemed far away enough.

The creak of a door snapped their heads around to peer down the dark pit of the staircase, but they could only stand frozen in horror as the shuffling of steps revealed a young servant girl, her dreamy secret smile slipping into abject terror at the sight of them.

"Oh, no, please don't—"

The girl screamed an ear-piercing sound as she fled down the stairs, shooting out into the courtyard to raise the alarm.

"Come on," Eve urged as she pushed the door open and they both burst out into the hallway.

The bells sounded, echoing a frantic warning throughout the castle loud enough to wake the dead. Brielle glanced down both directions, her mind in a panic as she tried to recall the nearest escape route.

"This way!" Eve yelled above the bells clanging in Brielle's ears.

Brielle didn't question it, she followed as Eve dashed down the hallway. Adrenaline coursed through her veins, charging her legs with unexpected speed and agility. How had this happened? How could everything change in the space of a heartbeat? They shot down corridors and around corners, but halted suddenly at the sight of four guards. Brielle shrieked as the guards locked eyes on them and bolted in their direction.

"In here!" Eve called, and they crashed through the nearest door, whirling quickly to shut it behind them, throwing both their body weights against it.

The door had a lock, but they did not have the key. The guards rammed the door with their bodies and Brielle screamed, the reverberations rattling her teeth. She glanced around the room at the familiar long oak table; they were in the council chamber. She could grab a chair and barricade the door, but to retrieve a chair she would need to leave the door.

The door erupted as the guards burst through and Brielle was flung to the ground. Eve had kept her footing, Brielle noticed with irritation, and already had a blade in her hand. She scrambled to her feet as a guard lunged for her, but she was not quick enough to retrieve any of her hidden blades before the man's meaty hands were around her throat.

His grip was crushing, his expression sickly satisfied as she kicked against him and clawed at his hands, her fingernails drawing blood. But he would not relent and she could not breathe and there was no air as black spots entered her vision.

She fought her panic to clear a space in her mind to think. Reaching into her bodice, she fumbled for the hidden blade and stabbed the guard through the neck. His eyes went wide, surprised, as he gurgled blood like a fountain. Sticky wetness splattered her face, her neck, and the distinct smell of iron filled her nostrils. Brielle watched, stunned, as his hands released their grip on her and his lifeless body fell to the floor.

She spluttered as her shaking hands moved to gently feel her raw, bruised throat. Her gaze locked onto the rich crimson pool of blood slowly seeping toward her feet, and she instinctively stepped backward. It was ironic that she did not want the man's blood on her shoes despite the fact that she was covered in it. Brielle looked up, dazed, to find Eve staring at her from across the table. Their eyes held for a moment, one that confirmed they were both still alive, before three more guards surged through the door.

Brielle's senses immediately sharpened and she swung her crossbow from her back, fitted an arrow, and aimed. Eve's dagger was faster than her arrow, but both met their targets with brutal efficiency. The third guard hesitated before launching himself at Eve, who moved fast to evade the swing of his sword.

Watching her repeatedly dodge his blows, Brielle realized Eve was out of weapons. She quickly loaded another bolt and lifted it to eye-level. She had never practiced hitting a moving target, but Eve must have known what she was doing because she dropped and rolled, giving Brielle an opportunity to let her arrow fly. It hit the guard's shoulder; not a fatal wound, but enough to distract him for a split second so that Eve could attack. In two maneuvers she had disarmed him, claimed his sword, and sliced his belly open. The sight of his entrails made Brielle want to hurl her own guts up. The smell of blood and tissue and organ was nauseating.

The warning bells ceased abruptly.

Brielle stilled at the sudden silence. Her eyes shot to Eve. "What does that mean?"

Eve shook her head and clutched the hilt of the sword tighter. They looked to the open door, but there were no more guards pouring through and she couldn't hear any sounds in the hallway.

"We should barricade the door," Brielle said, moving to collect a chair, but Eve held up a hand to tell her to stop.

She did. Eve turned her ear slightly to the doorway, listening intently, but there was only silence. Brielle reloaded a bolt and held it aloft, aimed and ready. They waited, eyes trained on the open door, barely breathing.

Citric rushed past the room, only to turn back at the sight of them. Relief immediately flooded Eve's face and her sword fell to the ground. She ran to him, flinging her arms around his neck, and he caught her in a one-armed embrace, while his other arm held a bloody sword. Brielle lowered her crossbow a little but did not dare to hope that they were safe yet.

"It's done, then?" Eve asked as she pulled away, and Citric nodded down at her, brushing a strand of hair from her face.

Eve beamed, her smile equal parts joy and relief. A smile Brielle had never witnessed on her before.

"The others?" Eve pressed.

"Securing the castle."

It was true, then. Somehow, against all odds, they had prevailed. She couldn't believe it.

"H-how?" Brielle stammered. "Did you kill the Butcher?"

Citric looked over at her as if he had only just realized she was there. "No. He ordered the King's Guard to stand down."

Brielle frowned. "Why would he do that?"

"He would do anything to save Henri's life," Eve replied smoothly as her smile turned cunning.

Brielle knitted her brows, confused. "Why would the Butcher care about Henri?"

Citric's eyes caught on something behind her and he moved past her to the oak table. His gaze was fixed on a sheet of glass inlaid in the middle of it.

"The sword of peace," he murmured darkly.

Brielle didn't notice Eve pick up a chair until she had hurled it into the table, smashing the glass into a million tiny shards. Citric didn't so much as blink, his eyes never leaving the sword. Climbing up onto the table, Eve bent down and carefully retrieved the sword. She laid it across both hands, letting the light of dawn from the high windows cast a gleam down its sharp edge. Then she turned and kneeled down on the table as she presented the sword to Citric.

Something was not right.

Brielle knew it, even as Citric took the sword and examined it carefully.

"Where is Henri?" she demanded. "What is happening?"

"Justice is being served, a wrong is being righted," Eve replied. Her expression was cold, but her words were triumphant.

Citric's eyes never left the sword as he said, "Generations ago, my people were the custodians of these lands. We lived in peace and prosperity for many years until one day a great army came against us. They did not approve of our way of life, our connection with the land, our ambivalence to your invisible, wrathful God. But most of all, they coveted what was ours. They slaughtered my people. The woodland was soaked in the blood of my ancestors, our homes were set on fire, our temples reduced to rubble."

The ruin. Citric had told them it was a grand house, but could it have been a temple?

"After the slaughter, the two men who led the army divided the lands into North and South and pronounced themselves kings. The Old Treaty was written to ensure that they never came against one another, that one side could never claim the entire breadth of our lands. Over time, the truth was lost, burned from history, buried underneath rumors of blood magic and vengeful spirits. But today, today will be recorded in history forever as the day that the rightful custodians of these lands reclaimed them."

Citric turned his gaze away from the glint of the sword to fix it firmly on Brielle. "The Old Treaty is over."

Thank you so much for reading my book! I hope you enjoyed it. It would mean the world to me if you could leave a review on Amazon, Goodreads, or BookBub. One of the most important keys to an indie author's success is book reviews. Book reviews give social proof to potential readers that it is highly likely they will enjoy the book. With so many options for books out there, book reviews are a must! Especially at launch time. By leaving a review, you are helping other like-minded readers to find my book and thereby are greatly assisting me in building my career as an indie author. So thank you!

If you enjoyed this book, you'll love the FREE bonus scene from Citric's point of view which you can get by signing up to my mailing list. It's easy, just go to my website at www.clairebutlerauthor.com and sign up!

https://www.instagram.com/clairebutlerauthor/

Clairebutlerauthor | Facebook

Clairebutlerauthor (@clairebutlerauthor) | TikTok

Claire Butler Books - BookBub

ABOUT AUTHOR

Claire wrote her first book before she knew how to write the alphabet. It consisted of scribbling on a page and having her sister illustrate the page next to it. She has since refined her books to include actual words. Claire has a background in Psychology. She loves writing young adult and new adult books because it allows her to explore coming of age themes, intense emotions, the formation and shifting of identities, the power of first love, and the enduring bonds of friendship. Claire lives in Australia with her husband and two children. She is obsessed with beaches, picnics, and sunshine. Often in combination with a good book. Her favorite authors include Sarah J Maas, Renee Ahdieh, Raven Kennedy, and Tahereh Mafi.

If you enjoyed this book, you'll love the FREE bonus scene from Citric's point of view which you can get by signing up to my mailing list. It's easy, just go to my website at www.clairebutlerauthor.com and sign up!

https://www.instagram.com/clairebutlerauthor/

Clairebutlerauthor | Facebook

Clairebutlerauthor (@clairebutlerauthor) | TikTok

Claire Butler Books - BookBub

ACKNOWLEDGMENTS

I would like to thank Page Turner Publishing - you are my dream company. Anthony, Jess, Suzie and Katrina, I am so glad I have you all in my corner. Thank you to my editor, Emily, for your valuable insights and suggestions. Thank you to Menna for being an amazing literary friend, storyline sounding board, and expert plot hole fixer. And lastly, but most importantly, I would like to thank you dear reader. I hope we meet again!

www.ingramcontent.com/pod-product-compliance
Lightning Source LLC
Chambersburg PA
CBHW030630120726
47904CB00006B/2097